THE
RED PLAGUE
AFFAIR

He took a step forward, and for a moment Emma thought Kim Rudyard might well strike her. The gold hoop at his ear sparked angrily, foreign charter symbols running golden under the metal's surface, and her own necklace, a large oval cameo held to her throat by a black band of silver-threaded lace, warmed dangerously. The entire room rattled once, as if the hotel had forgotten it was stationary and had temporarily decided to become a train carriage.

It was, she thought, so *easy* to unsettle a man. Even a dangerous player in the great Game of Empire could be made to stumble in a simple verbal dance.

Rudyard recollected himself with a visible effort. Emma was not surprised to find Mikal's warmth at her shoulder. "But," she continued, silkily, "perhaps I misunderstand you?"

"I hope you do." His white teeth showed in a smile that held no joy, a grimace of terribly amused pain. "Those *his kind* serve most often end envenomed. *Do* be careful. The Empire might hate to lose you."

Is that a threat? "I have no intention of being lost."

D0239423

THE
RED PLAGUE AFFAIR

Bannon & Clare: Book Two

LILITH SAINTCROW

orbit

www.orbitbooks.net

ORBIT

First published in Great Britain in 2013 by Orbit

A CIP catalogue record for this book is available from the British Library.

ISBN 978-0-356-50093-5

Typeset in Times by Palimpsest Book Production Limited,
Falkirk, Stirlingshire
Printed and bound in Great Britain by
Clays Ltd, St Ives plc

Papers used by Orbit are from well-managed forests
and other responsible sources.

MIX
Paper from
responsible sources
FSC
www.fsc.org FSC® C104740

Orbit
An imprint of
Little, Brown Book Group
100 Victoria Embankment
London EC4Y 0DY

An Hachette UK Company
www.hachette.co.uk

www.orbitbooks.net

To the strangers

Acknowledgements

As always, I am grateful to Devi Pillai, who did not throttle me during revisions, and Miriam Kriss, who told me I could indeed do this. I am indebted to Mel Sterling and Christa Hickey for putting up with me, and to my children for cheerfully going along with my research experiments. Special gratitude must also go to the ever-patient Susan Barnes and the incredibly tolerant Joanna Kramer, who both deserve some sort of medal. (And booze.) Last, as always, dear Reader, thank you. Come into another one of my little worlds, and let me tell you what happened next.

Historical Note

I regret to inform the Reader that I have, as they say, played fast and loose with History. Being a subjective wench in several regards, History did not seem to mind, but some who peruse these books may. I can only say that whatever errors and inaccuracies are contained herein, they are for the most part lovingly and carefully chosen; any that are not, are the regrettable result of cracks and defaults that occur even in the best Research For The Purposes Of Almost-Historical Fiction, and the fault of Your Ob't Servant, namely, the Humble Author.

And now, my best and most faithful darlings, my Readers, let me welcome you once again into Londinium, where the smoke rises, the sorcery glitters, and the clockworks thrum . . .

Chapter One

Not How Things Are Done

I am too bloody old for this.

    Archibald Clare spat blood and surged upward. He gave the struggling fellow opposite him two quick jabs to the head, hoping to calm the situation somewhat. Foul knee-deep semiliquid splashed, dark as sin and smelly as the third circle of Hell. Clare gained his footing, unwilling to deduce what deep organic sludge his boots were slipping in, and retched painlessly. Blood from his broken nose, trickling down the back of his throat, was making his stomach *decidedly* unhappy.

Where is that blasted Italian?

He had no worry to spare for Valentinelli. For Clare strongly suspected he had other problems, especially if what his faculties – sharpened by coja and burning like a many-sided star of logic and deduction inside his skull –

were telling him was truly so. If, indeed, the man in the long academician's gown struggling in Clare's fists, spluttering wildly and half-drowned, was not Dr Francis Vance . . .

. . . Clare would not only perhaps have quite a bit of explaining to do, but would also have been bested *again* by the sodding criminal bastard.

The man in Clare's grasp ceased thrashing quite so frantically. Since he was being held under some of the foulest sewage drained nightly into the Themis, it was not so amazing. However, Clare judged that his opponent was about to drown, and further judged his own faculties were *not* stunned by the knock on the skull he'd taken earlier that night. Which made his opponent a potentially valuable source of information from whence to deduce Dr Vance's whereabouts and further plans.

Besides, drowning a man in shite was not, as Emma Bannon would say archly, how things were *done*.

Now why should I think of her? Clare freed the obstruction from his throat with a thick venomous cough, wished he hadn't because the reek was thick enough to chew, and dragged the false Vance up from a watery grave.

Choking, spluttering words more fit for a drover or a struggling hevvymancer than the man of quality Dr Vance purported to be, Clare's bespattered opponent hung in his narrow fists like wet washing. Clare's chest was uncomfortably tight, a rock lodged behind his ribs, and he wheezed most unbecomingly as his trapped opponent tried gamely to sink a knee into the most tender spot of Clare's anatomy.

Bad form, sir. So Clare took the man's feet out from under him and dunked him again, boots slipping in the sludge coating whatever passed as a floor to this foul tunnel. The echoes held a peculiar quality that made Clare think this part of Londinium's sewers were built of slowly crumbling brick, which made them not quite as ancient as those built by the Pax Latium. *Newer* often meant *sturdier*, but not always. The Latiums had believed in solid stone even for a cloaca on the benighted edge of their empire.

An encouraging observation. Or not. He hawked and spat again, grateful he could not see the colour of whatever bodily fluid he had just thrown into the dark. His face would be a mask of bruising upon the morrow.

He hauled the man forth from the sewerage again, and wished his sensitive nose would cease its operation for a few moments. "Be reasonable!" he barked, and the echoes gave him more of the dimensions of the tunnel. Quite large, really, and quite a volume of almost-fluid moving through its throat. His busy faculties calculated the rate of flow and returned the answer that Clare was lucky it was a slurry; he would have been swept off his feet and drowned had it been any thinner. "Vance! *Where is he?*"

The besmeared visage before him contorted; there was a sharp tooth-shattering crack. Another odd sound rose under the plashing and plinking. What little unhealthy gleaming there was showed a rather oddly coloured face under a stringy mass of black hair, a hooked nose decked with excrescence, and rotting teeth as the man Clare had been chasing howled with laughter.

Dear God, what—

The laughter swelled obscenely, and the man in his grasp went into convulsions. More filth splashed, and Clare swore with a ferocity that would perhaps have shocked even Miss Bannon, who could – he had discovered – let loose torrents of language that would make even the ill-tempered drabs of Whitchapel blush.

Poison tooth, broken open. Of course. And the reek blocked his olfactory capability, so he likely would not discover what variety of toxin in time to halt its progress.

Dr Vance was not above sacrificing a hireling or two. They were pawns, and life was cheap on Londinium's underside. For the promise of a shilling, much worse than this murderous diversion had been committed – probably several times over tonight, in the depths of the city. Or even in the past hour.

Clare swore again, dragging the suddenly stiff body towards the tunnel's entrance. He now remembered falling off the lip of the adjoining tunnel, splashing into this fetching summer garden of a place with a bone-rattling thump. The rock in his chest squeezed again, his left shoulder complaining as well. Perhaps he had strained it, in the excitement. He had chased the good Doctor from one end of Londinium to the other over the past two days, and at least denied the man his true prize – or so Clare hoped.

"Eh, *mentale*." A flat, queerly accented voice, falling against the thick water without so much as an echo. "You are *loud* tonight."

"Poisoned tooth!" Short of breath and patience, Clare was nevertheless gratified to find the Neapolitan assassin, as usual, did not ask useless questions. Instead, sleek dark Ludovico Valentinelli splashed into the muck a trifle more gracefully than his employer had, and relieved Clare of the burden of his erstwhile opponent. A different foul reek arose.

The man had voided his bowels. It was, Clare reflected, almost a cleaner stink. Certainly fresher, though hardly *better*.

He took in tiny sips of the fœtidness and choked. "Damn the man," he managed. "*Damn* him!"

"Too late!" Ludo was, as usual, infuriatingly cheerful. "He has risen to Heaven, *signore*. Or to Hell, who knows?"

"B-bring the b-body." Why were his teeth chattering? And his chest was even tighter, iron bands seizing his ribs. "D-dissection."

Ludo found this funny. At least, he gave a gravelly chuckle. "You are certainly no *Inquisitore*." He hauled the corpse to the entrance, heaving it up with little grace but much efficiency. Then, the assassin splashed back to Clare, who was suddenly much occupied in keeping upright. "*Mentale?*"

How strange. I cannot breathe. Not that I wish to, down here, and yet . . . "V-v-val—"

He was still seeking to speak Valentinelli's name when the pain clove his chest and felled him. The thick darkness was full of things no gentleman would wish soiling his cloth, and Clare's busy faculties, starlike, winked out.

Chapter Two

A Duke to Chastise

Inside the stoic, well-bred walls of 34½ Brooke Street, Mayfair, Londinium, a quiet bustle of orderly activity was shattered.

"*Strega!*" a familiar voice bellowed, and Emma Bannon, Sorceress Prime, arrived at the bottom of the fan-shaped stairs in a silk-skirted rush. Mikal was there in his tails and snow-white shirt, easing a dead man's lanky frame to the floor, and the smell hit her.

Dear God, what is this? Her half-unbuttoned dress whispered as she flicked her fingers, a cleansing charm rising with a Minor Word and scorching the air of her parquet-floored foyer. Her dark curls, almost-dressed in anticipation of Lady Winslet's ball, tumbled about her face as she recognised the long, beaky-nosed corpse who, contrary to her expectations, drew in a rattling breath, clutching at his left shoulder and jerking his limbs in a decidedly odd fashion.

Next to him, pock-faced and hollow-eyed Ludovico Valentinelli was spattered with effluvium as well, but she had little time to wrinkle her nose.

Her other Shield, tall dark Eli, arrived at a run. He was further along in the dressing process than Mikal, since both of them were to attend her tonight. Still, his starched shirt was unbuttoned, and his jacket knocked askew.

Clare's breath rattled. *Angina. It is his heart*, she realised, the spark of life in Archibald Clare's body guttering like a candleflame in a draughty hall. "Fetch me *crystali digitalia!*" she barked, and Eli leapt to obey, taking the stairs three at a time. Her workroom would admit him, and he knew enough to take care with any experiments in progress – especially the æthericial commisterum. "Ludo, what on earth?" She did not expect him to answer.

"*Strega—*" The Neapolitan was almost beyond words, but Emma was already on her knees. She was barefoot, too – the ball would not start for some while yet, and she had intended to be only *slightly* late. Only fashionably so, as it were.

Later than her night's quarry. It was always advisable to surprise one's prey.

Mikal, his yellow irises bright in the foyer's dimness, spared the Italian a single glance, bracing Clare's shoulders.

A Major Word took shape on Emma's lips, sliding free whole and bloody, red sparks of sorcery fountaining. The four plain silver rings on her left hand fluoresced as she pulled stored ætheric force from them, heavy garnet earrings swinging against her cheeks warming and sparking as well. She would, in all eventuality, need the force she was expending later tonight – but just at the moment, she did not care. Her right hand, a large bloody stone in its antique silver setting flashing on the second finger, clamped to Clare's chest and her senses dilated. She located the source of the distress, feeling about inside his flesh with several nonphysical senses, and determination rose bitter-bright inside her.

Not your time yet, sir. Not while I am here to gainsay it.

The heart, determined muscle that it was, twitched under her ætheric pressure. She forced it into a rhythm that matched her own, exhaling sharply as her concentration narrowed. There was some damage, true, but all in all the organ had carried on gamely.

She was not surprised. He could be provokingly stubborn, her mentath. "The golden orb in the library," she heard herself say, from very far away. "And three surdipped hawk feathers, Mikal. Bring."

He did not protest at leaving her alone and distracted with Valentinelli, for once. Which was very good, because Clare's tired heart began to resist the pressure of her will, and the sorceress was suddenly very occupied in keeping Archibald Clare's blood moving at its required pace. At least her Discipline, Black though it was, gave her sufficient knowledge of the body's processes to keep extinction from Clare's doorstep in *this* instance.

I do hope his faculties have not been damaged. The flow of ætheric energy through her hands intensified, scorch-hot. The mentath, a logic-machine trapped in frail, weary flesh, coughed and convulsed again.

Strange, he looks old now. Perhaps it was merely that his colour was very bad. Then again, he was not a young man. He had been a vigorous thirty-three when she met him, but the years since had kept up their steady wearing away at him, drop by drop.

And Clare was congenitally unable to cease pursuing trouble of the most exotic sort. He was not engaged in a life that would permit much rest, and the wear and tear on his physicality was marked.

A chant rose to her lips, the language of Mending forced to her will – for her Discipline was not of the White branch, and Mending obeyed her only reluctantly. Still, she was Prime, and such a designation required a will that brooked very little bridle – and could force even the most reluctant branch of sorcery to its bidding.

A rolling sonorous roil, the entire house suddenly alive with rushing crackles, its population of indentured servants so used to the feel of tremendous sorcery running through its halls they hardly paused in their appointed duties.

Eli arrived, not breathless but with his dark hair disarranged. He measured out two tiny venom-purple crystals of the *digitalia*, dropped them into Clare's fishworking mouth, and clamped the mentath's jaw shut for a few seconds to make certain they would stay in. Then he settled back on his heels, watching the Sorceress Prime's face, alight with crawling golden charter charms screening her flesh as she half sang, her evening dress pulled askew and white shoulders rising from a silver and blue froth of gauze and lace. The charter symbols, ancient runic patterns of Wheel and Plough, Stone and Blossom and others less willing to be named or pronounced, invaded Clare's pasty skin as well, and finally Eli glanced up at the Neapolitan assassin. "Looks as if you've had rather a night of it."

Ludovico shrugged. For once, he did not sneer, perhaps a mark of his agitation. Or perhaps his lips were sealed by the filth coating him, smeared on his face as if he had bathed in a foul-ditch. Under that mask, his colour was very bad indeed – not that his sallow, ratlike features would ever win regard for blooming beauty, indeed. At least the dirt masked the pox scars on his cheeks.

Mikal reappeared, yellow eyes alight as he shouldered his fellow Shield aside. In one hand he held an apricot-sized globe of mellow gold; the three feathers, coated with a black tarry substance, shivered in his other. The sorceress, dark gaze full of a terrible blank _presence_, swayed slightly as she chanted. The charter symbols glowed crimson as they ran down her left side, clustering high under the ribs, crawling over the pale slope of one breast like a cupped hand.

A shudder ran through her swelling song, the mentath's filth-caked bootheels drumming the parquet as his body thrashed, and Mikal leaned forward, offering the globe and the feathers.

Who knew what objects would be required for any act

of sorcery? It was, by its very definition, an irrational art. Many sorcerers were magpies, since one could not tell what physical item – if any – would be required for a Work. Some Primes sniffed disdainfully and said the best sorcery was unanchored in the physical . . . but those of a practical bent understood that the ease of a Work moored in an object of reasonable permanence was in most cases a desirable thing.

Sorcery flashed, ætheric energy coalescing into the visible for a brief moment, and Ludovico Valentinelli crossed himself, breathing a foul wondering curse in his native tongue. His pox-pocked face, under its splattering of black matter, was flour-pale.

The globe and feathers were gone, their physical matrices picked apart to provide fuel for the impossible. The chant relaxed, swimming bloodwarm through air suddenly prickling and vibrating. Clare, his eyelids fluttering, was no longer ashen. A trace of healthy colour crept back into his lean, lax face.

Easily, softly, the brass syllables wound down from Emma Bannon's lips. She leaned over the mentath, cradling him, and breathed in his face. His body jerked again and the sorceress relaxed slightly, uncurling her mental grip from the repaired clot of fibrous muscle in his chest. One final stanza, her nose wrinkling slightly as the acridity of some drug burned her sensitive palate, and the language of Mending fled her.

She sagged, and the almost-bruising grip on her shoulders was Mikal's hands, fever-hot and hard with callouses.

Emma blinked, shutterclicks of dim light stinging her suddenly sensitive eyes, storing away the taste of whatever substance had been running through Clare's blood. *Hmmm. No wonder he has looked rather ragged of late. It tastes dreadful, whatever it is.*

Mikal's face was tense and set.

"He will live." It was a relief to hear her usual brisk tone. For a moment, she had almost been . . . had she?

Afraid. And that could not be borne, or shown.

"He will live," she repeated, more firmly. "Now, let us be about clearing up this mess. I have a ball to attend and a duke to chastise."

Lady Winslet's dowry had restored the fortunes of her husband's family, and though she was not taken into *quite* the highest echelons of Society, her taste and judgement were considered quite reasonable. She had redone a fashionable Portland Place address – one of Naish's, of course – in a manner most befitting her husband's title. Of late she had taken to inviting an astounding mix to her Salons, patronising certain promising members of the Royal Society, and had garnered much praise for her dinners. In a few generations, the Winslets would be very proud indeed to have invited such a petty bourgeois into their hallowed family tree.

If, that is, she managed to produce an heir. Barry St John Duplessis-Archton, Lord Winslet, was a dissipate scoundrel, but he had ceased gambling and now only drank to a religious degree that might preclude fathering said heir. He had a nephew who showed some signs of not being an empty-headed waste of a few fine suit jackets, but, all in all, Emma privately thought the Winslets' chances rather dim.

And no breath of scandal attached itself to Lady Winslet; she did not seem the sort to have a groom provide the necessary materials to make a bastard either. Very sad; had she been just a trifle less extraordinary she would have more chances of success against the ravening beasts of Society and Expectation.

All of that was academic, however, for Emma had known the Duke of Cailesborough would be at the Winslet ball. One of his current mistresses was attending, and further-more, Emma herself had carefully planted a breath of rumour that would interest him.

And he had taken the bait whole. Which led to her presence in this forgotten, cramped second-floor storeroom full of discarded bits of off-season furniture and rolled-up, unfashionable carpets. A single candle, stuck in a dusty candelabra probably dating from the time of the Mad King Georgeth, gave wavering illumination to the scene.

Eli straightened, exhaling sharply. He was not rumpled in the slightest, though there was a slight flush to his cheeks. Perhaps embarrassment, for the quality of Cailesborough's struggle had been quite unexpected.

Said Cailesborough, on the floor, trussed hand and foot and gagged with commendable efficacy with his own sock, glared at Emma with the one blue eye that was not swelling closed.

For a man of the aristocracy, he had put up a rather remarkable tussle.

That was immaterial. "Now," she said, softly, "what do we do with *you*?"

She had the dubious honour of addressing a Spaniard, moustachioed and of a small stature to inspire a touch of ridicule or pity, his right arm twisted behind him in an exceedingly brutal fashion by a silent and immaculate Mikal, who twisted his lean dark face and spat at her.

There was a creaking sound, and Mikal's other hand clamped at the small Spaniard's nape. "Prima?" The one word was freighted with terrible menace, and had Emma been feeling insulted instead of simply weary, she might have let her Shield do what he wished with the man. Mikal's eyes burned in the dimness, a flame of their own.

Outside the locked door, a hall and the cigar room away, the music swelled. Her absence would not be remarked during the waltz, but perhaps the Duke's would.

They will be missing him a very long time. A greater worry returned, sharp diamond teeth gnawing at the calm she needed to deal with this situation in its proper fashion. *Is Clare well? Resting comfortably, I should hope.*

She put the thought aside. He was as easy as she could make him, and she had other matters to attend to at this moment. Her regard for a mentath was one thing. Her service to Queen and Empire was *quite* another.

"On the one hand," she continued, suppressing a slightly acid burp – for Lady Winslet's cold supper tonight left a trifle to be desired – and clasping her hands prettily as she sank onto a small, handy-even-if-covered-with-a-dustcloth chair, "you are a diplomatic personage, sir, and Her Majesty's government does believe in observing proper forms. It would be a trifle awkward if a member of the august consulate of that pigeon Isobelia disappeared."

Don Ignacio de la Hoya went almost purple and cursed her in a whisper. He was emphatically not a Carlist, which was interesting indeed. The Spanish embassy had been rather a hotbed of anti-Isobelian sentiments for a long while, the round, benighted, silly Queen of the Spains had never had much of a chance against those who wished her a catspaw. Still, she was nominally in power, and Emma supposed the idea of royalty and majesty might have held a certain attraction for some of her subjects. Especially if they were as ill-favoured and ratlike as this specimen.

His throat had been almost crushed by Mikal's iron fingers, and now, the sharp stink of fear poured from him in waves.

The dustcloth would perhaps taint this dress. She should not have sat, and she was taking far too long over this part of the matter. Still, Emma tilted her head slightly and regarded the man. Don Ignacio writhed in Mikal's grip, and it would be merely a matter of time before he collected himself enough to raise a cry, bruised throat or no.

There was little chance of him being heard over the merriment and music, but why take the risk?

He stared at her, and the sudden spreading wetness at his crotch – it was a shame, his trousers were of fine cloth – sent a spike of useless revulsion through her. Champagne and terror were a bad mixture, and this man was no ambassador. He was a low-level consulate official, despite his *Don*; but, she supposed, even a petty bureaucrat could dream of treason.

"Did you truly think you could plan to murder a queen and go unnoticed?" She sounded amused even to herself. Reflective, and terribly calm. "Especially in such lackadaisical fashion? The weapons you brought for the planned insurrection will be most useful elsewhere, I suppose, so we may thank you for that. And *that* baggage . . ." She indicated the prostrate, struggling Duke with a tiny motion of her head, and Eli, well used by now to this manner of situation, sank a kick into Cailesborough's middle. He had not yet gone to fat, the Duke, but he was still softer than Eli's boot. ". . . well, he has some small value for us now. But you? I do not think you have much to offer."

Don Ignacio de la Hoya began to babble in a throaty whisper, but he told Emma nothing she did not already know of the plot. He had very little else to give, and fear would only make him too stupid for proper use. His replacement in the consulate was likely to be just as idiotic, but vastly less troublesome.

His heart, she found herself thinking. *What manner of substance was he using? The damage was much more than it should have been; thirty-five does not make a man old. Merely lucky, and somewhat better-fed than the rest.*

She brought herself back to the present with an invisible effort. Mikal read the change in her expression, and the greenstick crack of a neck breaking was very loud in the hushed room. The candle on the table guttered, but the charm in its wax kept the flame alive.

On the floor, the Duke moaned, his eyes rolling. He was to be delivered to the Tower whole and reasonably undamaged. For a bare moment Emma Bannon, Sorceress Prime in service to Queen and Empire, contemplated crushing the life out of him by sorcery alone. It would be messy, true, but also satisfying, and Queen Victrix would never have to fear this caged beast's resurgence. He had chosen ill in the manner of accomplices, but he was capable of learning from such a mistake.

The decision is not yours, sorceress, she told herself again. Cailesborough had been one of the few allowed near Alexandrina Victrix when she had been merely heir presumptive under the stifling-close control of the Duchess of Kent; of course he had not been a marriage prospect but he had no doubt been amenable to extending the Duchess's sway over her soon-to-be-crowned daughter. The old King's living until Victrix's majority had cheated the Duchess of a regency, and no doubt Victrix had cheated Cailesborough of some prize of position or ambition. Still, the Queen appeared to wish him dealt with leniently.

If the Tower could be called *lenient*.

De la Hoya's body hit a rolled up, unfashionable carpet with a thump, raising a small cloud of dust. Mikal glanced at her. "Prima?" Did he look concerned?

It had taken far more sorcerous force than she liked to lure them both to this room and to spring her trap. And the worry returned, sharper than ever. Clare was not a young man, and he seemed inclined, if not flatly determined, to do himself an injury.

"Bring the body, and the Duke." Londinium's fog was thick tonight, and it would cover all manner of actions. "The window is behind those dreadful curtains – and *do* make certain the Duke lands gently. Lady Winslet's gardens need no damage." She stood, a slight crackling as her finger flicked and a cleansing charm shook dust free of her skirts. The silver shoes with their high arches and spangled laces were lovely, but they pinched abominably, and her corset squeezed as well. *I would much rather have been at home tonight. How boring I've grown.*

"I'll fetch the carriage." Mikal paused, if she wished to tell him where they were bound. It was a Shield's courtesy, and a welcome one.

"We shall take both unfortunates to the Tower." *Though the body will go no further than the moat. The Dweller should be pleased with that.*

Eli bent and made a slight sound as he managed the Duke's bulky, fear-stiffened form. Mikal simply stood for a moment, watching her closely. She took back the mask of her usual expression, straightened her shoulders and promised herself a dash of rum once she returned to her humble abode.

And still, the worry taunted her.

Something must be done about Clare.

Chapter Three

Grief Is Unavoidable

Dark wainscoting, large graceful shelves crammed with books and periodicals, including an entire set of the new edition of the *Encyclopaedie Britannicus* – Miss Bannon's servants were, as ever, extraordinarily *thorough* – and the heavy oak armoire full of linens charm-measured exactly to Clare's frame. The rest of the room was comfortably shabby, rich red velvet rubbed down to the nub and the tables scattered with papers left precisely where he had placed them the last time he had availed himself of Miss Bannon's hospitality.

The oddity was the chair set by his bedside, and the sorceress within it, her slightness cupped in heavy ebony arms and her curling dark hair slightly mussed as she leaned against the high hard back, sound asleep, dressed in silver and blue finery fit to attend a Court presentation. Her childlike face, without her waking character to lend authority to the soft features, was slack with utter exhaustion.

Of no more than middle height, and slight as well, it was always a surprise to see just how small she truly was. One tended to forget as the force of her presence filled a room to bursting.

The other oddity stood at his chamber door, a tall man with tidy dark hair, an olive-green velvet jacket and curious boots, his irises glowing yellow in the dimness. The smell of paper, clean sheets, a faint ghost of tabac smoke, and the persistent creeping breath of Londinium's yellow fog alone would have told Clare he was in the room Miss Bannon kept for his visits.

Which had been rather less often than he liked, of late. The sorceress's company could not be called restful, precisely, but all the same Clare found it rather relaxing to have at least one person with whom he could feel a certain . . . informality?

Was *comfort* the more precise term?

The Shield, Mikal, did not stir. His yellow gaze rested upon Clare with distressing penetration.

Lucid. But very weak. He tested his body's responses, gingerly. They obeyed, grudging him as if he were an invalid. Fingers like sausages, toes swollen but movable, his chest sore as if a gigantic clawed hand had rummaged through the inside of his ribcage and left a jumbled mess behind.

Now for the important part. His eyes half-lidded, and he performed the curious mental doubling of a mentath. A set of mental chalkboards rose before his consciousness, and he began with the simplest exercises he had learned at Yton when his talent had truly begun to manifest itself. Mentath ability came to the fore during late childhood, scholarships were quite generous for any who showed considerable promise.

Said scholarships, however, were contingent upon that promise being fulfilled.

A quarter of an hour later, loose with relief but sweating from the mental effort, Clare let out a long, shaky sigh. His faculties were unharmed.

Miss Bannon, perhaps disturbed by the slight sound, shifted in the chair and fell back into slumber. Clare now had the opportunity to study her while she was deeply asleep, and it was so novel an experience he rather wished he had not been forced to forgo a portion of that time to making certain whatever had happened to him had not destroyed his capacities.

You are avoiding, Clare. It was angina pectoris. Rather severe, too.

Mikal's eyes had half-closed as well. The Shield leaned against the door, and he was perhaps almost asleep. Did he think Clare a threat to the sorceress?

She did rather manage to accomplish a fair amount of vexation. Especially to Britannia's enemies. And she did so with a disregard for her own safety likely to give the Shield, tasked with maintaining said safety, a bit of nervousness.

However, it was far more likely that Mikal was unwilling

to let Miss Bannon out of his sight for . . . *other* reasons. Quite personal considerations, one could say.

The question of Mikal had occupied Clare most handsomely at one time or another. Since the affair that had brought the mentath into the sorceress's circle – not that Miss Bannon had anything so social as a *circle*, it was rather the circle of her regard, which frankly interested Clare more – he had added tiny nuggets of information to the deductive chain Mikal represented.

Your heart, Clare. Do not become distracted.

He was clean, and in a bed which linens smelled of fresh laundering. The last event he remembered was the darkness of the sewers swallowing him whole. Slightly irritated, he shifted in the mattress's familiar embrace. How had he arrived here, of all places?

The answer was stupidly simple. Valentinelli, of course. Where else would the Neapolitan bring him? The man was as fascinated by Miss Bannon as Mikal was.

Or as you are. You are seeking to distract yourself from a very important chain of deduction. Angina pectoris. A severe attack. You could have died.

Yet here he lay, clean and safe. At least, it would take a great deal of unpleasantness before *this* house became unsafe.

Miss Bannon no doubt performed some illogical miracle, and is sleeping at your bedside. In that dress, she was no doubt a-hunting in Society for a traitor, turncoat, criminal, or merely one who intrigued too openly against Queen Victrix. Yet here she sleeps, and you are . . . comforted? Troubled?

The problem, he reflected, was that Emotion was insidious, and an enemy of Logic.

Item one: he had lost Dr Vance. Again.

Item two: the more-than-mild chest pains during the hunt for the blasted art professor were unequivocally symptoms of a much larger quandary.

Item three: Miss Bannon, breathing softly as she slumped in an uncomfortable-looking chair. She took very little care with her person, and it was not quite right for Clare to put her to such worry. It was not worthy of the regard he held for her, as well.

He had no family; his parents were safe in churchyard beds, and his siblings had not survived childhood. But had he been one of those blessed with surviving kin, Clare supposed he would have felt for them much the same way he felt for Miss Bannon. A rather brotherly affection, tinged with a great deal of . . . what was it? Worry?

He might as well worry about a typhoon, or houricane. Miss Bannon was eminently capable . . . but she was also strangely fragile, being female, and Clare was not behaving as a gentleman by putting her to such bother.

You are being maudlin. Emotion is the enemy of Reason, and you are still distracting yourself. Had he not been a mentath, Clare might have been tempted to stifle a groan. As it was, he merely swallowed the offending noise and set himself to exercise his reason, since his faculties appeared undamaged.

"Clare."

He almost started, but it was only Mikal, breathing the

single word from his place at the door. The gleam of his irises was absent; the foreign man – for Clare had deduced he was, in fact, of the blood of the Indus, even if he had been born on Englene's shores – had closed his eyes.

"Yes?" Clare whispered.

"You could have died."

I am not an idiot, sir. "Yes."

"My Prima greatly weakened herself to avert such an event."

Obviously. "I am most grateful."

Emma Bannon stirred again, and both Shield and mentath held their peace for a short while. When she subsided, sliding sideways to end propped against one side of the chair like a sleepy child during a Churchtide evening, Mikal let out another soft breath. His words took shape inside the exhale.

"She is . . . fond of you."

Oh? "Only a little, I'm sure." Clare shifted uncomfortably. Such swimming weakness wore on him; stillness was remarkably painful after a while. "Sir—"

"She is fond of very few."

"That I can believe."

Mikal arrived at the warning Clare had already inferred was his intention. "Do not cause her grief, mentath."

I am a fleshly being in a dangerous world. Grief is unavoidable. His answering whisper was as stiff as his protesting back. "I shall do my best, sir." Had he not just been reminded of his own perishability, in the most alarming way possible? And further reminded that he was not being quite correct in his treatment of his . . . friend?

Yes, Miss Bannon was a friend. It was rather like forming an acquaintance with a large, not-quite-tamed carnivore. Sorcery made for powerful irrationality, no matter how practical Emma Bannon was as a matter of course.

The Shield fell silent again, even the glimmers of his yellow irises quenched, and Clare lay in the dimness, studying one of Emma Bannon's small soft slumber-loosened hands, until fresh unconsciousness claimed him.

Chapter Four

Breakfast and Loneliness

The Delft-and-cream breakfast room was flooded with pearly, rainy Londinium morning light, translucent charm spheres over the ferns singing their soft crystalline lullabies. White wicker furniture glowed, and the entire house purred like a cat, content to have its mistress at home and the servants quietly busy at their various tasks.

"You could have sent me a penny-post," Emma remarked mildly enough, her hand steady as she poured a fresh cup of tea. "Or worn the Bocannon I gave you." Her back protested – sleeping corseted and slumped in one of the most uncomfortable chairs her house possessed was *not* likely to give her a happy mood upon awakening. She had chosen the chair deliberately, thinking its discomforts might stave off the resultant exhaustion of a night of hunting through the glittering whirl of a ball, waiting for her quarry to slip.

There was one duke fewer in Londinium this morning, and one more traitor in the Tower to be judged and beheaded as befitted a nobleman. The evidence was damning, and Emma knew every particle of it. Should Cailesborough somehow bribe his way free . . .

. . . well, there was a reason the Queen called on one such as herself to tidy loose ends, was there not?

Tidiness was one of Emma Bannon's specialities. It was, she often reflected, one of the few assets a childhood spent in a slum could grant one.

"I suspected you were rather busy yourself, Miss Bannon." Archibald Clare's lean mournful face was alarmingly pale. He accepted the cup, and there was no tremor in his capable, large-knuckled hands. "It seemed a trifle."

Oh, yes, Dr Vance, a "trifle". Very well. "No doubt it was." She poured her own cup, keeping her gaze on the amber liquid. "Did you discover what the trifle was after?"

"A certain artefact of Ægyptian provenance." Clare shifted, fretting at the rug over his bony knees. He was alarmingly gaunt.

Of course, he had not been a guest at her table as frequently as had been his wont, these last few months. She would have half suspected his friendship had cooled, had she not known of his obsession with Vance. "Hm." She decided the noncommittal noise was not enough of an answer. "Clare, if you do not wish to tell me, that is all very well. But do not oblige me to drag the admission from you by force. Simply note it is not my affair, and we shall turn to other subjects."

"Such is not the case at all." He shifted again. "I thought it would bore you. Your feelings on Dr Vance are known to me."

"My feelings, as you so delicately put it, are simply that you spend altogether too much time brooding over the man. Rather as a swain moons over his beloved." She set her cup down, delicately speared another banger with a dainty silver fork. Fortunately, her physical reserves were a fairly simple matter to replenish, and Tideturn's golden flood of ætheric energy had flushed her – and her jewellery – with usable sorcerous force. Any remaining exhaustion could be pushed aside, for the moment.

Clare's silence informed her she had hit a nerve. For a mentath driven by logic, he certainly was tender-skinned sometimes. A misting of fine rain beaded the windows, the droplets murmuring in their own peculiar Language as they steamed against golden charter charms.

"This artefact would not happen to be the Eye of Bhestet, would it?" She cut with a decided motion, her spine absolutely straight. *Tiny bites, as a lady should.* The ghost of a wasp-waisted Magistra Prima at the Collegia walked decorously through her memory: a familiar song of black watered-silk skirts.

Prima Grinaud had been a harsh teacher, but a consistent and ruthlessly judicious one. There was much to emulate in the woman, even if her cruelty was legendary among the Collegia's children. Primes were notoriously long-lived, but Grinaud seemed to be kept on this side of the great curtain of Being by sheer wormwood and gall.

Clare's silence deepened. He did look rather ill, she decided, glancing in his direction just briefly enough to ascertain this. *Perhaps I should not tell him.* Perhaps, instead, she could enquire as to the odd substance he had been dosing himself with? It had not tasted healthful at all.

He finally spoke. "Stolen. Of *course*. He must have given me the slip in Thrushneedle. Bloody *hell*."

"It was in the broadsheets this morning." And yes, she definitely regretted telling him. "The Museum is most embarrassed. Speculation is rampant as to the culprit. I am . . . sorry, Clare. If you like—"

"He is a *mentath*, Miss Bannon." Frosty, and polite, a tone he rarely used. He was pale, his eyes glittering harshly. The rug over his knees creased itself as he fidgeted precisely once. "Illogic and *sorcery* are not applicable tools to catch him."

Well, you've been doing a fine job of it with your vaunted deductions. She occupied herself with another nibble of banger. Greasy, satisfying, hot, delicious. Just what it should be. When she was certain she had a firm hold on her temper, she spoke. "Perhaps not. More toast? Cook remembers your fondness for kippers as well."

But Clare was staring morosely into his teacup. "So close," he mumbled. "And . . . ah, yes. Definitely in Thrushneedle. He was only out of sight for a moment, damn him. Even Ludo—"

"Yes, Ludovico." Irritation made her own manner sharper than she liked. "I told him to take great care with you, and *this* is what happens. You could have died, sir, and that would distress me *most* profoundly."

There. It was said. The entire breakfast room rang with uncomfortable silence. She speared another tiny piece of sausage with quite unaccustomed viciousness.

"I do not mean to be the source of distress." He still stared into his teacup as if he would find Vance's whereabouts in its depths. "I simply—"

"The man is not a danger to the Crown." She did her best to utter it as a simple statement of fact. "He is a thief. A passing-good one, a mentath who uses his talents for vice, but in the end, merely a thief. He is *not* worth such attention, Clare. Her Majesty would prefer your consideration turned elsewhere. You are, after all, one of the Queen's Own." She eyed the glittering ring on her second left finger, a delicate confection of marcasite and silver, ætheric force thrumming in its depths visible to Sight. "There are other matters to be attended to."

"I should simply let him go, after he has thumbed his nose at—"

"Clare."

"He stole from the Museum—"

"Clare."

"Damn it, the man is a menace to—"

"*Archibald.*"

He subsided. Emma found her appetite gone. She set her implements down and fixed him with a glare he might have found quelling had he not still been staring into his teacup. *Oh, for God's sake.*

"I would take it as a kindness," she informed him, stiffly, "if you would convalesce here. Ludovico was sent this morning to gather such of your effects – and such things pertaining to the cases you have been neglecting while you chase your art professor – as are necessary for your comfort during such an extended stay." She restrained herself from further lecture with a marked effort of will.

"I suppose the servants have been informed of my tender condition." He even managed to wheeze a little.

And furthermore informed that you are not to stir one step outside this house unless it is under my care and my express orders. "You suppose correctly. You have been fretting yourself absolutely dry over this Vance character, Archibald. Pray do not force me to immure you in your room like Lady Chandevault."

He finally looked directly at her, blinking owlishly, looking more mournful and basset-hound-like than ever. "Who? Oh, that. Miss Bannon – *Emma*. There is no need for concern. It was merely angina, which is common enough. I am not so young, and certain—"

Was she the only one to notice the lines at the corners of his mouth, the bleariness of his blue gaze? And the terrible fragility of him, hunched in a chair with the laprobe tucked carefully about him. Emma opened her mouth to take him to task and turn the conversation to what manner of substance he had been dosing himself with, but was interrupted by the door opening without so much as a polite knock to warn the room's occupants.

It was Mikal, his dark hair slightly disarranged and his coat somewhat askew. He must have been at a Shield's morning practice, for Eli was hard on his heels. "An envelope, Prima." Mikal's mouth was a thin line. "From the Palace."

"Ah." *So soon?* But treachery did not wait for mannerly visiting hours, she reminded herself. "Some fresh crisis, no doubt. Archibald, finish your breakfast. It seems there are other matters for me to attend to."

He looked strangely stricken, and sought to rise as she did. She waved him back down. "No, no. Please, do not. Concentrate on your recovery, or I shall be not only vexed but downright peeved with you. A fate worse than death, I'm sure." Her sally only received the faintest of smiles, but she had no time to remark upon his sudden high colour and the steely glint in his tired, bloodshot blue eyes.

For the envelope Mikal deposited in her hands bore a familiar hand on its front, and the seal – heavy and waxen – was Victrix's personal device.

The Queen called, and her faithful servant hurried to obey, leaving the mentath to breakfast and loneliness.

Chapter Five

With No One to Scold

Shut me up like a child, will you? Clare's pipe puffed fragrant tabac-smoke, furiously. He glowered at the grate, unable to enjoy the comforts of a charming, familiar Mayfair room. *There are other matters for you to attend to. More important ones, surely.*

He was, perhaps, being ridiculous.

Perhaps? No. You are definitely *being ridiculous.*

It did not sting so much that Miss Bannon had taken him to task. What pinched was that she was *correct* in doing so. He had been rather lax when it came to his duty to the Queen.

But Vance was such a damn nuisance. And it was *twice* now that Clare had been outplayed rather badly by the man. It most certainly did not help that there was no earthly reason why the sodding brute would want the statue of

Bhestet, carven from a single priceless blue gem. It was more of a gauntlet, a game, than an actual theft.

A game Clare had lost; a gauntlet he had not returned.

His pipe-puffing slowed, turned meditative. Tabac smoke rose in a grey veil, and near the ceiling it crackled, a charm activating to shape it into a globe of compressed mist, whisking it towards the fireplace and up the chimney. That was new, and he could almost see Miss Bannon's pleased expression when he mentioned that such a thing was dashed illogical but useful enough.

What was Vance, to him? Clare was one of the Queen's Own mentaths, his registration secure and his retirement assured by pension, since he had rendered such signal services during a few affairs of interest to the Crown. The first had, of course, been the most strenuous. And no few of the following affairs had involved Miss Bannon as well. They were rather an effective pair of operatives, Clare had to admit. Miss Bannon was very . . . logical, for a sorceress. Her capacity was admirable, her ruthlessness and loyalty both quite extraordinary, especially for a woman. Clare had his career, and Miss Bannon's regard, and his own not-inconsiderable list of achievements. What did Vance have? A chair at a university he had been hounded from, a dead wife and a respectable career gone . . .

. . . a criminal empire, and the Eye of Bhestet, now. And the satisfaction of winning.

Clare puffed even more slowly. Perhaps he should take a fraction of coja while he meditated upon the question of Dr Vance and his own response to the man?

At that precise moment, however, there was a token knock at the door, and Valentinelli slunk in, his pox-scarred face a thundercloud. He carried two Gladstones, and behind him trooped the cadaverous Finch supervising two footmen and a charm-cart carrying a brace of trunks.

Horace, and Gilburn. Clare found their names and the mental drawers holding their particulars with no difficulty. Like all Miss Bannon's servants, they had their peculiarities. Horace was missing half the smallest finger on his left hand, and Gilburn's slow, stately pace was less the result of decorum than of his Altered left leg – everything below the knee was gone, due to an accident Clare had not quite gained the details of yet, replaced with a tibia and fibula of slender dark metal chased with pain-suppressant and oiling charms; the limb terminated in a clockwork foot that was a marvel of delicate architecture. Miss Bannon had remarked once that she had contracted especially for the Alteration, since Gilburn had received great injury in her service, and the man had blushed, ducking his head like a schoolboy. For all that, he was quiet and well-oiled, and Horace often tucked his mutilated finger away or wore a glove with padding to hide it.

The more Clare saw of Miss Bannon's servants, the more he suspected quite a tender heart behind the sorceress's fearsome ruthlessness. Or perhaps Miss Bannon knew that there was no gratitude quite like that of a disfigured servant given back his or her pride and held to high expectations of performance.

And no loyalty like that of an outcast given a home.

It was a testament to the complexity of the sorceress's character that Clare could not quite decide which or what combination of considerations led to her policy.

"Eh, *mentale*." Ludovico dropped both heavy leather bags near the fireplace. "Where you want the trunks?"

"I am certain wherever those excellent fellows choose to set them will be *quite* proper." Clare made a small movement with his still fuming pipe. "Did you bring my alembics?"

"Am I your *donna di servizio*? Pah!" The Neapolitan made as if to spit, but visibly considered better of it. "Baerbarth will bring *those*. He is still packing."

Dear God. "I do not intend to abuse Miss Bannon's hospitality to such a degree—"

"Oh, what *you* intend and what *la strega* intend, they are not the same." Ludo waved one dusky, calloused hand. "I have letters, too." He toed one of the Gladstones and crouched to unbuckle it, keeping a wary eye on the two footmen. "Many, many letters."

Clare suppressed a groan.

"Will you be needing these unpacked, sir?" Gilburn said, laboriously seeking to disguise his heavy Dorset accent.

"Yes *indeed*." Valentinelli snorted. "*I* am not unpacking, and he is weak as kitten."

"For God's sake, I'm not an invalid!" Clare prepared himself to take issue with this treatment.

"Do you rise from that chair, sir, I shall make certain you reoccupy it just as swiftly." It was Clare's least favourite of Valentinelli's voices, the crisp consonants and upper-crust drawl of a bored Exfall student. The Neapolitan often employed such an accent when he felt Clare to be behaving ridiculously in some manner. "For the time being, we are abusing Miss Bannon's hospitality roundly." His tone changed a fraction as he dove into one of the Gladstones. "I thought we lost you last night, *mentale*."

"It was merely a trifle, my good man. Merely a bit of chest pain—"

"You make a bad liar, sir." Valentinelli nodded as the footmen began unbuckling the trunks. "Here, I bring your post to your chair, as good valet should."

I do not need any damn letters or *a thrice-damned Neapolitan valet. What I need is to catch Vance and put him in the bloody dock, and for you and Miss Bannon to cease this ridiculousness.* Still, duty called, and Clare's legs were decidedly unsteady. It was, he had to admit, a relief to have some of his effects brought to him. Except for the galling fact of Dr Vance's escape, a stay at 34½ Brooke Street did sound quite pleasant. Tonic, even.

But being treated like a child was insufferable. He sank into silence, even the soothing tabac smoke overpowered by quite reasonable irritation.

"Here." Valentinelli brought the lapdesk, a cunningly constructed item of wood inlaid with hammered brass. A fat sheaf of paper – envelopes, with varying handwriting, all addressed to *Mr Archibald Clare, Esq.* – landed atop it, and Valentinelli busied himself with exchanging the bowl of pipe ash at Clare's elbow with a fresh cut-crystal tray, then scooping up a pen, ivory letter opener, and a silver-chased ink bottle from the massive table in the centre of the apartment. "You are like *la suocera* with none to scold."

Clare could have cheerfully cursed at him, and perhaps would have, had they been at his own address. His landlady, the redoubtable Mrs Ginn, did not like Valentinelli, and Clare wondered what she thought of this turn of events.

With a sigh, he turned himself to the first envelope. It was addressed from Lancashire, the handwriting female and gently bred, even if the ink was cheap. Impoverished gentry, probably seeking some guess as to the whereabouts of a missing husband.

There were precious few surprises in any piece of mail he opened, and his faculties rebelled at the slow rot triggered by want of proper use. That was half the trouble – Vance and his exploits were, at least, *interesting*.

Another heavy sigh, and Clare opened the envelope. *Duty. Ever duty.*

Perhaps Miss Bannon's responsibilities weighed as onerously as his, but she certainly never seemed *bored*.

Dear Sir, I am writing to you in great distress . . . my husband Thomas has disappeared and . . .

Another deep, tabac-scented, involuntary sigh, and Clare set to work.

Chapter Six

One of Our Own

It was an occasion of little pomp, but great publicity.

"You may approach." Alexandrina Victrix, Britannia's chosen vessel, ruler of the Isles and Empress of Indus, sat straight-backed on her gem-laden throne, the Stone of Scorn underneath one leg glowing soft silver. The hexagonal Throne Room, its vast glass ceiling full of rainy Londinium mornlight, was nevertheless full of shadowed corners behind and between marble columns, and in one such corner was a deeper shadow.

Emma held the glamour soft and still, though an alert observer would catch any movement she made, or perhaps a gleam from her jewellery. True invisibility was difficult and painfully draining, but simply blending into shadow was so easy as to be childishly entertaining. Mikal was a soft-breathing warmth at her back, and Eli would be in the gallery above, moving silent as a fish in deep water.

He hunted best while drifting.

The Queen's dark hair frothed in ringlets near her ears, the back put up as a married woman's should be, and her soft face blurred like clay under running water. Her eyes had turned infinitely dark, tiny speckles of starlight in their depths as the ruling spirit of the Isle woke slightly and peered out of its vessel. The Queen's youthful figure had thickened, pregnancy swelling the outline of the girl Emma Bannon had sworn service to.

That oath was private and unspoken, and Emma was of the secret opinion that Britannia, as ageless and wise as She was, did not quite comprehend the nature of the sorceress's commitment.

Perhaps it was for the best. What queen would wish to know of the depths of service one born in the gutters could sink to?

Alberich, Prince and Consort, stood to the Queen's right, instead of using the smaller chair he was wont to occupy during interminable receptions or state business. The Consort, an aristocrat of Saxon-Kolbe, was a fine figure of a man with a lovely moustache and a dashing mien in the uniform he affected, but he took a dim view of sorcery in general and his influence upon Victrix, while of the moderating variety, was also . . . uncertain.

He, Emma thought, as she did every time she glimpsed him, *bears watching*.

There were few of the elect in the Throne Room for

this event, but at least two of them – Constance, Lady Ripley (christened "Constant, Lady Gossip" by the broadsheets) and the red-jacketed, portly Earl of Dornant-Burgh – could be counted to carry tales. That was their function, and Emma's shoulders were cable-tight under blue satin.

There, approaching the throne in a wide-sweeping formal dress of rose-coloured silk, was the reason for this concern: the Queen's formidable mother, the Duchess of Kent.

She was still a handsome woman, though growing much stouter as the years passed. An examination of her aquiline but pleasing face with its open, frank expression would lead one to believe her of a light and frivolous disposition, if one was extraordinarily stupid. There were plenty who ascribed to the view that the Duchess had been easily led by her comptroller Conroy into keeping Victrix under a stifling System of rules and etiquette that not so incidentally never allowed her contact with those her mother deemed unsuitable; others thought the Duchess's raising of the princess and later heir-presumptive merely suffered from a mother's natural but overly indulged desire to shield her child from all harm, real or imagined.

The truth perhaps lay somewhere between the two, on an island of ambition shrouded with syrup-sentiment and a frustrated will to rule. The Duchess would have made a fine prince of some foreign country, had she been chosen as a vessel . . . or a trouble indeed, if born a man.

Emma eyed the Duchess's stiff posture as the mother of the Queen made the merest courtesy demanded of a sovereign's family member. The necklace the woman wore, Emma decided, was far too gaudy to be anything but real gems; she was not wearing paste yet, this blue-blooded and cold-calculating princess. *Despite* Conroy's "management" of her estates and benefices, that was.

Victrix sat, utterly inhumanly still, only her eyes showing that Britannia was examining the woman who had given birth to her vessel, and examining her closely.

The sorceress's fingers tightened. The cameo at her throat warmed, ætheric force held in the piece responding to her mood. It would be so easy to strike the Duchess down, and she could even beg Victrix's forgiveness afterwards. Not every conspiracy threatening Victrix's rule had its origins in the Duchess's desire to bring her daughter back under her sway, true.

But the ones that *did* were . . . most troubling. There had been a certain affair involving a tower in Wales, a slumbering wyrm, and an army of unsleeping metal soldiers some time ago. It had also involved a Sorcerer Prime, and Emma's unease heightened another notch.

She *would* think of Llewellyn now, wouldn't she? There was a warm weight in her chest that grew a trifle heavier when she did. It was not the Stone that had been her private recompense for the affair, she had decided. Perhaps it was merely the consciousness of how close he had come to succeeding? Each separate part of that conspiracy had been working to different ends, but Llewellyn Gwynnfud's envisioned end had put the other parties to shame in sheer flamboyance and scope.

He would have been delighted to know she thought as much.

Victrix will not take it kindly if I kill her mother, no matter what the woman has done. And no matter if Britannia roundly approves.

Seen from this angle, the Duchess's beauty had faded considerably since her youth. Yet her eyebrows were the same high proud arches, and the long nose and decided chin were balanced by good cheekbones. A handsome woman, still.

Handsome enough to keep a lover, perhaps. Or her estates were certainly attractive enough to gain some attention.

Those in attendance had already noted that Conroy, normally his mistress's squire and shadow, was not present. If the pale-eyed, silk-voiced comptroller had decided to slip into the gallery to witness this exchange, Eli would neatly collar him . . . and Emma Bannon would have a small sharp chat with the man.

This was not Victrix's wish, but Emma had privately decided Sir John Conroy had become far too dangerous to wait upon handling. Perhaps it was arrogance on her part, to see so clearly a danger Victrix underestimated, and to set herself to drawing its venom. Or perhaps it was merely her duty. The two blurred together distressingly easily.

"Your Majesty." The Queen's mother repeated her courtesy, but more deeply. "It gladdens my heart to see my daughter."

Her words had an edge that only a sorceress, a lifelong student of tone and cadence and what remains unspoken, might hear.

No, that was not quite precise. It was also the tone a mother could use to chastise a grown child, treacle-sweet but loaded with private significance.

Emma's fingers twitched. At least Melbourne, nasty skinflint that he was, had given the young Queen her first taste of what passed for the freedom of rule. Victrix still believed most things possible, most things available, instead of seeing choice and circumstance narrow about her like a lunatic's canvas jacket.

Victrix raised her chin slightly. "Madam." Today she wore the Little Crown, its diamonds sparking as Britannia's presence spilled through her skin; she was not formally in state even though enthroned. To sit in state would have accorded the Duchess too much importance. At least Victrix had agreed when Emma made *that* observation. "We greet you."

We. Victrix hiding behind Britannia, or a sign that the ruling spirit was unwilling to take her gaze from a potential danger?

The Duchess's smile faltered slightly. "I would that I saw you more frequently, my dearest. But you have such important matters to attend to."

Emma was hard put to stifle a gasp. To speak so *familiarly* to Britannia might have earned one a spell in the Tower in less civilised days.

Victrix's head tilted slightly to the side, her features

shifting imperceptibly. To see the sweet face of a married-but-still-young woman age so rapidly, Britannia filling her vessel as the Themis filled its cold bed, was enough to send a chill through even the stoutest heart.

"Important matters." Victrix's fingers tapped the throne's arm, precisely once. She did not move to cover her belly with a protective hand, but it may have been very close. Rings glittered, scintillating not with ætheric force as Emma's jewellery might, but with a different brand of power. "Have you ever been to Wales, dear Mama?"

Emma's pulse beat high and hard in her throat. She had not expected this.

"Wales?" To her credit, the Duchess sounded confused.

"Dinas Emrys. A property of the house of Gwynnfud, or Sellwyth if you prefer their title." Victrix was pale now, and the depth of Britannia in her star-laden eyes spread, a haze of indigo fanning from the corners. Alberich made a restless movement, as if he longed to touch the Queen's shoulder, his white-gloved hand halting in mid-air and dropping back to rest at his side.

Good. If he did not respect her, we would have even more trouble. Respect was not quite enough, though. It would, she thought, do the Consort no end of good to outright fear his wife.

Sometimes a man's fear was a woman's only defence.

The Duchess was pale too. The lace of her cap quivered on either side of her face – she had affected a truly matronly headgear for the occasion. "I do not believe I have had the pleasure, my dearest." Not so vivacious now.

"I have not either, of late." Victrix's gaze swung away, roving over the few of the peerage who remained in the room – and her Chancellor of the Exchequer, Lord Craighley. The last Chancellor but one, Grayson, had vanished in mysterious circumstances; some whispered of embezzlement and of a retreat to the Continent. Others, very softly, whispered of sorcery.

It was Emma Bannon who saw to it they did not whisper overly loudly, or for very long. Sometimes it did not do to have the truth bruited about.

"I have not either," Victrix repeated, her tone sharpening. "But I think upon it often, Mother. The Sellwyths were treacherous *worms* of old, were they not?"

The Duchess of Kent trembled. It took a sharp eye to see, but Emma Bannon's gaze was indeed pointed, and she saw the quiver in the older woman's skirts. *Very well done, Your Majesty.*

"Alexandrina . . ." The Duchess's lips shaped a bloodless whisper.

"You may remove yourself from Our sight, Duchess." Victrix's tone took on new weight, and the shadows in the Throne Room thickened. Each gem on her chair or her person was a point of hurtful brilliance. "Thou'rt confirmed in thy titles and estates. But We shall not suffer thee in Our presence."

Emma loosened her fists, deliberately, one finger at a time. Had she truly doubted Victrix's ability to handle this confrontation? And so neatly, too.

The Duchess, to give her credit, paid a most steady

courtesy to Britannia. It was odd – the pale drawn look she wore now suited her, lending a shadow of slender youth to her features. Her dark eyes burned as live coals, and Emma wished she were more visible, so she could catch the lady's gaze. It was no doubt overweening pride . . . but she wished the Duchess knew she was witnessing this embarrassment.

The Queen's mother took the prescribed three steps backwards, her skirts swaying drunkenly. The shadow of Britannia retreated, pearly rain-washed morning light filling the vast glass-roofed expanse again. Victrix's gaze was no longer starred with the speckles of infinite night. No, it was human again, and her eyes were dark with very human pain.

"Mother," she said, suddenly and very clearly. "*I* am reconciled to thee. But *We* are not."

Well, Lady Gossip and Lord Tale-A-Plenty will spread that far and wide. Good.

Victrix rose, and there was a great rustling as all courtesied or bowed, and the Queen swept from the Throne Room on her Consort's arm. He murmured something to her, and Victrix's pained sigh was audible in the heavy silence.

Emma found herself smiling. It was, she suspected, not a pleasant smile, and she composed her features before allowing the glamour to fold itself away. There was no reason to remain in shadow now. It was against the spirit of Victrix's commands, and yet . . .

She needn't have bothered. The Duchess stalked from the Throne Room with her head held high, amid a wash of tittering whispers and buzzes. The morning's event would be digested and re-chewed in drawing rooms around Londinium by lunchtime, and halfway across the Continent by supper. Those who paid court to Kent, believing she had some influence, would fall away.

This will only make her next gambit more subtle and hence, possibly more dangerous. And where is her hangman? Is he about?

It was unlike Conroy to let an opportunity pass, and Emma had made certain that a delicate insinuation of the restoration of royal favour had dropped in his ear – and thus in the Duchess's. An effective feint, and satisfaction was had.

But he had not shown, which made the satisfaction tarnish slightly.

A tingle ran along her nerves. She raised her chin slightly, her gaze taking in the entire columned expanse of the Throne Room in one sweep. The brush of ætheric force retreated hastily, and her attention snagged on the opposite side of the room, where a gleam pierced another shadowed corner.

Another player, or merely an onlooker? Interesting.

She was now, after witnessing this exchange, to attend the Queen in private. There were other matters than a mother put firmly in her place requiring the attention of a Sorceress Prime in Britannia's service. Still, she lingered, allowing herself to become still and receptive, her consciousness dilating.

It was no use. The other sorcerer had felt her attention

shift, and was already gone. There was a side door close by, a twin to the one Emma stood near, and probably chosen for the very same reason she had selected this spot.

Something about such precaution did not quite sit well. *Bother.* It mattered little; if there were another player at the table, soon enough he – or she – would slip and show a hand. Emma shelved the question and gathered her skirts, Mikal's step leaf-light behind her as she set a course for the door.

With a murmur of thanks, Emma lowered herself into the wide, heavy chair Victrix indicated with a wave of one jewelled hand.

"*Do* sit, Miss Bannon, that was *quite . . .*" Quite what, the Queen paused, as if unable to just yet define. Now, she clasped her hands over her rounded belly, wincing slightly. She had just begun to show, and so soon after the last. At least there was no shortage of prospective heirs, though Britannia had shown little interest in any of them to date. "Quite . . ."

Uncomfortable? Liberating, and yet terrifying? I can only imagine. Emma contented herself with a simple, "Thank you, Your Majesty." *After all, I have no mother or father, merely the Collegia. I cannot imagine.*

The Prince Consort, his features pale and mournful behind the fine moustache, busied himself at a rather graceless mahogany sideboard. The hefty apple-figured drapes, overstuffed brocaded sophas and spindly gilt chairs were overdone, rather in the manner of a royal idea of what a respectable country gentleman's drawing room would contain, albeit envisioned without any proper visit to such a space to discern its peculiarities.

In short, it was very much like the doomed Queen Marette Antoinette's faux farm-village. The ruling spirit of France had not recovered from the bloody end its last vessel had undergone, and there were whispers that the freebooters first of the *Révolution* and then of the thrice-damned Corsican had slaughtered every child of the royal lines, both ancillary and direct, to keep Gallica from rising again.

Such things could happen without those strong, cunning, and yes, brutal enough to safeguard the vessel's person. No doubt another ruling spirit would rise, or Gallica would resurface eventually.

There were even whispers that some of the Corsican's line were showing . . . signs. Emma was still undecided whether judicious assassination should be suggested – oh, very delicately indeed. Victrix had certain regrettable qualms that would hopefully fade with the passage of time – and the lessons of ruling an Empire.

A weakened France was a help to Britannia, but not *overly* weak. Used as a shield and balanced against the Germans, not to mention Austro-Angary, she was a useful tool. A Gallican vessel sympathetic – or beholden – to Britannia, within reason, was an asset to be considered and planned for.

Emma folded her hands sedately. Victrix's long glittering earrings trembled as their wearer shook, and the sorceress averted her eyes, studying the curtains, counting the gold threads worked in stylised apple-shapes. The room was windowless, the drapes only softening bare stone walls. It was an apt metaphor for the illusion of absolute power. Trammelled in a stone cube, the ruling spirit of an Empire the sun never set upon was no more than a daughter reeling with helpless frustration and quite possibly a measure of despair.

Even the meanest of Britannia's servants were free to do things their monarch could not.

That is a dangerous thought. Turn your attention aside. Is it safe here? In the very bowels of Buckingham Palace, they could be reasonably certain of little physical threat.

Privacy was another issue entirely. Especially with a pair of unfriendly ears in the room.

Oh, the Prince Consort was not unfriendly to Victrix. Not at all. His animosity, tinged lemon-yellow and very visible to Sight, was directed to another quarter entirely.

"That went well." Victrix, softly. The Little Crown still perched, winking, atop her dark hair. She was pale, and her eyes were merely, humanly dark. "Rather well indeed."

Emma nodded. "Yesmum." Equally soft, her tone conciliatory and soothing as possible. She continued her examination of the drapes, the gaslamps hissing softly and their flames much better for her sensitive eyes than harsh sunlight.

"We think . . ." But the Queen did not continue. Alberich brought her a small glass – *vitae*, Emma discerned, smelling of lavender and threatening to unsettle her stomach. How anyone could drink *that* was beyond her. But it was a lady's draught, as popular now as ratafia had been during the time of the Mad Georgeth and his regent son.

Had Britannia felt the echo of her chosen vessel's madness? Did such a thing leach into the ruling spirit? Those she ruled might never know, and never know why Britannia chose not to leave Georgeth until the bitter end. Who were they to question the spirit of the Isles?

Who was anyone? Still, Emma found herself curious.

The Prince Consort sank into a chair at the Queen's side, picked up her small gloved and ringed hand, chafed it gently between his own. He cast a dark, disapproving glance at Emma, who affected not to notice.

"Emma." As if the Queen had to remind herself who precisely the woman sitting in one of her chairs was.

Now was the moment to turn her gaze to Victrix's face. So Emma did, wishing she had not left Mikal in the hallway outside. It would be . . . comforting, to have him close. Rather too comforting, and hence a weakness. She banished the thought, bringing all her considerable attention to bear. "Yes, Your Majesty. I attend."

"No doubt," the Consort muttered bleakly, as if he expected Emma not to hear.

"Alberich." Victrix's tone held a warning, but a mild one. "Lady Sellwyth is highly capable, and has earned Our trust in numerous affairs."

"Sellwyth. A worm's name." The Prince Consort patted her hand again. "You said so yourself."

An angry flush sought to rise to Emma's cheeks. She

quelled it, iron training denying flesh its chance to distract her. What would this princeling know of the battle atop Dinas Emrys, the knife sunk in the back of the only Sorcerer Prime who had ever matched her, and the danger she had averted? Had she failed . . .

. . . but she had not, and the little man was not the first to cast aspersions. *Sellwyth*, Britannia's fanged reward for her part in the affair, and an insurance that a possible key to the Colourless Wyrm's waking was in safe hands.

Safe, long-lived hands. Emma kept said appendages decorously loose in her lap. To take umbrage or even acknowledge the remark would overstep the bounds of propriety, but such a consideration did not halt her as much as it should. Instead, the genuine regard Victrix showed for the man made her refrain. *And* the fact that he seemed to wish to be a shield for her at Court and in the game of politics. Even though Britannia was the spirit of rule, there were still other factors to account for, and other centres of power to be balanced – and carefully stacked, so that the spirit of the Isle was not forced to certain acts.

No, the Saxon-Kolbe pretender to a seat less than an Englene county was not worthy of Emma's ire.

Still, this will be added to the list of insults I remember. Odd, how that list grows and grows.

"Alberich." The warning was less mild now. "Do not."

"Sorceress." The Prince Consort shook his head. But he subsided, and Victrix chose not to take him to task.

It was not, Emma reflected, that he found the arts of æther overly problematic. Charm and charter, sorcerers and witches, were to be found in his homeland as well. It was the fact of Emma's sex that gave the Prince Consort lee to insult, suspect and provoke her. She had long since grown as used to such treatment as daily exposure could make one.

"Emma." Victrix sighed, and Britannia rose under her features again. The sorceress held herself very still, but the ruling spirit retreated with an unheard rushing, a tide soughing back to the ocean's embrace. "One of Our Own is missing."

She absorbed the statement and its implications. "Sorcerer, or . . .?"

"A physicker. Merely genius, We believe. A Mr John Morris. You are familiar with a certain Mr Rudyard?"

Emma nodded. Her curls swung, and the rings on her left hand sparked slightly. *Dear old Kim. Lovely.* "He is visiting again, then." Master sorcerers and Adepts lived long, but not nearly as long as Primes, of course. Rudyard courted death with a disdain and ferocity matched only by his single-minded dedication to Queen and Empire.

Slum-children, both of them, and if Rudyard despised Emma for the fact of her greater talent and the insult of her femininity, she could easily despise him in return for his violent arrogance, since she knew its source.

The trouble was, that arrogance sounded an echo in her own self, much as Llewellyn Gwynnfud's had. And Rudyard, well, had been *quite* attached to Llew in his own way.

Had he received word of Lord Sellwyth's mysterious

disappearance? It was very likely. And equally likely that he would suspect Emma of having a hand in said mystery.

For God – and Kim Rudyard – would both know that no other Prime could have faced Llew and survived. Or was that her own arrogance, again? Such an unfeminine trait.

"He is at the Rostrand." The Queen's expression suggested she was mystified, and Emma was hard put to hide a smile. "We are told he has . . . a monkey."

I am certain he does. Half-smile, half-pained grimace, Emma dispelled the expression before it could truly reach the architecture of her face. "How droll."

"He was the one to discover the physicker's absence. He will have the particulars for you."

And that is very curious. Rudyard come to Englene's shores and discovering such a thing? "Yes, Your Majesty." Emma waited. *Is that all? A physicker absconding, a mere genius? Not even a mentath?* But she did not press further.

She never had, beyond *by your leave* or *if I may*. If she could not guess, she would wait to be told, and keep her thoughts to herself. The principle had stood her in marvellous good stead in dealing with royalty.

It was also of good use when dealing with enemies, or potential enemies. Which covered a great deal of the globe's surface, no doubt.

The Prince Consort was breathing heavily through his nose, a huffing that denoted both unease with the proceedings and disdain for this common-born hussy who dared to sit, even when invited to do so, in the presence of Britannia.

Finally, Victrix nodded. She smoothed the fabric over her rounded belly, her fingers stippling over the loose corseting recommended at this juncture for supporting the distension of generation. "That will be all. Should you find Mr Morris, bring him to Our presence. But gently. We require him whole."

"I shall be as a mother cat with a kitten." Emma did not move. What would it feel like, to swell and split with a screaming little thing, a new life? Did she choose to breed, she would find out . . . but not yet. Though it was held to be a woman's highest happiness, she could forgo a little longer. "By your leave, then, Your Majesty?"

"Most certainly." Victrix's sigh was heavy. Even the Little Crown weighed terribly, and what was it like to host a being as ancient and headstrong as Britannia? Was it like a sorcerer opening himself to his Discipline, and becoming merely the throat a song moved through? At least a sorcerer knew the song would recede, and was trained to bear the shock of being simply an empty cup.

Emma Bannon rose, paid her courtesy. She did not acknowledge the Prince Consort. She left the room with a determined step and a rustle of skirts, uncaring if he took offence. It would serve the petty little man right.

Victrix wishes me to find a man. I should find Clare's doctor as well, and make them both happy.

She was, she realised, quite unsettled. It was not Alberich of Saxon-Kolbe's shot across her bow that worried her.

It was the fact that Conroy had not been in attendance this morning, and the Duchess of Kent had been far too easily disposed of.

I smell a rat. Later, of course, she would chide herself for being so exercised over what could have been coincidence . . . but at the moment, Emma Bannon was distracted, and in any case, how could she have known? Even a Prime could not tell the future with a certainty.

For now, she had her orders, the die was cast, and she winged towards her prey as a good merlin should.

Chapter Seven

An Admirer

Clare relit his pipe. Fragrant tabac smoke lifted, the charm near the ceiling crackling into life again. Afternoon light slanted through the window, past heavy wine-red velvet drapes and quiescent-glowing charter charms bleached by the sun's glow.

They had finally left him in peace. Valentinelli was no doubt in the kitchen, stuffing his pocked face and tormenting broad genial Cook; the footmen had gone about their business. The comfortable, dark-wainscoted room felt much smaller now, since his effects were unpacked over the table and into the capacious wardrobe. A full set of alembics brought by Sigmund Baerbarth – Horace would notify the cadaverous butler, Finch, to procure larger stands for them – and several of his journals were stacked higgledy-piggledy. Perhaps, if Miss Bannon wished him to remain hutched for a long period of time, she would make a workroom available? The sorceress's domicile often seemed larger inside than out, and there were curious . . . crannies, that sometimes seemed to change position.

His long nose twitched at the thought, as if he had detected an unpleasant odour. The irrationality of that thought was an itch under the surface of his skull. Once more he confined the irregularities of 34½ Brooke Street to the mental drawer of complex problems not requiring a solution at the present juncture. Several of Miss Bannon's peculiarities filled even that capacious space to over-flowing.

There was a reason mentath and sorcerer did not often mix.

Clare puffed, and turned his attention to the most inter-esting letter – the one he had left unopened, setting it aside to savour.

It was a joy to have something unknown. The paper was heavy, linen-crafted but not bearing any of the character-istics of a maker Clare was familiar with. Privately made, then? Perhaps. The ink was bitter gall, and a ghost of . . . yes, it was myrrh, clinging to the envelope's texture. It had not been franked, either. Left with Mrs Ginn, for Clare spotted a telltale grease-spot on one corner; the redoubtable woman had been called from her pasty-making, no doubt. Although, Clare allowed, it could merely have been slipped into the postbox, for it was addressed to him very plainly, in a cramped hand that was certainly a gambit meant to disguise the sender. Male, from the way the nib dug into the paper. The simple trick of writing with one's left hand, unless Clare missed his guess.

Oh, this is delicious.

The seal was old-fashioned, a blob of scented wax. Clare inhaled delicately. Yes, that was definitely a breath of myrrh.

A church candle used for sealing. And not just any church, but Reformed Englican of the Saviour. *They* used such a blend of incense in their rituals; and there were only three of their ilk in Londinium, unless Clare had missed one springing up in the last ten years.

Oh, careful, Archibald. Candle-wax is not enough to build a cathedral of reason upon. Remember your own words upon the matter of Assumptions, and how dangerous they are.

The wax crackled and creaked. The symphony of its breaking proved its provenance, but a candle could be stolen. Or the envelope could have been left in a church to absorb its aroma.

Who would go so far?

He suspected. Oh, how he suspected! Another man, not a mentath, would have called the sensation a glorious tension, rather as the moment before a beloved yielded to his embrace. A swelling, a throbbing, a pleasurable itch.

He drew the letter forth. Expensive, to use an envelope rather than writing the address on the outside of a cunningly folded missive. But what was expense, between rivals or lovers? And the envelope would rob him of a deduction caught in a missive's folds.

He sniffed the folded paper, again, so delicately. That same breath of myrrh, with an acrid note that was not the gall of ink.

Sewage. Oh, your escape was closer than I suspected. Good.

A single page, and a message of surpassing simplicity.

Dear Sir, your genius is much appreciated. Please do me the honour of considering me your Friend, not merely a Galling Annoyance. I remain, etc., An Admirer.

Clare's entire frame itched and tingled with anticipation. He closed his eyes, and his faculties burned inside his skull like a star. The two sentences were layered with meaning; even the shape of the letters had to be considered.

"My dear Doctor," he whispered, in the smothering quiet of his invalid's room. "Another game? Very well."

The Neapolitan eyed him narrowly. "I know that look, sir."

"Hm?" Clare absently knocked ash free of his pipe, blinking. "I say, is it afternoon already?"

"*Ci.*" A pile of broadsheets thumped on the cluttered table, and Valentinelli turned slowly in a full circle, his flat dark gaze roving over every surface. "And you are up to mischief."

"I have been sitting here quietly for some hours, my good man." *Merely exercising my faculties in different directions, readying them for another go at the good Doctor.* "Very quietly. Just as an invalid should."

"Ha!" Ludo's hand whipped forward, flashing an obscene gesture very popular on Londinium's docks. "You complain and complain. *La strega* wish to take good care of you, sit and grow fat."

"I do not do well with idleness. You have been my man long enough to know as much." Even to himself he sounded peevish and fretful.

"Today I am not your man. Today I am your *dama di compagnia*." A sneer further twisted his dark unlovely face. "She leave you in Ludo's hand because you are foolish little thing. I told you, a *pistole* would have solved all problems, *pouf*."

You think that if you repeat yourself, I will suddenly agree? "I wished to *catch* the man, not kill him."

"So I shoot to wound. You must have more faith, *mentale*. It is your silly teatime. *La Francese* sent me to collect you."

"Madame Noyon is too kind." Clare stretched, the armchair suddenly uncomfortable as his lanky frame reminded him he had been wrapt in a mentath's peculiar trance for far too long. The flesh, of course, was no fit temple for a soul dedicated to pure logic.

Not that a mentath was purely a logic engine. Their faculties only approximated such a device; sometimes, Clare was even forced to admit that was best. The pursuit of pure logic had dangers even the most devoted of its disciples must acknowledge. Still, it was a frustration almost beyond parallel to feel the weight of physical infirmity as age advanced upon him.

He did not mind it so much as he minded the fear – and yes, it *was* fear, for a mentath was not devoid of Feeling – of the infirmity somehow reaching his faculties. Dimming them, and the glory of logic and deduction fading.

That would be uncomfortably like the Hell the old Church, and even the Church Englican, did spout so much about.

It took him far longer than he liked to reach his feet, setting his jacket to rights with quick brushing movements. His knees were suspiciously, well . . . wibbly. It was the only term that applied.

Ludovico watched, far more closely than was his wont.

"Good God, sir, I am not about to faint." Clare took stock. He was respectable enough for tea, at least.

"You look dreadful." But then the Neapolitan waved away any further conversation. "Come, tea. At least *la Francese* will have *antipasti*. Ludo is hungry. Hurry along."

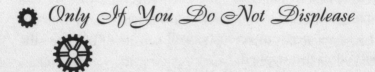

Chapter Eight

Only If You Do Not Displease

The Rostrand was not an old hotel, but it was fit for visiting royalty. Very few of Englene's natives would stay in its luxurious wallow; it was far too *Continental*. The walls were sheathed with kielstone, which meant the native flow of æther would not overly discommode foreign guests with any sorcerous talent. And, not so incidentally, so their own alienness would not create stray harmful bits of irrationality.

Rudyard was not a foreigner, precisely. He had been born in the glare and monsoon of the Indus. Which was practically Empire, true . . . but it still made certain of his talents unreliable when he ventured beyond the subcontinent's borders.

How that must irk him.

It was no great trick to locate him in the coffee room

off the cavernous overdone lobby with its glittering chandelier overhead sparking and hissing with repression charms. Mirrors in gilded frames reflected fashionable plumed hats atop women's curls, the height of Parissian fashion favouring dark rich jewel-colours this year, and men in sober black, a faint look of ill-ease marking every foreigner no matter how expensively dressed. The gaslamps were lit, their light softening each edge and picking out nuances of colour sunlight would bleach. The morning's glamour had not made her overly sensitive, but she still blinked rapidly. Even the rainy light outside was too much, sometimes.

The French were much in evidence today, and Emma's trained glance stored faces while her obedient memory returned names for some of them. Some of the guests here bore watching – the Monacan Ambassador, for one, oiled and sleek and quite fashionable to have in a drawing room lately. His tiny principality did not rate him such importance, and there were certain troubling rumours about his proclivities, both personal and professional, that would require attention sooner or later.

The coffee room was sun-bright and pleasant, done in a rather Eastern style. Sky-blue cushions with gilt tassels, a splendid hookah in a nook by a chimney – most likely defunct, a relic of some travel through a pawnshop – and cages of well-bred canaries cringing under a lash of high-pitched noise.

No, it was not difficult to locate Kim Finchwilliam Rudyard after all. For the small monkey, the ruff around its intelligent little face glowing silver, was screeching fit to pierce eardrums and shatter every single mirror and glass in the Rostrand's atrium.

Several harried employees fluttered about carrying different items perhaps meant to appease the howling beast – or its master. Who sat, apparently unconcerned, in a large leather chair near one of the fireplaces, one of the day's broadsheets open before his lean tanned face.

His cloth was sober and surpassingly fine, his waistcoat not disguising the taut trim frame beneath and his morning coat no doubt the finest the Burlington Estate could produce. Not for him the snappish newness of Savile Row; Rudyard's taste for the most conservative of fashions was an involuntary comment upon what he no doubt fancied was a hidden desire. To be more of the Isle than Britannia Herself would have suited him royally, for all Rudyard was a young and bastard son.

A nose too hawk and cheekbones too broad, a skin deeply tanned by the Indus's fierce sun – but not enough to be native of that dark-spiced country, no. Later he would be as seamed and rough as a nut, but for the time being, he was merely unusual. A gold ring very much like a Lascar's adornment dangled from one earlobe, and his hair was too fair for the Indus and the wrong manner of dark for Britannia. He wore no moustache, and though his colour was not muddy as so many half-castes were, the exotic on him was a dangerous perfume.

She did not see his *kukuhri*-knife with its hilt of sinuous dark carven wood, but that did not mean he was not armed.

Emma took her time approaching him, taking note of the various glances and exclamations from the Rostrand's staff. Mikal touched her shoulder, a fleeting pressure, and she nodded.

Of course he is armed somehow. And you can tell he is of the Indus. I wonder if you will recognise more of him?

The question of how to deal with the screaming monkey was solved as soon as the creature sighted her. For it froze, its mouth wide open and sharp ivory teeth gleaming, its wide white-ringed eyes fixed on Emma.

No, not on her, but over her left shoulder. At Mikal.

Well, that is very interesting.

The sudden silence was almost shattering. The top edge of Rudyard's broadsheet trembled slightly, and Emma came to a halt at a polite distance, eyeing the monkey. It was an odd little creature, and idly she wondered if Victrix would enjoy such a pet. The shrieking might even be a side benefit, to drown out her Consort's gruff-grumbling displeasure. Did the expense of obtaining one balance the satisfaction to be had in its presentation?

Like Clare, she would have to postpone the question for further analysis. Her lips twitched slightly, and she dispelled the rising softness from her features, schooled them into an appropriately firm expression.

The broadsheet's top edge quivered again. Rudyard inhaled, smoothly and slowly.

"Like old dark wine." His baritone, lightly accented, was pleasant enough. "Sorcery's spice, and the dust of the grave. Can it be?" The paper lowered and Rudyard's odd hazel eyes, more gold than green, surveyed her from top to toe. Emma suffered it, the slight well-bred smile frozen to her face. "It can. Well, well." He unfolded himself in a leisurely manner and rose, and rose – he was quite *provokingly* tall.

"Sir . . . *sir*." A rotund man in an ill-cut suit and moist paws for hands bustled officiously into range. "Sir, that *creature*—"

"Is enticing indeed, but I doubt you would wish to lay hand upon it. A poison bloom is she." Rudyard's teeth, just as white as the monkey's, gleamed in a smile, just their tips showing. "The female of her species is deadly."

"As is the assault upon the eardrums from your charming companion," Emma cut in, her tone light, arch, and amused. *Let us see how easy you are to provoke this time. It should lighten my mood immensely to darken yours.* "We shall require champagne, despite the hour, and a private room."

Rudyard's eyebrows lifted. You could see the echo of military bearing in his straight back, weight evenly balanced and his boots sharp-shining. He had been slated for a sepoy's life before his sorcerous talent had manifested itself. "Business, then. Very well."

"Sir . . ." The man – steward or head concierge, perhaps, with an incredibly harried air – next appealed to her. "Madam, that creature, the *creature*—"

She had very little patience for soothing him, though it was perhaps her female duty to do so. "I believe it is called a monkey, and it shall accompany us. Hurry along now, and prepare a private room. Champagne, and some light refreshment."

The man paused, taking stock of her jewellery, her frock, the charming and very expensive hat perched on her curls. Emma suffered this second examination with much less grace than the first, smoothing one gloved wrist with her opposite fingers. "I am not accustomed to such bold treatment, Mr . . .?"

He actually took a step back, paling as he realised his survey of her person was not genteel at all, and further taking note of the quality of her dress and posture, as well as her accent. "Yes. Of course, madam. Happy to. If you will follow me? Harold, champagne! Mr Bruin, refreshments to the Rose Room! I do hope you shall find it accommodating, Mrs . . .?"

"*Miss* Bannon. Mikal, my card." She held Rudyard's gaze with her own. The monkey still had not made a sound, but now it scrambled up the tall man's clothing and perched nimbly on his muscular shoulder. Its fur brushed his hair, and the contrast between the two textures was striking in its own way.

The concierge paled still further as he took in Mikal's leanness as well, the Shield's olive-green velvet coat and the knives worn openly at his hips, and finally realised – for he was no Clare, able to discern the facts of a situation at a glance – that Emma was not merely Quality but *sorceress*, and one powerful enough to require at least one Shield. Mikal produced a cream-coloured *carte* with a flick of his fingers and an unsettling, brilliant, white-toothed smile.

A curious crystalline silence, full of rustling, filled the

coffee room. Rudyard finally took notice of her Shield as well, and his colour underwent almost as interesting a change as the hapless little hotelier's.

The Indus sorcerer said something very fast and low, and – wonder of wonders – actually gave a half-bow, the monkey riding his shoulder with queer grace and managing to stay in place during the entire manoeuvre. It was the first time Emma had seen Rudyard perform such a gesture without a mocking edge, and she cocked her head, replaying the odd words.

No language I know, and not a language of Discipline. Some tongue of the Indus, perhaps?

Even more shocking was Mikal's reply. Her Shield sounded faintly pleased, but the edge to his tone was quite as intriguing as the words themselves. At least he spoke good Englene. "You are forgiven, *Kshatriya*. But only if you do not displease her."

"Your kind have no power on these shores. Nevertheless, I shall endeavour to be pleasant." Rudyard's eyes were suspiciously round, and he very carefully retreated, the broadsheet dropping from nerveless coppery fingers. When he blanched thus, he appeared paradoxically more Indus than Isle, and Emma's pulse leapt before her training flexed itself, controlling her heartbeat and glandular functions so she could act without her body's cries disturbing her concentration. "Come, Bannon." Rudyard reached for his brow, as if to lift a hatbrim, and visibly collected himself. "Your servant, ma'am. In every way."

It was a very good thing she was accustomed to the

Indus sorcerer's mercurial temper from their dual studies at the Collegia, for her jaw was suspiciously loose as the hotelier croaked a pale polite word and managed to bow and scrape the entire way to the Rose Room, whose only claim to roses was the overblown cabbagey herbage on the wallpaper. She observed a decorous pace, glad the coffee room was almost deserted, for this was a scene she would have rather avoided.

If Mikal's presence would frighten the Chessmaster of Lahore, it would certainly make questioning him much less tiresome. And perhaps, she reflected, it was time to turn her attention to the matter of her Shield's provenance.

She had put off that particular question long enough, and that it chose to rear its ugly head now was simply to be expected. The walk did her some good, therefore, since Emma Bannon's hands were, for the first time in a good while, not completely steady.

"Morris? Is that all?" A flute of champagne, bolted as common water might be and followed with a draught from a silver-chased flask, had done wonders to steady the half-Indus. Still, he was rather pale, and his tone far less biting than usual. "What a relief."

The monkey sat in his lap, shivering. Its fur bristled, grey sheen quivering with light that did not sting her eyes. Was it some manner of *animus*? She had read of the Indus sorceries of animal avatars, sometimes employed in place of a Shield to care for a sorcerer's physical well-being. She had never actually witnessed one, and probing at the creature with her non-physical senses would be . . . impolite.

Besides, it might make the man more difficult to handle.

"A guilty conscience, Kim?" She held her own flute, but had not sipped of it yet. The bubbling liquid within trembled slightly, and she studied its fluid gleaming. It was a good pose, and would perhaps hide her discomfiture.

Rudyard did not like being addressed by his Christian name – as an Indus boy instead of a *sir* – and Emma used the resultant pause to marshal her thoughts and calculate her attack. Mikal was at the door, arms folded and his yellow eyes half-lidded, his manner perhaps a trifle too tense to be called his habitual calm.

Perhaps the half-Indus sorcerer discommoded him.

The Chessmaster was a fortress, certainly. But Rudyard could be breached with relative ease. The problem was retaining enough civility to use him as a resource later.

Rudyard's face actually twisted, and he darted her a glance of such venom she was almost cheered to see it. "In the Great Lady's service, Bannon, such a thing is not uncommon. If you possessed such a thing as a *conscience*, it might well be uneasy."

She tilted her head a fraction. "Women are generally held to be creatures of sentiment and morality, albeit frail." *And your hatred of us is well known.*

"You are not properly a woman, are you? Not with *that* over your shoulder, and a Prime's will in you." But his voice dropped, and the monkey, its clever face a mask, grabbed his shirt-front with one tiny hand and patted at his lean dark face. "Never mind. Morris's working quarters are in Bermondsey. Faithgill Street. Twenty-seven, I believe."

Just outside the Black Wark. A chill traced its fingers down Emma's back, but her face gave no indication. She stored away the fascinating titbit of *that over your shoulder*, and continued studying her glass. "I see. And when was the last time you saw the good physicker genius?"

"When I returned from Keshmir, some weeks ago. He was engaged upon a commission that . . . overlapped with some of my concerns."

Emma waited.

Rudyard sighed, shook his head. "A problem of some bloody tribesmen, among others, and how to make them docile." Now he looked weary, lines appearing as he sagged briefly into the chair's embrace. "Some benighted folk do not see the benefit of being under Britannia's . . . protection."

In other words, rather dirty business you don't care to speak of, even if it is your duty to Queen and Empire. And this genius has some part in it. "I see."

The half-Indus sorcerer's head jerked up. He poured himself another generous measure of champagne. The monkey rode his lap with some aplomb, still silent. "How penetrating of you. Since you grasp all the complexities, let me add some advice, which you will no doubt ignore. Science for its own sake is as deadly as sorcery for its own end. The genius Morris, unprepossessing as he is, is a most dangerous man."

Most intriguing. "What, pray tell, is his speciality?"

"She didn't tell you?" His laugh was bitter as heavy day-old tea. The monkey hunched down, then half-turned, one beady little ancient eye fixed on Emma. "Poor Em, thrown into a *snake*-pit, blind. He's a genius of Biology. His speciality is tiny things, and he was working with an Alterator named Copperpot – a cracked man, to be sure. That's all I know. Go and see what you can accomplish, Bannon."

"Thank you." She set the alcohol aside, untasted. It was a shame, but her stomach had curdled. Passing too close to the Black Wark was not a thing to be desired, especially since Mehitabel's temper was extraordinarily uncertain. Not that it had ever been sweet . . .

. . . but the wyrm had cause to hate her openly now. It mattered little, Emma would brave much worse than a young wyrmling's ill-temper if necessary.

It was not quite craven to be glad that today, she did not have to, was it? Merely . . . wise.

"Good day, then, Mr Rudyard." She twitched her skirt aside as she rose, and for once, the man leapt to his feet instead of languidly unfolding. His face had suffused itself with ugly colour, and the monkey scrambled to his shoulder, a squeak escaping it.

"It's *good day*, is it? Something in return, *Emma*. What of that?" He pointed at Mikal with two spread fingers, rather as Valentinelli would avert ill-luck. "Do they know, at the Collegia?"

"My Shield was *trained* at the Collegia, sir. He is

properly native born." The cut was a trifle unjustified, but the idea of the Collegia perhaps investigating Mikal's background more thoroughly was a pinch in a sensitive spot.

Shields were taken young, and some of them, found or caught in the slums rather as Emma herself had been, were of uncertain parentage. The Collegia became mother and father to them as well as to sorcery's children, and their fleshly parents – if found – given remuneration. Some hopefuls even brought their babies to the Finding Festivals four times a year or to a sorcerer who could perhaps sponsor them – and add a shilling or two more to the recompense, ridding themselves of a mouth to feed in the process. "Are there none so well-trained in the Indus as to catch your fancy, that you must make eyes at mine?"

He took a step forward, and for a moment Emma thought Kim Rudyard might well strike her. His taste in lovers was easily indulged in some of the sinks of the Indus's dust-hazed cities, if *lovers* was a proper term for it. The gold hoop at his ear sparked angrily, foreign charter symbols running golden under the metal's surface, and her own necklace, a large oval cameo held to her throat by a black band of silver-threaded lace, warmed. The entire room rattled once, as if the hotel had forgotten it was stationary and had temporarily decided to become a train carriage.

It was, she thought, so *easy* to unsettle a man. Even a dangerous player in the great Game of Empire could be made to stumble in a simple verbal dance.

Rudyard recollected himself with a visible effort. Emma

was not surprised to find Mikal's warmth at her shoulder. "But," she continued, silkily, "perhaps I misunderstand you?"

"I hope you do." His white teeth showed in a smile that held no joy, a grimace of terribly amused pain. "Those *his kind* serve most often end envenomed. *Do* be careful. The Empire might hate to lose you."

Is that a threat? "I have no intention of being lost." She nodded, for that mannerly mark was all she would give him. If he was determined to be a rude beast, she was under no injunction to grant him more. "Thank you, Kim. You're a dear, sweet boy." The urge to pantomime a kiss at him rose and was ruthlessly quashed. "Good *day.*" She turned on her heel, and Mikal stared past her for a moment. Her Shield's face wore a grinning grimace to match Rudyard's, and for a moment her breath caught in her throat.

There was a soft thump behind her, and Kim Rudyard made a curious, hurt little sound. Emma glanced back when she had reached the door, and found that he had gone to his knees.

The limp body of the monkey lay against the Rose Room's pink carpet. The thing lay on its side, its face turned towards her and its gaze, curiously filmed, had pinned itself to Mikal's back. Was it dead, or merely stunned?

I did not do that. Perhaps it was not an *animus* after all. Foreign creatures did not take well to the Isle's clime, and the thing's screeching no doubt had fatigued it. She fought the urge to curl her fingers in – a lady did not go about with fists clenched. She kept her head high and swept along at her accustomed brisk pace. Her Shield, trailing in her wake, said nothing.

Rudyard had recognised something about Mikal. Her own research and suspicions, while not quite inconclusive, now had a new direction to turn.

But first she would find this errant genius of Biology, and return him to Britannia. And she realised, once she had exited the Rostrand's glitter, that Rudyard had not mentioned Llewellyn.

Curious, and unsettling. It was turning out to be a dreadful day.

The bone-rattling ride in a hired hansom – for she had left her own carriage at home today, wishing to slip anonymously about – passed in almost complete silence, Emma staring thoughtfully out of the small window. Thankfully, it was Eli's duty to ride with her, as Mikal ran the rooftop road. The new Shield, for she still thought of him as "new" despite the considerable time he had spent in her service, was laconic in nature, and did not disturb her reflections, well used to her moods by now.

Emma roused herself as the hansom slowed, the driver chirruping to his mud-coloured clockhorse. Hooves struck the cobbles, and she glanced at Eli, whose attention was seemingly taken by the hem of her dress.

"Eli." As if reminding herself who he was. "How long has it been, now?"

"I couldn't say, Prima. Two years? Three?"

"Unlike you to be so imprecise."

"My former . . ." He halted. For all his dangerousness, he was still at bottom a quick-fingered ill-at-ease Liverpool bravo, who must have been a dark-eyed urchin on the Collegia's training grounds.

"Dorian asked you that, implying he would rid himself of your service? Charming of him." Emma sighed. "You are a good Shield, Eli, and *much* more suited to my temper than his. There's no danger of that." She chose her next words carefully. "I wish you to be very . . . observant, in the next few days."

As usual, when there was a task to accomplish, he brightened. "Glove, or Recall?"

"Neither. Merely . . . observe." *I am about to do something I may regret.* "It is Mikal. I wish your thoughts on him."

"I have thoughts?" He sounded honestly puzzled, and a flash of irritation boiled through her. But then he nodded, a curious expression crossing his almost-handsome face. "I shall observe him, Prima. Most closely."

"But without—"

"Yes. I am not *quite* thick-headed, though I am no mentath."

"I am no mentath either, Eli. We are in good company. Thank you."

He darted her a bright glance, and for a moment she wondered if he knew the nature of the . . . relations between Mikal and herself. And if he thought it likely she sought to replace Mikal in those particular relations with a more tractable Shield. Some of Emma's peers delighted in setting their complement of guards at each other in such a fashion, forcing them to vie for position within the closed circle of sorcerer and those who protected.

I am Prime. It is beneath me to act in such a fashion. Even though other Primes did not have the same . . . reluctance.

The hansom jolted to a stop and Emma alighted, Eli's hand warm and steady through her glove. Mikal appeared as the driver, a lean iron-spined old man in a tattered royal-blue coat and a voluminous red and yellow knitted scarf, popped the whip smartly over the clockhorse's dull flanks and drove his contraption away with a clatter and a grinding neigh of protest. The clockhorse was due for an oilbath, and Emma devoutly hoped the driver would give the poor creature one sooner rather than later.

To the west, a colossal lifting smudge was the perpetual cinderfall of the Black Wark. Daylight was the best time to enter that region of Londinium, but Emma was still secretly grateful she did not *have* to.

Twenty-seven Faithgill was a large slumping building, the district here sparsely populated due to the titanic stink from the Leather Market and the slaughteryards. Nearer the Wark, the clockhorse pens, where equine flesh was married to tireless metal in service to industry, gave out its own stench of coppery blood, terror, and the smokegloss of Alterative sorcery. The warehouses here would be full of spare bits for mechanisterum, to be hauled into

Southwark and given function before being shipped out, gleaming proudly, down the Themis to the sea.

No few of the vast boxlike structures would be stuffed with meat laid under slowly unravelling sealcharm, dripping ice and great fans wedded to cool charms to keep the interior of such buildings frigid. Catmeat and poor viands, true, but Emma always wondered how many of Londinium's finest ate this un-veal, unknowing. It was a good thing her own Cook was a canny marketer . . . and happy in her employ.

Mikal's face was a thundercloud, but she dared not acknowledge it. Instead, she gazed upon the rotting two-storey edifice, its brick crumbling and its timbers slumping dispiritedly. It looked to have been built in the time of Henry the Wifekiller, a vessel of Britannia who had paradoxically hated women almost as much as Kim Rudyard. Henry had also hated the Church, and had garnered the support of sorcery's children – even the females – by expelling the worst of the Inquisition from the Isle's shores along with the scarlet and black plague of Popish filth.

"I rather hope he is at home," she remarked, merely to break the tension. The sky was a mass of yellow cloud, Londinium's coal-breath holding the city under a lens. Perhaps after Tideturn it would rain. "Though it seems unlikely."

Both Shields gave her astonished glances. She shook her head, her curls bouncing against her ears and her peridot earrings swinging, a reassuring weight. "Never mind. Mikal, if you please. Eli, with me."

Her caution was almost useless. The inside of the warehouse consisted of two rooms – Morris's living quarters were tucked behind a sagging partition, spare as a monk's. A pallet, a small empty table that might have served as a desk or bedside table, and a single easy-chair in some hideous moth-eaten black fabric, and that was all. No wardrobe, no washbasin.

No means of storing food.

The workroom bore evidence of being lived in, but it was also full of disorder. Smashed glass smeared with various crusted substances lay everywhere, corroded brass fittings broken in piles on the floor, and scorching over everything as if a cleansing fire had been attempted. Emma wrinkled her nose at the stench. How had anyone *breathed* in here? More glass crunched like silver bones underfoot, and she did not bother to tell the Shields to move cautiously.

Later, she wondered if she should have. But she was too occupied with the new attention Eli was paying Mikal, and the deepening ill temper Mikal was barely – but thoroughly – keeping in check.

It was, indeed, a dreadful afternoon.

Chapter Nine

Most Singular And Unnatural

Miss Bannon's childlike face was unwontedly serious as she cut into her chop. "It is a puzzle, and one I should be glad of your help in solving."

"A physicker gone astray. Hmm." Clare applied himself to his own plate with a will. Miss Bannon's table was always superlative, and the graceful silver epergne had the air of an old friend. Even the carved gryphon legs holding the aforesaid table level, shifting occasionally as currents of sorcery or tension passed through the room, had become familiar. "Faithgill Street? Bermondsey?"

"Yes. Number twenty-seven. Very hard by the Leather Market." She was a little pale, and her tone had lost some of its usual crispness. Another might not have remarked upon it, but Clare's faculties had seized upon the tiny details as a distraction from the weary retreading of ground connected to Dr Vance.

And besides, he could flatter himself that after this much time he . . . did he? Yes. He could say he was well-acquainted with Miss Bannon.

He could even say he *knew* her. As much as a man could ever be said to know a woman whose trade was the illogic of sorcery.

"Very hard by the Black Wark." He paused again, as if thinking. The idea of that quarter of Londinium – the falling ash, every angle fractionally but critically off, and the *thing* that crouched inside its confines – tried to wring a small shudder from him. He controlled the movement, thinking of the equations he had arrived at to explain the range of degrees by which everything in the Wark had subtly *shifted*, and by consigning everything inside those ranges to a definition of "variable" soothed his nervousness most admirably.

"Yes." A tiny line had begun between her dark eyebrows. "Though during daylight, the Wark is . . . not very dangerous."

The last time we ventured into that place, we barely escaped with our lives. And when I had a moment to reflect later, I arrived at the conclusion that you were the one most at risk. But he contented himself with a noncommittal, "I see," and another pause, as if he needed further deliberation.

He sat, as usual, at Miss Bannon's right hand. Valentinelli beside him was applying himself to his plate with fierce, mannerly abandon. On Miss Bannon's left, Mikal ate slowly, rather in the manner of a cat who does not quite need the sustenance but likes the taste. Eli, dark and silent, had a high flush to his cheeks. Some manner of embarrassment between the sorceress and the men set to guarding her from physical danger, perhaps? The younger Shield merely toyed with his food, and Clare turned his attention in another direction.

"A genius of Biology. Hrm. Well. It seems he wished to stay hidden. That quarter of the city is rather notorious in that respect. And . . . the house was quite sound, you say?"

"Quite reasonably so, except for a great deal of broken glass in what I took to be his workroom. Shattered alembics and other curious pieces. Metal wiring, some brass pieces I took the liberty of sketching . . ." Miss Bannon lay her fork and knife down, with delicate precision. She took a sip from her water goblet, though a glass of mannerly hock stood by her plate; she held to the Continental custom of champagne as a dessert instead of to accompany the roast. "There are also some pieces in the workroom I have made available for you. Since I rather rudely assumed you would be disposed to shed some light on the matter."

"Quite disposed." The smile that stretched his lips was not unfamiliar now. "And you anticipated my likely request for such a space."

Across the table, Eli laid his own cutlery down. He had hardly touched his meat, and that was unlike him. The man liked his roast, and indeed ate such a goodly portion Clare was surprised he was not round as a partridge by now.

Of course, the daily sparring practice with Mikal was enough to keep anyone trim. Clare only occasionally partook of *that*, and the Shields treated him with a consideration he might consider insulting if he had not seen them in action against others of their ilk.

To see the Shields fight in deadly earnest was . . . distressing.

"Anticipation. A woman's sorcery." She toasted him with the water goblet, and he was surprised by the answering smile rising across her features. For someone with such a decided air, her face was oddly young, and yet Clare only sometimes saw flashes of the girl she must have been. "Mr Finch will show you to the workroom whenever it suits you."

"I take it this physicker is a challenging quarry." The salad, also in Continental fashion, had a tart tang that vied with the hock, but not displeasingly. "Since you are prepared to spend more than a day in seeking him."

She accepted the compliment with a slight queenly nod. "Any effects which might have told me the direction of his flight were quite provokingly absent. Questioning his neighbours led to nothing, as there were none. He has very few friends, and no tradesmen to question either, since any deliveries to said house left no scrap of bill or list."

"Very few friends?" *Speaks the sorceress who has none. Except, perhaps, myself.* As strange as it was, it seemed she valued his person far more than she valued even her fellow sorcerers. She had plenty of acquaintances, the better to hunt Queen Victrix's enemies in Society and elsewhere.

But very few ever saw behind the mask of manners and flashes of practical temper she chose to show.

She touched her glass of hock, thought better of it. "His disposition is said to be unpleasantly pedantic."

Is it now. "The same could be said of my own."

"You are *difficult*. Not *unpleasant*." The sally was pale, but she was attempting to put him at ease.

And that was troubling. It was not at all her usual manner. "I am heartened to hear as much."

"His personal effects were thoroughly absent as well. There was not a scrap left behind to practise a sympathy upon, and I do not wish him alerted if he has engaged another of my kind to help him hide. I prefer to surprise him, since Her Majesty wishes him taken alive." She paused, as if waiting for him to comment. When he did not, she forged onward. "And undamaged."

His eyebrows threatened to rise. "She made a special point of those strictures? To you?"

"She did."

"Very interesting." He nodded, slowly. "The Crown requires information from him, but does not wish you to extract it."

"Insulting, but perhaps precautionary. Mine is not to question Britannia."

Was she aware of the clear note of pride ringing through the words, or the tilt of her head expressing even more pride in her chosen servitude? Perhaps not. "And the good physicker's disappearance was exceedingly well-planned. Which means he is in possession of something very valuable, something that could perhaps be used against our ruling spirit."

"Or Her vessel," she was quick to remind him, though her expression was suddenly very thoughtful. "Which concerns me more. Britannia . . . endures."

"And may She ever." The mumble was reflexive. Clare contemplated for a few further seconds, savouring every particle of the course before him. At least Miss Bannon did not press him – she knew that when he was ready, he would speak.

He did not, however, have the chance. For Eli pushed his chair back and rose, stiffly, his flaming cheeks and bright glassy gaze suddenly very pronounced.

The entire dining room drew a sharp breath. Or perhaps it was only Miss Bannon, whose earrings swung, spitting pale sparks, the profile on her large cameo running with pale foxfire as her mouth opened, her question – or irritable reproof – also unvoiced.

Eli collapsed, falling to the floor in a heap, and began to convulse, his entire body jerking to some music only its strained and tortured muscles could hear.

"High fever." Clare's sensitive fingers found the pulse in Eli's wrist, high and thready. "His heart is racing. No, those will do no good, cease waving them about."

The smelling salts vanished, one of the footmen whisking them away. Miss Bannon stood, her arms crossed over her midriff and a curious look on her childlike face. "It is not sorcerous," she said, numbly. "I cannot find its source . . . Archibald, what *is* it?"

Mikal's hand was on her shoulder, and the older Shield gazed down with a peculiar expression. Almost . . . amazed. And there was a flash of something very like fear; was this some dreadful fate that befell certain Shields? No, for Miss Bannon would know of its provenance and treatment.

Clare simply stored the observation away for later, being more occupied with the event before him. "I do not know yet." He peeled back one eyelid, stared at the fascinatingly thin greasing of blood over the white underneath. "Most interesting. Ludovico! Fetch my case, the one with—"

"Already here, *mentale*." The Neapolitan squatted on Eli's other side; he and Mikal had carried the fallen Shield into the adjoining cigar room, for the use of men during dinner parties Miss Bannon rarely, if ever, hosted. There was a soft confusion in the corridors – servants sent hither and yon, and the walls themselves resonating a trifle, as if feeling the pale, wide-eyed sorceress's distress.

"I can sense nothing," Mikal murmured, clearly audible. "Prima . . . *Emma*."

Do keep her calm, sir. "He was well enough this morning." Clare opened the small black Gladstone with a practised motion. "Let me see, let me see . . ."

Cholera? No, entirely wrong symptoms. Not flu, or dropsy – there were swellings under the chin, ruddy and vital, and when Clare touched one in the axillary region the sudden galvanic jerk running through the unconscious body informed him the bulges were painful. He next tried the inguinal fold, unconcerned at Miss Bannon seeing him handle the patient so familiarly. The same response, the same swelling. "Most intriguing."

"Burning up." Ludovico pressed his fingers to Eli's sweating forehead. The Shield's dark hair was sopping now, and the smell of his sweat was curiously sweet. Almost sugary.

"We shall need to make him comfortable. And ice, to bring the fever down." Clare settled on his heels, considering.

"How much ice do you require?" Miss Bannon's skirts made a low sweet sound, and Clare realised she was trembling.

Most unsettling. She was by far the woman least likely to engage in a display of fear or sentiment he had ever known. "Perhaps an ice bath? We must send for a merchant or charmer—"

She waved one small hand, visibly collecting herself. Her rings – two of plain silver, another a large ruby with a visible flaw in its centre that held a point of red light – glowed under the soft gaslight, and for a moment the atmosphere of the room chilled. "You shall have everything necessary or helpful. I shall also send for a physicker. Mikal, please inform Mr Finch to do so. Ludo, be a darling and tell Madame Noyon we shall need water boiled, and a tub brought to Eli's room. And you . . ." She pointed at one of the footmen, broad brawny Teague. Horace did not wait upon the table tonight. "Bring Marcus in to help carry him. Move along now, boys."

The Neapolitan and the Shield sprang into motion, and

Miss Bannon approached swiftly. She knelt, tucking her skirts back with a practised hand, and the edge of her new perfume – bergamot and spiced pear, odd but not unpleasing – brushed Clare's face. "I cannot Mend him effectively if I do not know what ails him. I cannot find a source for this distress." Her gaze was fastened to Eli's face. "In the absence of that, anything you need to discern the cause shall be provided. Archibald . . ."

"Don't fear, Emma." His hand clamped around Eli's wrist as the younger man began to thrash. "But do move back, he may harm you."

Physicker Darlington was a round jolly man in the long black stuff-coat of his trade, a throwback to the time when priests were the only legal medical professionals. At least he did not wear the bird-mask that had also been usual in those days, to protect from ill humours. Instead, he sported fine ruddy muttonchops and a gin-blossomed nose, and Clare caught a faint iron tang of laudanum in the man's scent.

To soothe his nerves; perhaps it is why he smiles so. "The swellings are of particular concern. They seem quite painful, and he is only semi-conscious."

"*Emma . . .*" the Shield moaned. "*Prima . . .*"

"I am here," she said from other side of the bed, quietly but with peculiar authority. "*Pax*, Shield. I am here."

He subsided, lapsing back into his delirium. The bed with its green-vined counterpane was narrow, and the Shield apparently had a fondness for botanical prints. His room was small but very well appointed, and Clare thought it was tiny because Eli preferred it so. The closeness perhaps reminded him of some childhood comfort.

Darlington felt the patient's pulse, and Clare's estimation of the man rose a notch as he noted the quality of the man's touch. His blunt fingers were surprisingly delicate, and he preferred the Chinoise method of secking several "levels" of heart's-gallop, gathering information from each. The round man peeled back one of Eli's eyelids, just as Clare had, and almost recoiled from the thin film of blood over the eyeball. "*Most* unusual." He glanced up at Emma, his gaze bloodshot but bright blue. "Are you certain there is no sorcerous origin to this?"

Miss Bannon's gaze did not move from Eli's contorted features. "I can find no breath of sorcery about his illness. If there was, I would have already dispelled it."

"Well. Hrm. It is not consumption, not cholera . . . It is no doubt a miasma, or a form of pox, and a rubescent one at that." He tested one of the swellings again, and the Shield's body twitched. "Ice to bring the fever down. A preparation of laudanum to ease him and make him quiet. I shall lance one of these boils and see what manner of substance is contained therein."

There was another quiet commotion – a copper tub was being hauled through the door, and servants behind with buckets of steaming water. The tub was set just so, and Miss Bannon gestured. Gilburn and the black-haired Marcus set about stripping the Shield, being careful when he flinched, and Miss Bannon's fingers flicked. Sorcery hummed, the sound indistinguishable from the low contralto tone in her throat until her voice turned into words. "He shall not struggle so, now."

"I *say* . . ." Darlington glanced at the sorceress. "*Do* leave his undergarments in place!"

The hum vanished, replaced with the unsound-crackle of live sorcery. "I hardly think he is capable of shame, in this state." But Miss Bannon nodded, and the buckets, sloshing with catch charms to keep the water in place during its transport, were emptied with murmurs over the tub. It was quick work to fill it, running feet in the corridor from the washroom down the hall, and the house trembled again. Her small right hand sketched a symbol in empty air, and it flamed with a cold blue radiance; she uttered a short word Clare could not . . . *quite* . . . remember once it had been spoken.

The copper tub creaked alarmingly, and frost traced tiny sharpfeather patterns on its sides. Horace and Marcus heaved, and thin threads of sorcery sparked and crackled as the deadweight of an unconscious body was eased.

"Gently," Miss Bannon murmured. "Let me adjust . . . there."

"Fascinating," Clare breathed. "You do not require an ice wagon then."

"Any competent charmer could do the same." Miss Bannon's gaze was fixed, a ringing in the air like a wet wineglass's rim stroked gently but firmly. "Do test it, physicker, and see if it . . . yes? Very good. Ease him in."

A splash and a howl as the shock of temperature change

met fevered skin. Clare might have winced, but he was observing events and effects with great interest. The physicker busied himself with a tray of shining implements, selecting a few that looked more like instruments of torture and laying them aside.

"Well, whatever comes from those swellings will give us a clue. A most singular illness." Darlington clicked his tongue twice, testing the sharpness of a lancet. "*Most* singular."

"There may be other remedies." Miss Bannon's queer flat murmur as she kept the sorcery steady was chilling. "You two shall keep my Shield alive while I pursue them."

Clare did not have the heart to tell her that he already doubted, very much, whether the Shield would survive the night. Later, he thought he had perhaps done both her and the young Liverpool man a grave disservice . . .

. . . but at that moment, all he felt was slight impatience, waiting for the body to be brought from the ice bath so he could gather more valuable data.

Chapter Ten

Coldfaith

The great Collegia, the massive main heart of Londinium's – and hence, of the Isle's – sorcerous population, seemed to stand on empty air. Charm-tangled lattices of support and transferral cradling its tiered white-stone edifices were clearly visible to Sight, but to the ordinary it appeared that the Collegia and its parklike grounds merely . . . floated. It drifted in a slow, majestic pattern above Regent's Parque, a nacreous glow in the dusk. Tideturn had come and gone, the golden flood of ætheric force sweeping up the Themis and filling every charmer, witch and sorcerer with a fresh charge to be used in service to their fellows – or in service to their selfish desires.

Emma normally almost-enjoyed visits to the Collegia's grounds. Tonight, however, she cursed inwardly and monotonously as she moved along a path of white crushed shell, her stride so energetic even Mikal sounded short of breath.

"Prima." Again, he attempted to engage her attention. "*Emma*. Listen to—"

"Cease your chatter." Sharper than she had ever addressed him, and breathless besides. "I am in a very great hurry, as you can see."

"The sorcerer. Half-Indus, correct? As you suspect I am. I would tell you—"

"No." She halted, her skirts snapping as her forward motion was arrested. Turned on one heel, and faced him fully. A curl had come free, it fell in her face. That was almost as provoking as his continued attempts to speak. "I do *not* wish to *know*, Mikal." *How much plainer can I be?* "Especially if such knowledge will force me to act in a . . . certain manner. Look about you, look where we *are*. Have you no sense?"

He stared at her, yellow irises alight in the gloaming. She studied him afresh, this Shield who had come to her service in the worst of ways.

"I have often wondered," she continued, in a much more well-bred tone, "why you killed Miles Crawford."

And there was another wonder: that she could say the name so calmly, robbing it of its power. Still, the memories rose – to be restrained, helpless, while another sorcerer prepared to tear one's ætheric talent out by the roots, was a thing almost guaranteed to drive a Prime past the brink of sanity. A Prime's will did not take a bridle lightly, if at all; it was that ill-defined quality of resolve that *made* a Prime, along with the ability to essay a split of focus and fuel into more than one Major Work at once.

To feel the bonds again, to hear her own despairing cries, to hear the sounds Crawford made as his throat was slowly crushed while water dripped and uncontained sorcerous force hummed its unformed song . . . it was enough to make one shudder, and it took all Emma's considerable willpower to quell the unwelcome movement.

Here between the House of Mending's white bulk and a low, sorcerously smoothed stone wall bordering a tidy herb garden, Mikal studied her for a long moment. Finally, his tongue crept out and wet his lower lip. "How long you have waited to ask me. I thought you knew."

That is quite irrelevant. "Answer me, Shield."

"He *hurt* you." Soft, sharp words, as if he had taken a strike to the midsection. "Is that not reason enough?"

It is not a reason I may credit, though I might wish to. She tucked the errant curl behind her ear, smoothing her hair with quick habitual motions. It displeased her to be dishevelled. "Surely you can see that Rudyard's dark hints would give me pause."

A short nod. "Nevertheless."

"What I wish not to know may still make me cautious, Mikal. Have I released you from my service? No. That should inform you of my continued trust in your capability." *It is not a lie*, she reminded herself. *He is capable, at least.* "Now come along, and do not be foolish."

She did not think it would soothe him, but it seemed

to. He followed in her wake, and she turned the corner. The House of Mending's front bloomed before her, its fluid lines pleasing even though the rivers of golden charter symbols held in its stone shivered uneasily at her presence.

For Emma Bannon's Discipline was not of the White, of which Mending was an honoured branch. Her sensitive eyes watered and stung slightly, and it would only be worse inside.

Never mind that. Eli requires aid. She moved forward, her back prickling instead of steadily warm with the consciousness of a Shield's presence. If Rudyard had meant to make Emma distracted and cautious, he had succeeded admirably.

The larger danger was, of course, that Rudyard would drop a quiet, envenomed word among her enemies . . . and Mikal's. There was no shortage of those, to be sure. The suspicion that Mikal was perhaps heir to a bloodline that should not under any circumstances be trained in the discipline of Shield was dangerous, for the only remedy – since he had *already* been fully trained, through what oversight Emma could not guess at, since there were many tests to avert such an occurrence – was a quick, nasty murder with all the force of law and Law behind it.

Even a Prime's absolute right over Shield and possessions could be . . . overcome . . . in cases of Law. Were she to halt and cogitate upon the problem, Emma would arrive at exactly where she had every other time she had considered this particular eventuality.

Even if Mikal was not what she suspected, she had

enemies enough; singly they were trifles, but together their collective force could rob her of Mikal's presence – and rob *him* of his very life.

I do not wish to set myself against every Prime in the Empire just yet, thank you, she might have said, were she possessed of breath and patience to spare. Which she was not, at the moment.

In any case, it was a calculated risk, bringing him onto the Collegia's grounds now.

I do not care what he is, she told herself. *I have trusted Mikal, and he has done nothing to change that. It is ridiculous to think that such an event as one of* those *could be trained as a Shield. It is simply not possible; the Shield tests are thorough and most thoroughly applied, as well.*

Then why had she asked Eli to watch him?

The Menders took bleaching as a matter of pride, hanging their Hall with swathes of pallid material and affecting spotless white-charmed linen. Marlowe had called them *whited bobbers* for their bowing and scraping to the Inquisition, a thing that had not been forgotten even today. Another name was less polite, and had to do with the process of bleaching involving vast quantities of urine and nasty herbs, not to mention charms that reeked of more urine and sulphur.

To be so pure required a great deal of stink. The Black, of course, did not seek to hide such rot. Or at least, Emma did not.

If you had a conscience, Kim Rudyard had sneered, and

she pushed the thought away. She blackened herself in Victrix's service, for while Britannia's current vessel had other sorcerers, including Primes, to work her will, she had none as thoroughly determined as Emma to do anything at all that might be required for that will to work. And if for that she was held in disdain, well, it would not kill her. It might even be useful.

Careful, Prime. Do not lie to yourself. Of course some insults sting. Else you would not keep such a list of those deserving repayment.

The Hall resonated as she stepped over the threshold, and the glare scoured her eyes. Hot water leaked down her cheeks, but she had not brought a veil.

She would not give them the satisfaction.

The entrance hall was hung with that rustling pale material, charter charms of Mending glowing golden on their rippling fluid lengths. The traditional white stone altar, carved with spirals and alive with golden light too close to sunshine for Emma's comfort, shifted uneasily in its seating. On its other side, the young student on receiving duty let out a squeak as the pressure-front of a Prime rippled through the sensitised air.

"Good evening." Emma came to a halt. "I require Mr Coldfaith, young one. Where is he?"

It was not quite polite, but there was no use in etiquette at this point. A fresh tear trickled down her cheek as she waited, her foot all but tapping under her skirts.

The student, a weedy young man with a prefect's patch and a bad case of spots that almost masked the fume of talent he gave off, swallowed visibly. He would no doubt be a Master Sorcerer, or more, someday. If he survived the Collegia. "Erm. Yesmum. Well. Sir is . . . well, he's . . ."

Emma grasped her temper in both mental hands and squeezed. *A lady must not shout.* She modulated her tone accordingly. "I am aware of the lateness of the hour, young one. If you are unable to point out Mr Coldfaith's location I shall go door to door through this House to find him. It is *quite urgent.*"

"No need to frighten the poppet," a deep bass rumbled from behind fluttering white. "Hullo, Em."

"Thomas." The tightness on her face was, she supposed, a smile. "I've something rather dire."

"No doubt. *C——x'y.*" The Word rolled free, silent thunder shaking through every bone and particle of stone, and the light dimmed.

Emma blinked, shaking her head slightly. It wasn't necessary for him to do such a thing, but it was, she supposed, a way of bringing home that he was Prime as well. And far more powerful than she. Though he would never stoop to duel, or unbend enough to act in any way unfitting the greatest Mender since Isabella de la Cortina – the Mad Hag of Castile herself might have been moderated by his influence.

No, Thomas Coldfaith was completely useless. And if it irked him to have no manner of pride in blood or matters of honour, none would ever know – except Emma herself.

Does he still feel the same? she wondered, not for the first time, as he moved past the fluttering material.

Mender he was, but no Mending would untwist his spine or remove the hump. One shoulder hitched on a muscled bulge higher than the other, his face almost a ruin except for two large liquid black eyes; he bore the stamp of Tinkerfolk in his colouring and dressed to it as well, in bright, oddly placed odds and ends. He was a scarlet jay among the Mender's monochrome, and the gold glittering at his thick throat and twisted fingers was an unwelcome echo of Rudyard's glimmering hoop.

Crow-black hair and those lovely eyes, skin scarred worse than Valentinelli's pox markings and his left arm twisted as it dangled from his high-hitched shoulder, fine legs that would have been the envy of many a man in the Wifekiller's time, when hose was the accepted means of clothing such appendages. His fingers were spidery, and his teeth picket-misshapen.

Such was the price Mending had demanded from its favoured Prime. Or perhaps the childhood accidents and beatings that twisted and so marked him had demanded it, and the Mending had rushed into him like water into a battered cup. *The light still shines, even though the vessel be oddened*, he had remarked once, and Emma, laughing, had kissed his bone-thick, fever-warm brow.

You and your light. What good has it done you? She had not missed the quick flash of hurt in his dark gaze then, but she had thought it of little account. Not until later, when she had seen him staring across the room at the last great Charmtide Ball of her school years, his face an open book in that moment – as Emma trod the measures of a dance in Llewellyn Gwynnfud's arms, laughing and blithe.

She did not often regret, but sometimes . . . well. And *after* that ball, Kim Rudyard and Llew had engaged in a screaming row inside the boys' half of Merlinhall.

Kim would be happy to know he has unsettled me. "Thank you." She found herself straightening her gloves, and forced the motion to cease. "I hoped you would be here."

"I am where you find me." Flat and ironic, his unamused smile showing the yellowed, stumplike teeth. "Fetch some tea, Straughlin, there's a lad. We'll be in my library." The Mender's hands tensed, knobs of bone standing out at each knuckle. Then he shook them out, his slight grimace so habitual she winced inwardly as well.

They must still pain him. There was a hot rock in her throat. "Thank you, but I may not be here long enough to partake. Time is short, and—"

"For a Prime, you are very rushed," he observed, mildly, as the student stammered out something affirmative and scurried away to fetch tea. "Bring your Shield. He looks like Folk, he does."

He's not. "He may be." She left it at that. It was polite of him to acknowledge Mikal – so few would, now. Since he had done the unforgivable, and was suspected of murdering the Prime he had been sworn to. "There is an illness. As far as I can tell it is non-sorcerous. It struck very suddenly, and—"

"Still the same." He had retained the irritating habit

of interrupting her. "Nothing ever Mends in a hurry. Come."

"I see." Thomas settled himself in the chair made specially for his twisted spine. His library was tall and narrow as he was broad and twisted, huge leather-bound books on the rosy-tinted wooden shelves vibrating with contained secrets. Plenty were Greater Texts of the White Disciplines – Mending, Making, Naming – though strictly speaking Naming had no colour, it simply served to *describe*. Mending's major branches were somewhat evenly represented: the Trismegistusians, Hypokratians, even the almost-Grey Hypatians and the somewhat-embarrassing Gnosticans, who saw illness as something to be celebrated and sometimes fostered instead of treated.

Some of the smaller texts were jewel-bright and precious, herbals and treatises on the body and its humours, a folio of anatomical drawings from the great Michael-Angelo's corpse-studies, studies of various illnesses and illustrations of the body's attempts to cheat Death of its prize.

No novels, like those stacked on Emma's bedside stand. Nothing light or frivolous. A globe of malachite atop a straining, muscular bronze Atlas stood to attention on a desk with three precisely stacked piles of paper upon it; an inkwell and three pens in an ebonywood stand straight as rulers.

Thomas tapped his fingers once on the right arm of the chair, set lower than the left and curving further inward to support him. "Swellings, you say? At the armpit, the throat, and . . ."

"The inner hip. The physicker mentioned lancing them to see what they hold." Emma kept her tone even. He was disposed to listen, but also indisposed to move quickly. "It was so sudden."

"I see." This time he drew the two words out. They were not a question; they served to mark his place in the conversation while he thought.

The itching irritation inside her skin mounted another notch. *I have not the skill to Mend this. Tell me you do. Tell me you know what it is.* "I rather fear for him."

There. It was said. A shocked silence filled the library. Thank God there was no pale linen hanging from the vaulted white-stone ceiling; her impatience, tightly controlled, might have escaped her and shredded it. Or turned the strips to glass. Wouldn't *that* be a sight.

"Ah." Thomas's eyelids lowered a fraction. "And so you come to me."

Mikal, at the library's door, was deathly silent. She could sense his attention, and a sudden weary consciousness of being a woman in a world of silly but powerful men swamped her. They had to make everything so *difficult*.

And while Thomas perhaps wished to revenge himself in some small way for her treatment of him, Eli was suffering. A Shield, *her* Shield . . . and she was all but helpless.

Dear God, how she hated such a feeling. Was that why she served Britannia so faithfully?

Did she even wish an answer to that question?

She stood, ignoring his sudden twitch as if he would rise as a gentleman should. Gathered her skirts with numb hands. "Yes. It was rather foolish of me; I thought you would have some idea of how to combat such an illness."

"Combat? No. But Mend, perhaps. Emma—"

"I have had," she informed him, stiffly, "rather a trying day. I am concerned for my Shield. It is my duty to care for him, even as he risks death in my service. Which you disagree with the very *principle* of, well and good, but not all of us can wall ourselves up in our books and our mighty pacifism."

"Emma." Weary in his own turn now, as if she were a tantrum-throwing child. He succeeded in rising, with a walrus-lunge. His very gracelessness, and the placid acceptance of his body's failures, was yet another irritation. "I did not say I would not help."

Then help, and cease being a hindrance. "No, but while you reach a decision on the matter, my time is more profitably spent gaining every inch of aid I can muster." *I will not see another Shield die.*

If she thought of Crawford, she had to think of the four men who had vainly tried to protect her from him. And paid with their lives. Their twisted bodies, and the smell —

There was a flutter of movement as Mikal stepped aside, and a tremulous knock at the door. It opened to reveal the white-faced prefect, his spots glaring red. Why hadn't someone taught him the charm to rid himself of such annoyances, dear God? It was child's play for a *Mender*. There was a silver tea tray in his trembling hands, and from the look of it, someone had told him who she was.

Emma. You are being ridiculous. She took a deep breath.

Her corset, familiar as it was, cut most abominably, but it reminded her to stand correctly. The library was full of a rushing noise, but perhaps it was only the blood soughing in her ears.

Movement. Thomas had crossed the space between them, in his peculiar lurching way. "My God." A breath of wonder. "There is something you care for, after all."

Did you ever think there was not? But saying *that* was out of the question. Instead, she examined his countenance.

It would not have been half so horrid if his eyes had not been so beautiful. The Mending in him shone out, pale ætheric force behind the coal-blackness of his irises and pupils, luminescent jet beads. Those eyes belonged on a Grecquean urn, or to one of the marvellous statues of the great Samaritan, Simon Magister, who had swayed a crowd from a deranged prophet's ravings with beautiful sorcery. The language of Making even held a story of how one of the statues had fallen in love with an apprentice of the great Magister, and become flesh when he uttered her name . . .

. . . only to catch her dying beloved in her newly supple arms, for he had spent his entire life in those syllables to give her breath.

The story did not end, it merely halted, as if even a Great Language could not express what came next. Perhaps one of the Grey Disciplines had their own ending. Among the Black, the Magister was accorded high honour for several of his . . . *other* . . . researches.

Her teeth were clenched in a most unladylike fashion. "Of all people, Thomas, *you* should know how much I care." *And how little it matters when duty calls*. Though she could not fault him for thinking her cold and faithless. She had merely been young, and Llewellyn . . . and once again, the memory of a much younger Kim Rudyard rose, grinning and capering like a wraith. He had merely been finishing his studies, since any drop of good Englene blood, no matter what the admixture, was entitled to at least an Examination at the Great Collegia, the beating heart of the Empire's sorcery. No doubt in the Indus he was a *sahib*; just as among Menders, Coldfaith was a prince.

It did not seem to satisfy either of them. Her own dissatisfaction seemed a pittance compared to theirs; perhaps it was her sex that insulated her from such longings.

Oh, Emma, you are engaged upon untruths with yourself. Do not. "I am sorry for disturbing your rest. I shall be going now." Very evenly, very softly, her lips shaped the words, and she watched familiar pain rise in his gaze again.

"Emma—"

But she quickened her pace, and swept through the door. The teapot chattered on the tray, and she paused only long enough to speak the charm that would rid the boy of his spots, spitting each syllable as if it pained her and feeling the small words of Mending, a Discipline not her own, bitter as ash on her recalcitrant tongue. They were only a few – it was a child's charm – but when they passed, she found Mikal's hand on her shoulder, and the bright glow of the Hall's light stung her eyes so badly she was not ashamed of the tears.

Chapter Eleven

No Tongue Fit For It

Archibald Clare half lay, collapsed in the chair, staring at the grate. The coal burned grudgingly, hushed crackles from the charm drawing its breath up the flue scraping his sensitive ears.

He had spent many an hour here in the comfortable sitting room, conversing with Miss Bannon. The pale wainscoting was an old friend, and the paper above it, with its restful pattern of geometric gilt on sky blue, was particularly fine. The door was flanked by tall narrow tables, each holding a restrained alabaster vase with a plume of snowy ostrich feathers; the carpet was fashioned to seem a twilit pond with water-lily pads scattered thickly across it, clustering in the corners. The furniture, on slim birch stems, gave glimmers of paleness adding to the fancy, and two large water-clear mirrors held soft dancing luminescence in their depths, so the room was never entirely in shadow.

For all that, it was hushed and soothing, and it had the added benefit of being near the front door, so he could hear when Miss Bannon returned.

He had lost track of how long he sat there, staring at the coal as it grew a thick white coat.

The familiarity of the soft vibration running through the walls roused him from his torpor. He had never asked Miss Bannon if every sorcerer's domicile recognised the return of its inhabitant so joyously, trembling like a well-trained but excited dog. Perhaps he should. Her answer might be instructive, though often her replies clouded the issue rather than clarifying.

How can I explain sorcery logically? Mr Clare, that is akin to asking the deaf to explain music, or a fish to explain dry land. There is no tongue fit for it but that of sorcery itself.

His faculties were wandering. He shook his head slightly, heard the front door's opening, Mikal's murmur. No servants hurrying to greet her – would she guess?

". . . hear his heartbeat," Mikal said. He opened the door for her, and a very pale Miss Bannon stalked into the sitting room. Stiff-backed and dry-eyed, she nonetheless looked . . .

He groped for words, among all those he knew the permutations of. Yes, that was it. That was it precisely.

Emma Bannon looked as if she were weeping without tears.

Clare gained his feet slowly. They regarded each other, and the sorceress's childlike face grew set and still. And even paler, the delicate blue traceries of veins under her skin showing. A map of fragility, stunning in so iron-willed a personage.

His words did not stumble. "I sent the physicker home. After . . . Miss Bannon. *Emma*. You'd best sit down."

"He is dead, then." Quiet, each word edged with ice. The coal fire flared, its hissing whisper threading through the sentence. The entire house jolted, as if a train had come to rest, and Clare sighed. His chest pained him slightly, as did his joints.

"The boils burst. It was . . . there was a great deal of blood, and coagulated matter. Darlington admitted it was quite outside his experience; he was most vexed. The disease . . . we are not certain it is such, though it seemed . . ." For quite the first time in his life, Archibald Clare ran short of words, staring at Miss Bannon's small face.

Not much had changed. A ha'penny's worth of shifting, perhaps. But it had somehow altered the entire look of her. A pinprick of leprous green flared in each of her pupils, and Clare was suddenly aware of the nips and gnawings of exhaustion all through him. His collar was askew, and his hair was disarranged, and he had failed to roll his sleeves down. Where was his jacket? He no longer remembered.

Miss Bannon, still silent, studied him, rather as an astronomer would peer through a telescope. Her stillness was . . . uncanny.

"I drew samples." Clare decided that Eli's dying screams – *Prima! Emma!* – were best left undescribed. "The work-room is well-appointed, thank you. And I have examined the bits from your absent genius." He drew in an endless breath. "I am afraid we may have, erm, rather a problem."

She was so pale. Even in the midst of the affair with the dragon and a mad Prime, she had never looked thus. The burning coal whispered, mouthing a song of chemical reaction giving birth to heat. The sorceress's hair rose on a slight breeze from nowhere, curls over her ears stirring gently. Her hat was askew, Clare noted, and that pinprick of vaporous green in her pupils was almost as disturbing. She was normally so fastidious in matters of dress.

He forged onward. "The only conclusion I can draw is that this . . . illness . . . is somehow connected to the crusted substance smeared inside the glass canisters. Its source appears to be . . . Eli had suffered a small cut to his hand from the broken glass, and it is likely the . . . substance . . . was introduced. It is perhaps toxic – I took all appropriate caution, mind you, I suspected something of the sort – and, well. This genius Morris, he would not be engaged in manufacturing some manner of poison, would he? The implications are . . . distressing." *To say the least.*

"Poison?" A thin breath of sound. "His hand – a cut from the glass? You are certain?"

"It is the only conclusion I may draw at the moment. It presents very much as an illness, but it cannot be . . . I do not know." He searched for something to say. Why was this so difficult? He should be able to present the symptoms, explain his conclusions, and . . .

The damned angina intensified, but it was all through his chest instead of clustered high on the left. It was not, however, a physical ache. And its source was not his own organs of Feeling, but the look on the sorceress's face. The frailty of her shoulders, and those glimmers in her eyes. She would not weep, of course. Miss Bannon would not ever allow herself to do such a thing where it could be witnessed.

Perhaps he should have taken a fraction of coja to sharpen him, to make this less . . . messy.

"His body?" A shadow of her usual brisk tone, but he was heartened by it nonetheless.

"The cellar. Mr Finch said you would wish for it to be placed so."

"Yes." A single nod. Her earrings swung, the peridots flashing with far more vigour than the dimness of the room should allow. "Do *not*."

Mikal's hand fell back to his side.

"I am not quite . . . safe," Miss Bannon continued, in that same ghostly little voice. "Please do rest, Archibald. I am grateful for your pains in this matter, and I shall be calling upon your services tomorrow. We shall hunt this man, and I am not at all certain he will be returned to the Queen alive." A slow, leisurely blink, the green pinpricks staying steady though her eyelids closed, and Clare found he had to look away.

It simply was not *right* for such a thing to be seen.

Miss Bannon turned, sharply, and the house held its breath. She passed through the door like a burning wind, and it swung shut behind her, pulled by an invisible hand. Mikal, a curious expression on his lean face, stared after her.

My Prima has a temper, he had remarked once.

Her footsteps passed down the hall, and she must not have been able to contain her fury. For a single cry rent the nighttime quiet of 34½ Brooke Street, a sound of inhuman rage that would have blasted the house off its foundation had it been physical. It passed through Clare's skull without bothering to use his ears as a portal, and he staggered. Mikal's hand closed about his elbow, warm and hard against skin crackling with the dried blood from Eli's final convulsions, and the Shield steadied him.

"She will tear him to pieces," the man murmured, almost happily, and Clare was too shaken to enquire whom he meant. It was, in any case, perfectly clear.

The physicker Morris, wherever he was hiding, was about to find there was no hole deep enough to shelter him from Miss Bannon.

Morning rose grey and fretful over Londinium. Tideturn came slightly past dawn, soughing up the Themis's sparkle and spilling through the streets, filling the city with gold even the unsorcerous could see for a bare few moments.

Clare, roused from slumber by the consciousness of the hour more than by any real desire to be ambulatory, yawned and entered the breakfast room rubbing at his eyes in a decidedly ungentlemanly fashion.

"*Guten Morgen*, Archie!" Sigmund Baerbarth, round and ruddy as ever, his seamed head a boiled egg's proud dome, absently waved a teacup, its contents dangerously close to spilling. "I bring you letters."

"I say, good morning. More mail?" *Let me have breakfast first, old man.*

Baerbarth's face was grimed with soot, wiped clean hurriedly, and his fabulous sidewhiskers were tinged with black particles as well. "Serious, yes. *Frau* Ginn send for me, tell me hurry to you. Is from a man in top hat, she said. Very urgent. He pay her to give to you."

"Really." His skin chilled, reflexively. *It cannot be. Too soon.* "What did he pay?"

"Guinea." Sig set his teacup down, digging in his capacious pockets. Everything about him was rumpled and grimed with that same black dust.

A guinea, eh? "You have been at your *Spinne* again, haven't you." The huge mechanisterum spider was Baerbarth's true love, though he was also quite fond of Miss Bannon. *Un Eis Mädchen*, he called her, and paid her extravagant compliments. Yet he was forever taking the damn *Spinne* apart and putting it back together, with improvements and refinements.

Even a genius who had failed the notoriously difficult mentath examinations in his own country needed an obsession.

"She works!" Sig crowed, wiping his fingers on his jacket. "Archie, I make her work. She even make steam. Like tiny cloud for her to ride on." He kissed his blunt fingertips, then dug in his pockets some more. "Ah, here. Urgent letter. Important. But *Fräulein Eis Mädchen*, she said not to wake dear Archie."

"Miss Bannon? You've seen her this morning?" He accepted the missive – heavy paper, a folded envelope, a wax seal. *So soon? Well, well.*

"*Ja, ja.* She go out. All in black. Is *in Trauer*, the *Fräulein*?"

Her variety of mourning is likely to be rather difficult for all concerned. "I rather think so, old man." Clare settled himself, blinking as the rain fingered the windows. Londinium's yellow fog hunched under the lash of cold water. "Bit of bad business yesterday. Sig, did Mrs Ginn say anything about the gentleman who delivered this? Other than his hat?"

"Fine hat, top hat with feather. Blue coat. Muddy boots." Sigmund nodded, his poached-egg eyes behind their spectacles swimming a bit. He applied himself to the plate before him, heaped high with viands. Two different kinds of wurst, good plain bangers as well, and eggs. It was a wonder the lot of them didn't eat Miss Bannon out of house and home. "River mud. Saw it on the steps. *Mein Sohn*, he bring home mud like that every day."

Chompton, Baerbarth's assistant, a lean dark half-feral lad with an affinity for clockhorse gears, mudlarked about in the Themis, scavenging bits of mechanisterum and other things for Baerbarth's experiments – and to bring a few pennies in for his employer. If not for the young man's vigilance, Sig would no doubt be cheated of every farthing; the Bavarian was *incredibly* easy to separate from his coin.

"Ah." Clare settled himself further in the chair. The breakfast room, blue fabric and cream-painted wicker, was perhaps the most openly womanly of all Miss Bannon's chambers. He would not have put it past her to have weapons hanging in her boudoir; this and the sunroom were the only concessions to femininity she allowed herself.

The thought of a moment or two spent examining Miss Bannon's bedroom was extraordinarily pleasing. Such deductions he could make from, say, the shade of her draperies, or the contents of her—

Impolite, Archibald. He busied himself with arranging some provender on his plate. Sig was already snout-down in his own.

The door flung itself open just as Clare lifted the envelope again. Valentinelli stamped in, followed by a ghost-grey, burning-eyed Mikal. Who was dishevelled as he rarely appeared, hair disarranged and his shirt unbuttoned, a strange stippled pattern on his bare chest Clare did not have much time to examine before the man pulled the fabric closed, buttoning swiftly.

How very odd. Burns? No, too regular. I wonder —

"She did not tell *me*," the Neapolitan assassin snarled. "*La strega* go where she pleases. Threaten me again, *bastarde*. Ludo will answer."

Wait. Clare's jaw felt suspiciously loose. "Good God. Miss Bannon left without you?" She did not often do so, and with Eli . . . well.

The contours of this affair were beginning to take a shape Clare did not quite like.

Mikal cast him a single, venomous yellow glance. "Well before Tideturn. *He* saw her off."

"She go out in a carriage, black feathers and hats. *Ludo*, she say, *I do not wish to be followed. Tell Mikal.*" His imitation of Miss Bannon's softly cultured tones was almost uncanny. "I do, and he accuse me of—"

"I do not *accuse*," Mikal disputed, hotly, and a galvanic thrill ran through the entire house. The Shield turned on his heel, towards the door, and the betraying twitch in his shoulders told Clare he had been perilously close to sending his fist into the wall.

How intriguing. Clare settled himself to observe what would follow most closely. He was not disappointed, for shortly after, the mistress of the house appeared, her black watered-silk skirts dewed with droplets of gem-glittering rain.

She was in deep mourning, even a crêpe band at her throat holding a fantastic teardrop of green amber, softly glowing with its own inner light. High colour in her cheeks, and the slight untidiness to her hair, bespoke some recent exertion. Her rings were very plain, for once – bands of heavy mellow gold, one on each finger of her delicate, lace-gloved hands. Her earrings, long shivering confections of gold wire and small garnets, made soft chiming sounds as she halted, taking in the breakfast room with one swift glance.

"Good morning, gentlemen." She sounded exactly as usual, and that was the first surprise.

The second was the breath of sick-sweet smoke overlaying her perfume. Clare's sensitive nose all but wrinkled;

he took careful note of the circles under Miss Bannon's wide dark eyes and the decided set of her child-soft chin. There was a single tear-track on her cheek, brushed impatiently away, the lace of her glove had scratched and reddened. The redness rimming her eyes as well completed the picture of a woman fiercely determined not to let her grief consume her . . . but the mourning she wore all but flaunted it.

It was a response he would not have expected. His estimation of her character shifted another few critical degrees. Even after all this time, apparently, she could still surprise him.

Bother. He tucked the letter out of sight as he rose, and Sig dropped the wurst he had speared with a dainty silver fork as he hurried to his feet.

"*Guten Morgen, Fräulein.*" Sig's broad beaming smile was a flag. "Lovely, lovely. I bring Archie his mail, and supplies!"

"Thank you, Mr Baerbarth." Her small answering smile was a ghost of itself. "Ludovico, good morning. Mikal, have you had breakfast?"

"No." The Shield's face was a thundercloud. "I was too busy worrying for my Prima."

"Then by all means, please partake. I shall require you in readiness very shortly. Mr Clare? I have some rather—"

He had the most illogical desire to take her to task. "Have *you* had breakfast, Miss Bannon?"

The sorceress paused, her head tilted and the drops of rain caught on her dress each glimmering a slightly different shade. "No," she admitted, finally. "I have not. There were other matters to attend to." *And there still are*, her tone said, *and that is that*.

"I would take it as a kindness if you would join me," Clare persisted. "I would also take it as a kindness if you accept my services in finding this Mr Morris and bringing him to Her Majesty, as I am now quite intrigued. It is a fascinating puzzle."

She considered him, and he perceived how carefully Mikal was observing this interchange. Valentinelli, his back to the wall, had his eyebrows drawn together and one hand held oddly low at his side. There was a spark in the Neapolitan's gaze Clare had not seen in a long while – rather like a cat's expression as it crouches before a mouse-hole.

"Very well." Miss Bannon crossed the room with a determined air, her dainty boots click-tapping with their accustomed crispness. He had, Clare reflected, grown quite fond of that sound. "Do sit, gentlemen. Let us have a civilised moment before the day begins."

Mikal followed her, and Valentinelli peeled himself from the wall. Was it . . . yes, it was. The Neapolitan appeared slightly disappointed, of all things. What had he expected the sorceress to do?

The letter was a weight in Clare's pocket. To be caught with two items deserving his faculties was an unexpected gift, and as he settled to breakfast, Miss Bannon sinking gracefully into the chair a silently fuming Mikal held for her, he allowed himself a moment of quiet gloating.

Miss Bannon's next words, however, gave him much more to think upon.

"As a matter of fact, Mr Clare, I had hoped to see you before I left the house again. Do you think I might borrow dear Ludo from your service? Temporarily, of course."

"I stand right here, *strega*. You could ask me." Ludovico actually bridled, dropping into a wicker chair with a grunt that was only partly theatrical.

"Mr Clare is your employer. Please, do see if you can break another piece of furniture, I rather had the idea of replacing the entire house."

"If you like, Ludo break everything." His accent had thickened, and he looked well on his way to as foul a temper as Mikal.

"That will not be necessary, but thank you. I require you for something different today. We shall be visiting a certain sorcerer, and perhaps he will want . . . convincing, to give us whatever information he possesses." The smile that settled over her face was chilling in its good-humoured savagery, as unguarded an expression as Clare had ever seen. "And you are so *very* good at convincing, my *bastarde assassino*."

A pained silence descended on the breakfast table. Even Sigmund had ceased his chewing, staring at the sorceress.

Clare coughed, clearing his throat. "Yes, well. Quite. Some tea, Miss Bannon?"

The whip crackled, the matched black clockhorses with their ribbon-braided manes hopped, and Miss Bannon's carriage jolted onto Brooke Street. The sorceress sat bolt-upright on the hard red cushions, her right index finger tapping occasionally as she stared out of the window, her face set and bloodless.

"Who is this sorcerer?" Clare settled himself more securely – Valentinelli, jostled next to him, looked ill at ease with the sudden motion. Even the best of carriages jolted one about unmercifully, especially when its owner had told her coachman, *quickly, please.*

Said coachman, Harthell, a wizened nut of a man, was as adept at sailing a carriage through traffic as an experienced sempstress at threading needles. Shouts and curses outside, the carriage yawed alarmingly, then righted itself as the whip cracked again.

"Hm?" She stirred slightly, her hands decorously laid in her black-clad lap. The breath of smoke and roasting on her had faded, and her bergamot perfume was wearing through. It was easy to deduce she had consigned Eli's body to some form of flame; perhaps it was traditional to do so? Or perhaps it was a hygienic measure? "Oh. His name is Copperpot. He is a Master Alterator; I was at the Collegia this morning and took the liberty of checking the Grand Registry. His address was not quite correct, but there were enough traces at his former residence for me to acquire the location of his new domicile, which Harthell is following a tracer towards. It is quite possible there will be . . . unpleasantness."

Oh dear. "Dare I ask what manner of unpleasantness?"

"The usual manner, when we are hunting a conspiracy.

The quarter I received information from about Mr Morris had some dark hints, and he has quit his hotel. Perhaps he returned to his employment overseas, the better to avoid any further questioning."

"Ah." Clare absorbed this. "So, blood, screaming, and sorcery. And *Signor* Valentinelli here . . ."

"Is to convince the sorcerer to tell all he knows." Valentinelli's grin was wolfish. He now looked supremely happy, even jolted and tossed as they were. "And even things he does not think he know, he will tell."

"Quite. I do not wish him dead until he has told all he knows, and I do not wish to question his shade, as such an operation takes precious time we may not have." Her lips compressed, and Clare's faculties woke and stretched more fully, inferences from her choice of words turning the picture several shades darker and more complex. "There are other considerations, as well."

Oh, you are never boring, my dear Emma. "I see."

"Good. By the way, Clare, you did not show dear little Sigmund the items from Mr Morris's home, did you?"

"Of course not. Sig would be of no use in . . . ah. I see."

"Precisely." Her hands clasped each other now, the lace digging and scratching as her fingers tensed, and she had gone quite pale. "I believe the fewer people who know of this affair, even in our small circle, the better."

"Good heavens." He could feel the blood draining from his own cheeks. "Surely you don't think Sigmund—"

"Of *course* not." Irritated now, she made a small gesture,

easing her shoulders inside her dress, leaning into the rattling turn. "I merely wish him to be . . . safe. He did not see Eli's . . . well. We witnessed an event that no doubt has grave consequences. Mr Baerbarth does *not* need to be party to those consequences." Another pause. "Ah. We have arrived. Come, gentlemen."

Chapter Twelve

Led to Regret

Timothy Copperpot, Master Alterator and possessor of a very fine flat overlooking Canthill Square, was at home. Not only that, but he welcomed their visit with almost unbecoming enthusiasm. His narrow, nervous face bore a rather startling resemblance to a terrier's, since his whiskers were cut to resemble that animal's headshape.

"I say! Delighted! Charmed!" He was not sweating, and did not seem in the least put out that they had arrived unannounced. "Was just about to leave for the workshop, but would much rather a visit with another of the ætheric brethren. Tea? Something stronger?"

"Tea would be lovely, thank you." *This cannot be so simple.*

He had two Shields – even a low-level Alterator would need them for handling overflow if an Alteration went wrong or began twisting, the ætheric charge warping under concentrated irrationality. The idea of marrying flesh to metal was faintly distasteful, even if Emma could see the financial benefits available to those who could master the requisite Transubstantiation exercises. And Copperpot was no back-alley metalmonger; his cloth was fine and his flat was a wide, airy, pleasant one, on the third floor. His Shields – one dark, one fair – were neatly dressed, and they both eyed Mikal with a fair amount of apprehension.

Which meant they ignored Valentinelli, since the Neapolitan did quite a lovely job of slouching along behind Mr Clare, whose mournful basset face had brightened considerably as he glanced about the sitting room.

The curtains were pulled back, the coal fire built up and quite pleasant, the wallpaper a soothing blue and the wainscoting clean. Copperpot's taste ran to brass and a touch or two of the Indus, and Emma's gorge rose hotly, her breakfast staging a revolt. She quelled it with an effort, taking the seat Copperpot indicated with a smile and murmured thanks.

"Harry, old boy, do bring some tea, and the savouries! Had a spot of brekkie, of course, but never say no to more." The Alterator's delight seemed entirely unfeigned; to Sight he was a cheerful bubbling of low red, tang-tasting of the molten metal he charmed on a daily basis. The blond Shield glanced again at Mikal and hurried out of the room. Valentinelli hovered behind Clare, the very picture of a solicitous manservant to a not-quite-elderly-but-no-longer-young gent.

"Quite. I appreciate your hospitality." She tilted her head slightly as Clare settled in an easy-chair, Copperpot dropping into what must be his accustomed seat near the grate. "I do beg your pardon for the impoliteness, but I must come straight to the point."

"Oh, please do, then. Happy to help in any way, Prima! You have some work that needs doing, a spot of Alteration, or . . .?"

"I wish it were so simple. I must ask you about a certain genius, a physicker, Mr John Morris . . ." She left it open-ended. His response would tell her a great deal.

"Morrie? Oh, yes. Bit of a prickly chap. Had me make him lovely bits of metal and glass. Canisters, according to a set of drawings. Wonderful things, really. Tricky work, had to stand a great deal of pressure inside without leaking. Did he recommend me?"

You poor man. "He did, very highly." She settled her hands carefully in her lap. The dark Shield was not watching her. His attention was wholly occupied with Mikal. Clare leaned forward, his narrow nostrils flaring as his gaze roved every surface in the room. "How is his holiday progressing?"

"Saw him off to Dover this morning, matter of fact. A Continental tour, just the thing for his nerves. Rather raw, poor Morrie."

Dover? "He works too hard," she murmured. "Dover? I thought he was to be in town longer."

"No, no, he'd finished his masterpiece, he said. Saw him off at the station; made certain the canisters were loaded correctly and all. Taking two of them along, to show the Crowned Heads of Europe. *Quite* the thing, maybe even a patent!"

"Your maker's mark on the brass fittings," Clare interjected, suddenly. "The crowned cauldron."

"Too right!" The terrier-man beamed with pride. His fingertips rubbed together, and ætheric sparks crackled. "You've seen them, then? Pressurised canisters. A mixture of fluid and air, made into a fine mist – but it couldn't be steam. It couldn't be heated. Quite a puzzle, but Copperpot never gives up." He waved one finger, wagging as if to nag an invisible child. "I told him, I would make him a *thousand* once we found the right design!"

"Did you?" Clare leaned forward, and Emma could have cheerfully cursed him. She did not wish the quarry alerted just yet.

"No. Merely twelve, but the right design! Two sent overseas, with him. He said he'd show the remaining ten in Londinium, an Exhibition, he said, but I don't know . . ." Copperpot's smile faltered. He glanced nervously at Emma. "I say, what is it you're after, Prima? More than willing to help, but—"

"Master Sorcerer Copperpot." Emma's spine was rigid. An onlooker would not have been able to tell how her heart, traitorous thing that it was, had begun to ache. The chunk of amber at her throat warmed. "I regret this, I truly do."

Mikal *moved*. The dark Shield went down with the greenwood crack of a neck breaking, a sound that never failed to make Emma's heart cringe within her. Clare let out a sharp yell, Valentinelli was a blur of motion, and in short order the blond Shield, alerted too late, was down on the carpeting with Mikal's fingers at his throat. He had burst through the door, no doubt to save his master – who sat very still, with the edge of a knifeblade to his carotid and Valentinelli breathing in his ear.

"*Bastarde*," the Neapolitan whispered. "Move, or cast one of your filthy sorceries, I slit your throat."

"I advise you to believe him." Emma rose. Her skirts made a low sweet sound, and the curtains, fluttering, closed themselves without the benefit of hands. A Master Sorcerer was no match for a Prime, but still, caution was required. And the morning's light should not shine on this work. The sudden gloom was a balm to her sensitised eyes. "Now, Timothy – may I address you as such? Thank you. Timothy, Mr Clare and I require you to be absolutely truthful. And if you are absolutely truthful, you will survive this encounter."

It pained her to lie, but the man's face had turned cheesy-pale. He would be of absolutely no use if he knew the likely outcome of the morning's visit.

Britannia wished Morris taken alive, but she had said nothing about *this* man. And Emma was of the opinion that leaving behind anyone to be questioned was rather a bad idea at this juncture. It was *necessary*, she reminded herself, because she did not know if Kim Rudyard had left for his own part of the globe . . . or if he was still in Londinium, with a plan that hinged on some canisters and a certain physicker.

Clare glanced at her, but he did not, thank God, give voice to his plain certainty that she was being misleading.

"Mr Clare?" She kept her tone level. "Please question him thoroughly. I hope you don't mind if I interject every so often? Oh, but before you begin, one small thing . . ."

Mikal's fingers clenched. The crunch of cartilage collapsing was very loud in the hush. Emma's low hummed note caught the sound, wrapping the flat in a smothering veil.

It wouldn't do to have the neighbours inconvenienced.

The dark Shield suffocated, his heels drumming the floor, and Mikal glanced up. His gaze, yellow as the Ganges-dust of Indus, met hers.

Now that she had the attention of every man in the room, the business could begin. "What time did Mr Morris leave for Dover? And do tell me, what ship was he to board?"

Copperpot's eyes rolled. He was sweating now, and Valentinelli's hand was steady. The Neapolitan watched her too, his smile as tender as a lover's.

Ludo enjoyed this sort of thing far more than was quite *right*.

Timothy did tell them all he knew – which was quite a bit more than she had expected. And quite possibly, far more than the Alterator *knew* he knew. Clare grew paler and more agitated with each raft of seemingly innocuous or hopelessly complex questions, and Copperpot's visible hope that he would leave this flat later whole and breathing was uncomfortable to witness.

If you had a conscience, Bannon, it might well be uneasy. Rudyard, damn him, had been utterly correct.

Clare looked rather green. His glance studiously avoided the stained armchair before the low-burning coal in the grate. "Are you familiar with the Pathogenic Theory?"

"Arrange it . . . yes, that will do." Emma shook her head. The silence cloaking the flat was well-laid; she checked its charter knots one more time, humming a sustained note that turned into the burring un-noise of live sorcery as she tweaked its contours, delicately, rather as she would smooth a dress's wayward fold. "No. I am not familiar, Clare."

"Illness – or at least, some illnesses . . . good God, man, did you have to do that to his hands?" The mentath shifted uncomfortably, tugging at his jacket and reaching for his pocket. His fingers brushed the material, then returned to the chair arms.

"When Ludo asks, he tell the truth." The Neapolitan settled the corpse's legs. "Ask *la strega*, she know."

"I am rather occupied at the moment." Emma sighed. Three bodies; she would have to expend rather more ætheric force than she liked tidying this mess up. "Do go on, Clare. Pathogenic theory? Is this Science?" *For if it were a branch of sorcery, we would not be discussing it thus.*

"There are beings invisible to the naked eye that may cause some illnesses. Science has suspected for a great while, but required proof – optics, and in particular, a certain Dutchman gave us the means of—"

"Do not become distracted. Perhaps you should wait in the carriage." There *was* rather a large bloodstain. "Put the Shields . . . yes, thank you, Mikal."

Mikal crouched easily over the bodies, his hands loose but his jaw tight. He did not question, but he was far too tense for her to believe the danger had passed.

"I am not *distracted*. Was it truly necessary, Miss Bannon?"

Damn the man. "Was Eli's death *necessary*, sir? Do not ask such silly, useless questions." The words had altogether far more snap than she was accustomed to hearing in her own voice. "We are dealing with some manner of poison, in canisters that will spray it in a fine mist. It must have been a virulent one."

"Perhaps not poison. The trouble taken to keep the temperature of the mist so rigidly controlled rather speaks against it. And poison does not *spread*. It is not a genius of Biology's likely method." As well as green, the mentath was decidedly pale. "Tiny organisms, Miss Bannon, are a possibility. The canisters are only a first step. No doubt the mist produced, drawn into the lungs . . . It would make precious little sense unless this Morris was certain the infection would spread."

Emma's hands dropped. She regarded him, the curious sensation of clicking inside her head as a piece of the puzzle fitted into place turning her to ice.

Small things, Rudyard had sneered. *Go and see what you can find.*

"Dear God. A weapon . . ." She halted herself with an

effort. Her lips were numb. In the closely packed streets of Londinium, such an infection could spread with hellish speed. And if its result was what Eli had suffered . . . "Eli . . . how . . .?"

"The crusted substance – introduced under the skin through the cut on his hand. There is much I can only surmise." Clare could not look away from the blood-drenched armchair. Even when Valentinelli hefted it with a grunt and dragged it to the arranged bodies, the mentath's blue gaze followed. "The canisters are no doubt already placed in public areas, in order to maximise the initial exposure." He blinked as the coal fire shifted, ash falling with a whisper. "And Eli had some few hours before he evinced symptoms. The first cases could be wandering the streets now. And infecting others."

"While the good physicker hies himself to the Continent and to whatever paymaster has turned him." *D—n the man. Oh, I shall give him an accounting soon enough. A right round one, too.* And *Rudyard. No matter how he hates me, this is quite beyond.*

It almost, she thought, bordered on the treacherous. *Almost*, and yet it was not in the Chessmaster's usual vein. This physicker genius was canny enough to hide his intent from Rudyard, if he had laid his plans with such care.

Clare's forehead furrowed. "I do not know if he has been turned. It seems unlikely."

She had to remind herself that her mentath did not say such things lightly, and that he was in all likelihood correct when he bothered to venture such an opinion. "Why?"

"To turn a man against his own country requires some manner of frustration, and Morris does not seem frustrated. Rather, he seems to be following a very logical path to its inevitable conclusion. He has made somewhat of a discovery and is testing it in grand fashion. Really, it is a magnificent and elegant—" He took note of her expression, and halted. "Ah, well. Yes. Clearly he cannot be allowed to proceed. But I do not find much evidence for *treachery*. Merely misguided genius."

"Yes. I was warned of that." *When next I see dear old Kim, I shall not be polite at all. First his monkey, if it still lives, then him.* "Mr Clare, can you find those canisters?"

"The sorcerer . . . yes, he has given me some ideas. Unknowing, of course."

"And discern the exact nature of this threat, poison or otherwise?" Did Britannia, Emma wondered, know the shape and danger of this weapon? The ruling spirit was ancient and wise, but Victrix was headstrong, and Science was new. Or was this a pet project of some minister gone astray?

I do not know nearly enough of the roots of this matter. She took a deep breath, seeking to still her quickening pulse and banish the prickle of sweat under her arms and against the curve of her lower back.

"I believe I may." He even sounded certain, thank goodness.

"Very well, then. I shall leave that in your capable hands."

"And meanwhile?"

Why do you ask, sir? "I shall be travelling. The man must be stopped."

"And brought to the Crown's justice?"

"Possibly." She did not sound convinced, even to herself. "He may be too useful for justice, Mr Clare." *No matter how I long to watch him die as my Shield did.*

She was rather becoming entrenched in the habit of lying to herself, was she not? It was an awkward habit for a Prime.

Awkward, and dangerous.

"As we are?" Thoughtfully, as he slowly rose. "Or am I?"

For a moment, she could not believe she had heard such a question. Her temper almost snapped. *I am standing over a pile of corpses, Archibald. Now may not be the proper time to accuse me of plotting* your *murder.* "If you are asking whether I would—"

"No. I do not think you would. Forgive me, Emma."

Too late. It is said. The pain in her chest would not cease. *And were you a danger to Britannia, I may well be led to regret.* "Certainly. Take the carriage, and Ludovico. Find those blasted canisters. And *do* be careful. For whatever you may think, sir, I am most loath to lose you."

Perhaps Clare would have replied, but Emma's attention turned inward, and threads of ætheric force boiled through her fingers. If she concentrated on the demands of the task before her, she could easily push away the jabbing beneath her ribs. It was perhaps merely her corset. A mentath's judgement should not sting so – he was only a man, after all.

Oh, Sorceress Prime, lying to yourself is very bad form indeed.

Chapter Thirteen

Don't Go that Way, Sir

Valentinelli, examining his dirty fingernails, looked supremely unconcerned as Miss Bannon's black carriage jolted into motion. In fact, he was humming an aria from *Ribellio*, of all things, and off-key as well.

It was, Clare reflected, like sharing a cage with a wild animal. Familiarity had allowed him to overlook just how dangerous the Neapolitan could be.

And Miss Bannon?

It was a very good thing mentaths did not often wince. For if they did, Clare was certain he should be wincing now at his own idiocy.

It was not the credence given to a controversial theory; there was no other way to account for the peculiarities the case presented. It was the flash of pain on Miss Bannon's features, swiftly smoothed away, when Clare had wondered aloud.

He had *meant*, of course, that Miss Bannon's value far exceeded his own in the current situation. It was quite likely that the Crown depended on her loyalty far more thoroughly than Miss Bannon ever guessed. Empire was maintained by those like her – proud servants, all.

Clare had often speculated upon the nature of the sorceress's attachment to Britannia's current incarnation, but had consigned it to the mental bureau-drawer of mysteries deserving close, thorough, and above all, *unhurried* contemplation at some later date. She did an excellent job of hiding her origins, did Miss Bannon, but he had the advantage of close acquaintance. The ghost of childhood want and deprivation hung about her, and her attachment to the Queen bespoke a battle against such a ghost within a person's character more than an avowed duty to Empire.

No doubt Emma would hotly dispute such a notion, or give it brisk short shrift. But Clare thought it very likely – oh, very likely indeed – that it was not Victrix the sorceress sought to insulate from harm. It was instead a young girl who had been saved from the spectre of a short brutal life in a rookery or worse, plucked from the gutter and set in the glitter-whirl of sorcery's proud practitioners. Of course nothing less than serving the highest power in the land would do for such a child's powerful wanting in a sorceress's body, and of course she would see an echo of her own struggles in Victrix's dangerous first years of reign.

In any case, this morning Miss Bannon had apparently not taken his meaning correctly, and Clare consoled himself with the thought that she was an exceedingly logical woman, and would not take umbrage at his indelicacy. Would she?

And yet, he had never quite seen her look . . . *hurt*, before.

The morning crush of crowd and other conveyances had thickened during the few hours spent in Copperpot's well-appointed flat. Rumblings, shouts, and curses filled the close-choking Londinium air. The wheels ground more slowly, and Clare's busy faculties calculated the likely rate of the sickness spreading and the resultant chances of sufferers surviving the boils.

Could the Shield have spread the disease? Perhaps. Physicker Darlington? No, there was no break in his skin . . . but still. Clare cursed inwardly. If the canisters dispensed a form of highly infectious illness, Eli may well have served the same purpose. Certainly very little of Morris's behaviour made sense unless he planned the sickness to spread from sufferer to sufferer.

Another jolt, and the carriage ceased its forward motion. There was a great deal of shouting and cursing – a blockage in the street, perhaps? Sunk in thought, Clare barely noticed when Valentinelli stiffened.

The carriage door was wrenched open, and Clare's short cry of surprise was drowned by Valentinelli's much louder bark. A confusion of motion, and the Neapolitan was thrown back, an elegant half-hand strike to the man's throat folding him up quite effectively. The attacker, stocky but long-legged in black, his top hat knocked askew, drove another fist into Valentinelli's groin, a swift blow that made Clare inhale sharply in male sympathy.

There was a click, and the door pulled closed. The man, with a speed that bespoke long practice, levelled the pistol at a cursing, writhing Valentinelli.

Clare coughed, slightly. "Well. A pleasant surprise."

Francis Vance, Doctor of Art and mentath, had a wide, frank, disarming grin. His moustache was fair but his hair had darkened as he aged, and one of the odd qualities of the man was his ability to change appearance at a moment's notice. He required no appurtenances to do so, merely his own plastic features. His eyes were variously hazel, gold, or green, depending on his mood, and at the moment they were quite merry. "Hullo, old chap."

"I *kill* you—" Valentinelli was not taking this turn of events calmly at all.

Clare cleared his throat. "Ludovico, please, he merely wishes to talk. Or he would have shot you with that cunning little pistol. A Beaumont-Adams, is it not? Double-action. And you only have two shots."

"Very good." Vance's smile broadened a trifle. "Two are all I require; normally it would be merely *one*. Your Neapolitan here is most dangerous, though. I have a high idea of him."

So does Miss Bannon. "You are not the only one who does. To what do I owe this pleasure, sir? I have been a trifle too busy to return your letters."

"If you *could* reply, I would be in Newgate by now. As it is . . ." Vance gauged Valentinelli with a sidelong look. The assassin had ceased sputtering and half lay, curled against the carriage's wall, glaring balefully at the uninvited guest. "I do apologise, *signor*. I did not think you would offer me a chance to speak."

"You were correct," Valentinelli snarled, and Vance's eyebrows raised a fraction.

"Indeed. You are *most* singular. Anyhow, Mr Clare, I have come to offer you my services."

"I would engage *your* services?" A queer sinking sensation had begun in Clare's middle.

"Oh yes." Vance apparently judged the moment to be less fraught, as he tucked the pistol away. His entire posture bespoke tense readiness, though, as Valentinelli slowly uncurled. "You are pursuing a certain Morris, are you not?"

Dear heavens. Clare's stomach was *certainly* sinking. "And you are as well? No. You cannot be. For one thing—"

"He came to my attention; I neither engaged nor funded him. His project is unprofitable, to say the least." Vance's smile faded. His changeable countenance became a statue of gravity. "For another, even *I* have some scruples, faint and fading as they are. This is dirty pool, old boy. Very dirty indeed."

"I see." Clare's mouth was dry. Of all the turns this case could take, this was perhaps the most surprising.

And he had not foreseen it. Perhaps his faculties were dimming.

"No, you do not. Yet. But, Mr Clare, might I suggest you tell your driver to direct us to Bermondsey? It seems a particularly profitable place to begin."

* * *

Londinium's sky wept, a fine persistent drizzle tinted a venomous yellow as the sun began its slow afternoon descent. Between the buildings the fog rose in streamers, tamped down by the rain's catlike licking, the Themis breathing its vapour into street-arteries. Valentinelli slumped next to Clare, staring balefully at the mentath who had struck him.

Vance appeared at ease, having taken the entire seat for himself. "What do you know of Morris?"

Clare suspected he had gathered his faculties as much as he would be allowed to. "A genius of Biology. No more than thirty-three, and quite a disciplined student, though he failed any and all requisite mentath testing and consequently paid for his schooling by neighbourhood subscription and—"

"His childhood, Mr Clare." As if Clare were at Yton again, and Vance a patient instructor.

I rather do not like this fellow. "Londinium born and bred, south of the Themis in every respect until he was sent to school. I deduce his father died while he was young. His mother rather coddled him, and his schoolfellows did not like him."

"Consequently, he took refuge in his art. And in one other thing." Vance nodded. His eyes had darkened to hazel, the gold flecks in them shrinking. He observed a catlike stillness, but Clare had no doubt the pistol, especially filed by a gunsmith to rob the trigger of any stutter, would make short work of any obstacle in his path.

Clare's faculties helpfully supplied the answer. "Ah.

Religion." A few more scraps of information came together inside Clare's skull. "A Papist, quite possibly."

"Most certainly." Vance looked pleased. "And today is Monday."

Of course it is. What does that have to do with— But the carriage slowed its forward motion, Harthell calling and clicking to the clockhorses in the peculiar tongue of coachmen, and from the sound of the traffic outside, Clare decided they had reached Ettingly Street in Bermondsey.

There is a church of the Magdalen here. I wonder . . . "The Magdalen was Morris's church?"

"He visited regularly. Papists *can* be faithful, you know. Come, gentlemen." Vance's countenance had turned graver, and he now looked at least ten years older. "Let us discover if he was praying to a saint, or to Science."

Valentinelli's flat dark gaze met Clare's, and the mentath shook his head slightly. *No, my canny Neapolitan. Do not kill him. Yet.*

And Valentinelli subsided, his capable fingers retreating from the knife in his sleeve.

Chapter Fourteen

Above Your Notice

The stables were full of susurrus. Feathers rasped dry-oily against each other, and the clacking of sharp beaks snapping closed was like lacquered blocks of wood struck sharply together. The keepers, lean men in the traditional red bracers and high boots, were hard at work. They went in teams of two, one pushing the barrow, the other selecting chunks of red, dripping muscle and sawed-white bone, hefting it with an experienced grunt over the stall doors.

Gryphons were, after all, carnivores.

Emma stood very still, her hands knotted into fists. The smell – raw meat, the tawny flanks simmering with animal heat – scorched her throat, and the beasts craned their necks to see her, in the flat sideways way of birds. One hissed angrily, its feathered foreclaws flexing, and wood splintered.

"Best wait outside, mum." The head keeper, young for his post and with a livid scar across one wrist, shook his head. The beads tied into his hair made a clacking, just like the beasts' beaks. "Fractious today. And, well. Sorcery."

"Stay, Prima." Mikal, standing before her, did not precisely seem *small*, but he did look a very slender protection against the tide of feathers and gold-ringed eyes. "All is well."

No, all is not well. Gryphons do not forget.

"Ssorceresss." The sibilants were cold with menace. "*Deathsssspeaker.*" A black gryphon, a little smaller than its fellows but apparently the one appointed to communicate for them in this matter, clacked his beak twice. How the creatures used human language without lips to frame the syllables was a mystery, and one neither Science nor sorcery could solve. A dissection could have perhaps shed some light on it, but a gryphon's corpse was impossible to come by.

Theirs was a savage tribe, and it consumed its own dead. To be left uneaten by its fellows was the worst fate that could befall them, and Emma Bannon had caused one of their own to suffer it.

I had no choice. But gryphons did not understand such things. Or they would not, where a sorcerer was concerned. For of all the meats the beasts consumed, they liked sorcery-seasoned best.

"Speak to me, winged one," Mikal said, pleasantly enough. His back was tense under its olive velvet, though, and his feet were placed precisely, his weight balanced forward, his hands loose and easy. "My Prima is above your notice."

A ripple went through them, glossy, muscled flanks tensing. Emma set her jaw more firmly, and stared at Mikal's back.

Entering the stables was never pleasant. Even the smell of the creatures was dangerous, causing an odd lassitude that made anyone with ætheric talent prone to miscalculation. The effect on those without capacity, or on animals, was not so marked, but still enough to ensure wild gryphons did not often go hungry. They were Britannia's allies, and drew her chariot; they were also crafty, and exceedingly vicious. A better symbol of Empire than the ruling spirit conveyed by such beasts would be difficult to find.

The black gryphon moved forward. It had finished its meal, and an indigo tongue flicked, cleaning the sharp beak with a rasp. Traces of blood dappled its proud face, and the gold of its irises was a new-minted coin. The pupil of its nearer eye, black as ink, held a tiny, luminescent reflection. Over the reflection's shoulder peered a white-faced sorceress, her hair smartly dressed and the amber at her throat glowing softly as she held herself in readiness.

"Why are you here, *Nagáth*? We are hungry, and *that* issss prey."

"She is my Prima, and you will not taste her flesh. I require two of your brethren to fly swiftly at dusk, wingkin."

A sharper movement passed through the serried stalls and the overhead perches. If they decided to attack en masse, perhaps not even Mikal could hold them back. Emma had thought, when she had visited the Collegia that morning to consign Eli to the Undying Flame, to visit the barracks and select half a dozen Shields.

And yet, she had not.

Thrent. Jourdain. Harry. Namal. All murdered by Crawford. A litany of her own failures, men who had risked their lives in her service and paid the last toll. Now she could add another to that list, could she not? *Eli.*

Did Britannia feel this aching, when her faithful servants fell? Or had so many passed through her service that she no longer cared, and saw them as chess pieces – pawns could be lost, castles taken . . .

. . . and even queens could be replaced.

A dangerous thought.

"We ssssshall not carry *her.*" This from another gryphon, tawny with dappled plumage, its gaze incandescent with hatred. Its foreclaws gripped the top of a stall door, and the two keepers before it stumbled back, one of them with a dripping haunch clutched in both hands like an upside-down tussie-mussie for a sweetheart.

Mikal did not move, but a new tension invaded the air. "You shall carry whom I *command* you to carry. *Y béo Dægscield.*"

The ancient words resonated, the stable a bell's interior, shivering. The gryphons went utterly still.

I am Shield.

Their compact with Britannia was antique, true. But their compact with the brotherhood who guarded the workers of wonders was even older, brought from other shores with the wandering conjurers of the Broken City. Mordred the Black had given shelter to that brotherhood on the Isle's shores during the Lost Times. Mordred claimed descent from Artur's left-hand line; none knew the truth of that claim, none cared to dispute it, either. The Collegia itself, only recently tethered above Londinium, was a wonder of Mordred's age, its black gatestones crawling with crimson charter charms the first things laid. There was said to be a mist-shrouded mountain the Collegia had torn itself from the side of, long ago. A craggy peak whispered to have held another school where thirteen students were admitted, but only twelve left, and the last – either the best or the worst, according to which set of legends one excavated from antique dust – was taken as a toll.

"You are Sssshield." Grudging, the black gryphon lowered its head.

Mikal's tone softened, but only fractionally. "I would not ask, were the need not dire. Britannia requires, wingkin."

They moved again, restlessly, as the ruling spirit's name passed through them.

"*And we ansssswer,*" the chorus rose, as one.

So do I, gryphons. Emma's throat ached, the dry stone lodged in its depths refusing to budge. *So do I.*

A thickly painted statue of the Hooded Magdalen smiled pacifically from her knees, beaming at the wooden, writhing holy corpse nailed to the *tau* above the altar. Clare blinked, his sensitive nose untangling odours – wax, incense of a different type than that perfuming the letter still in his pocket, old stone and damp, the ash of breathing, beating Black Wark close by providing a dry acid tang.

The church had stood before the Wifekiller's time, and those recalcitrant or conservative enough to remain under the command of the Papacy in matters of faith had preserved it fairly well. Well enough that Valentinelli, Neapolitan that he was, murmured a phrase in his native tongue and performed a curious crossing motion.

Clare caught Vance's glance at the assassin, and knew

the other mentath was storing away tiny bits of deduction and inference. Rather as he himself would.

He turned his attention away, examining the church's interior. Pews of old dark wood, each with a rail attached to its back for those who chose to kneel, the *tau* corpse lit from underneath by a bank of dripping candles. The altar was a tangle of dying flowers on a motheaten red velvet cloth; four confession-closets stood along the west wall, empty. On a workaday Monday, the stone-and-brick pile was full only of echoes. Generations of nervous sweat and the effort of pleading with uncaring divinity had imparted its own subtle tang to the still air, warmed by candle-breath. Another bank of candles crouched within a narrow room tucked to the side, under icons both painted and sculpted.

Vance exhaled, a satisfied sound. "Where would you say, old chap?"

Clare caught the first note of unease in the other mentath's tone. *Ah. You are not as certain as you would like me to believe.* "Certainly not the basement. Or the tower." He took his time, enjoying the sensation of pieces of the puzzle fitting together with tiny, satisfying unheard snaps. *Not under the altar, either.* He turned, smartly, and his steps were hushed as he entered the domain of the saints. Valentinelli drifted after him, and Clare was absurdly comforted by the Neapolitan's presence.

Vance had surprised the assassin once. Clare did not think such an event likely to occur a second time.

Paintings and small statues, the saints with their hands

frozen in attitudes of blessing and the thin crescents or circles of haloes about their heads worked in gilt, stared with sad soot-laden eyes. Clare stood for a moment, thinking.

He is a genius, not a mentath. He is the prey of forces within himself he cannot compass, and they have driven him. The initial impulse came from another quarter, but he made the quest his own. Clare nodded thoughtfully, tapping his thin lips with one finger. Ludovico, well used to this motion, stilled. Vance breathed out softly, perhaps in appreciation of the symmetry of this small room, a tiny gem of proportions tucked away inside the larger church. A pearl of a room, nestled in an oyster's knobbled shell.

"Only one possible choice," Clare murmured.

Under the painting of Kosmas and Demian grafting a leg onto one of their hapless patients – spoons and medicine boxes worked in gilt-drenched paint, the sufferer's mouth an elongated O of pain and the blood faded to a scab-coloured smear – was a shelflike table, its top a rack for a bank of small, cheap candles. The smoke from their tainted tallow was almost as foul as the yellow fog of Londinium's coal-breath: a miniature cousin.

Clare sighed. It was a sound of consummation, and he twitched aside the rotting cloth skirting the table's spindle-legs.

There, in the darkness, nestled in its hole, the canister sat. Perfect blown glass, still trembling with the breath of Alterative sorcery that had purged it of contaminants and occlusions, and the top, brasswork chased with charter symbols that winked out as he exhaled, their course run and their charge exhausted. Gears ringed the small perforated spigot at the top, each glowing with careful charm-ringed applications of neatsfoot oil.

"Ah," Clare murmured. "I see, I see. Here, before the saints of physickers. You *are* a doctor, after all."

"Not of Medicine," Vance corrected, somewhat pedantically.

Miss Bannon would not like you at all, sir. The thought, absurd as it was, comforted him. And how irrational was it, such comfort? To be a mentath was to largely forgo comfort.

Except the older Clare became, the less willing he was to believe such a maxim.

"Not of Medicine, no. But of Biology, that great clockwork of Life itself. Morris believes in the divine hand. He is merely a fingernail-paring upon it."

"Very poetic," Vance sniffed. "That is the mechanism?"

It was Clare's turn to become pedantic. "It is *a* mechanism. One used to contaminate those who came to pray to the saints of Physickers for aid. There are nine more scattered through Londinium, and there" – he pointed at the clockwork's bright-shining face – "there, you see, is the reason why we are too late. He set it to exhale just after Mass, when the devout would be praying to their saints. Then they go forth from the church, and carry death with them. The beast is loose."

"Dear God." Vance had actually paled. Clare ascertained as much with a swift glance, then returned to studying the clockwork.

To measure off time, rather as one would measure boiling an egg. Very clever. And then . . . yes, pressurised, and there is the release. And it comes out. Not steam, though. High temperature presumably deadens the effect.

He heard the soft thump and the sounds of struggle, but it was a predetermined outcome. Valentinelli had a matter of honour to avenge, and Clare perhaps should be grateful that the Neapolitan remembered Clare required the damn criminal taken alive.

"*Bastarde,*" Ludo breathed, rather as he would to a lover, as Vance's struggles diminished. If a man could not inhale, he could not fight, and when respiration was choked off by Valentinelli's capable, muscle-corded forearm, even the most canny criminal mentath in the history of Britannia ceased his frantic motions very soon.

"Be careful with him, my dear Italian," Clare murmured. "I rather think I need his faculties to solve this puzzle."

"He is a motherless whoreson," the assassin spat, apparently unaware of the irony of such an utterance.

"That may well be." Clare sighed and reached forward carefully, touching the smooth, cold glass of the canister with one dry fingertip. "But at the moment, we have *much* larger problems."

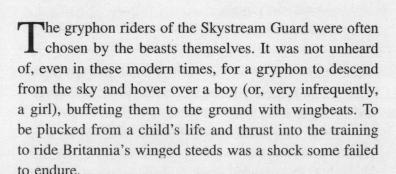

Chapter Sixteen

Barely, But Sufficient

The gryphon riders of the Skystream Guard were often chosen by the beasts themselves. It was not unheard of, even in these modern times, for a gryphon to descend from the sky and hover over a boy (or, very infrequently, a girl), buffeting them to the ground with wingbeats. To be plucked from a child's life and thrust into the training to ride Britannia's winged steeds was a shock some failed to endure.

Those who did found themselves with new names, scrubbed and shaven like a Collegia orphan, and drilled intensively before being allowed to see one of the creatures again.

Gryphons did not forgive a single mistake, and their riders had to be naturally resistant to the strange aura of lassitude that dropped over their usual prey. There was a martial practice of movement – the Shields were taught this, in addition to their other training – that allowed a rider certain advantages against even such a large, winged carnivore, and certain tricks with their traditional longcrook with its sharpened inner curve allowed them to direct the beasts.

The riders sometimes even slumbered with their charges, and there were stories of deep attachment between Guard and beast; from the gryphons they learned peculiar charter symbols that did not seem to disturb the æther but were nonetheless effective. Among the Skystream there were charioteers as well, those who could hold two or more of the beasts in check while they drew one of Britannia's shield-sided conveyances.

A gryphon chariot was light and afforded little protection from the elements. Boudicca had not been the first vessel to ride one into battle at the head of her armies, but it was said she had been the one to design better chariots. Certainly very little in their manufacture had changed since her ill-fated reign, and a citizen of the Isle from her time – or even Golden Bess's rule – would instantly recognise the high sides, rounded back and the queer metal-laced reins crackling with strange charter charms. Geared wheels and runners, cunningly designed to shift as the terrain made necessary or flight made *un*necessary, were alive with crawling coppery light.

Mikal leapt lightly into the chariot, his hand flicking out to take the reins from the charioteer. Muscle came alive on his back as the two gryphons – both tawny with white feather ruffs, their beaks amber and their wings moving restlessly – tested his control.

Shields, made resistant to the aura of lassitude by their membership in their ancient brotherhood, could commandeer a chariot. Carefully, of course, and only if the need was dire. Of course, very few of sorcery's children would consider such a conveyance under even the worst and most pressing circumstances.

There was no *time*. Rail to Dover and a ship from thence would simply not do. And the sooner Emma laid hands on the man, the sooner she could . . . do whatever was necessary.

"Prima," Mikal said, his head turned to the side. The gryphons heaved, and he stiffened, wrapping the reins in his fists. They settled, grudgingly – a Shield's strength was sufficient.

Barely, but sufficient.

The charioteer hopped down, his boots, with their curious metal appurtenances to keep them fastened to the chariot's floor, clanking briskly. He offered his hand, and Emma stepped gingerly up. She almost fell onto Mikal as the gryphons heaved, hissing their displeasure at being bridled and their further rage that they would be bearing her.

If Eli had been there, he would have buckled her in. As it was, the dark-eyed boy with an old, white claw scar down the side of his shaven head slid the straps over her, bracing her back against the front of the chariot and snugging the oiled leather across her shoulders and hips. Mikal slid the toes of his iron-laced boots through the iron loops on the floor and tested them as he kept the gryphons contained.

The charioteer glanced at her and she nodded. Anything she said would not be heard over the angry screeching. Unlike the Skystream, Mikal wore no goggles; his eyes hooded as Emma reached out, her gloved hand settling on his boot. A simple charm sprang to life, vivid golden charter symbols crawling over his cheeks – they would keep the wind from stinging his flesh too badly, and trickles of ætheric force would slide into him, easing the strain. Had she another Shield or two, they could have shared the burden.

But she did not. And now she wondered if her penance would be the death of her, and of her remaining Shield as well.

How strange. Her cheeks were wet, though they were not flying yet. *I do not believe Mikal can be killed.*

What a sorcerer could not compass was a weakness. To think the unthinkable was their calling; to lose the resilience of intuition-fuelled phantasy was to begin a slow calcification that was, to any Prime, worse than death and the precursor of annihilation.

"——!" Mikal yelled, and the charioteer sprang aside lightly as a leaf. The back of the conveyance latched shut, and gears slid. The great doors before them were inching open, and late-afternoon light scored Emma's tender eyes behind the leather and smoked glass of the goggles. The things were *dreadful*, but at least they kept the light at bay.

The chariot's runners squealed as the gryphons heaved. The ascending ramp, bluestone quarried and charm-carried across the Isle long ago, bore the scars of generations of gryphon claws and the scrape of numerous chariots, its slope pointing at a filthy-fogged Londinium sky.

Emma shut her eyes. The chariot jolted, and she felt the moment Mikal slightly loosened his hold, both psychic and physical, upon the beasts.

Motion. The straps cut cruelly as the beasts lunged, runners ground against oiled stone, and the great shell-shaped doors – their outsides still bearing the scars of the Civil War and Cramwelle's reign of terror – had barely finished creaking wide enough before the gryphons dragged their burden into the sky. The chariot's gears and wheels spun gently in empty air, the temperature dropping so quickly Emma's breath flashed into ice crystals before her face. Her stomach, left behind, struggled to keep up, and her fingers clamped on Mikal's ankle.

No, I do not believe in his mortality. And yet I am afraid.

Chapter Seventeen

A Process of Discovery

"We will not be torturing him. Why do you insist on making me repeat myself?" Clare tested the knot. No room for error when it came to their guest.

"He deserve it, *mentale*. A finger. One little finger, for Ludo's honour."

"I *can* hear you, you know." It was difficult to gauge Vance's expression under the blindfold, which was more a nod to Valentinelli's sense of propriety than an actual deterrent to Vance understanding which quarter of Londinium his captors had repaired to.

"Good." Ludovico was unrepentant, to say the least. He laid the flat of the razor-sharpened, slightly curved dagger along Vance's naked cheek.

A thorough search of the criminal's clothing and person had turned up several extraordinarily interesting items. One in particular had caught Clare's attention, and he slipped the small statue, cut from a single violently-blue gem, into a bureau drawer, deliberately making noise. There was no point in seeking to misdirect.

"You may return that to the Museum, Clare." Vance did not move a muscle. His tone was as if he was at tea, instead of with a sharp edge pressed to his flesh. "A sign of good faith, don't you think?"

"Ludo, fetch your instruments." *I sound weary.* Well, he *felt* weary. There were some terrible choices to be made soon. "We will in all likelihood not need them, but best to be prepared, don't you think?"

"*Ci.*" The Neapolitan was happier than Clare had ever heard him. "Do not start without me, *mentale.*"

"Wouldn't dream of it." He watched Valentinelli slink through the workroom's door, closing it with only the ghost of a click, and untied the blindfold. "My apologies, sir. He is . . . overzealous."

"But useful." Vance opened his eyes. He examined Clare from top to toe, then his gaze passed through the workroom Miss Bannon had placed at Clare's disposal.

Stone walls, sturdy enough to withstand all manner of experimental mishaps, showed grey and smooth, charm-brushed. One reached this room at the bottom of a long flight of stairs, and Clare had wondered if it was Miss Bannon's attempt to ease his mind at the incidence of such unnatural material in the walls and floor. The roof was heavy timbers, more than high enough for racks to dangle from them, hangman shapes with sharp and dull hooks Clare had not begun to fill yet.

The tables were heavy, solid pieces more likely to be found in a butcher's shop despite their fresh-scrubbed appearance, and the racks of alembics and other experimental minutiae gracing their surfaces were sparkling new. Clare's older glassware and materials did not look precisely shabby next to such equipment, but there was a glaring difference between the worn and the just-bought. Two capacious bureaus stood to attention, ready to receive larger items and racks. The desk, set with its back to one corner so Clare could see the door as he wrote, was a quite heavy oaken roll-top, with enough pigeon- and cubbyholes to satisfy the most magpie of mentaths.

"Very useful," Clare agreed. Whatever deductions Vance would make from the state of the workroom, he was welcome to them. "My hope is that you will prove likewise useful."

"If not, the Neapolitan prince is allowed to exercise upon me? Bad sport, old man." Vance's grin was untroubled. His eyes were now a cheerful hazel, and his moustache twitched slightly as he passed his gaze over the room's interior again.

"Almost as bad a sport as poisoning a decoy." Clare folded his arms, leaning one hip against the closest table, and examined his guest in return. He very carefully did *not* touch his pocket. "Or financing the lamentably missing Mr Morris."

"I did not *finance* him." Vance actually *prickled* at the notion, his eyes narrowing. A ghost of colour suffused his shaven cheeks. "He sought to engage some of my fellows in this work. But it is not *profitable*, and once I realised what he was about—"

A weapon, Miss Bannon said. Now gone astray. Madness, sheer lunacy. "And when was this?" Clare weighed every word, testing them for duplicity. "Your pangs of unprofitability, when do they date from?"

"Very recently, sir. I regret to say, very recently."

"It is, of course, an illness. Microscopic."

"Yes. And highly communicable. The Pathogenic Theory is borne out by my own experiments."

Yes, let us hear more about those. "You were working with Morris, and realised it was unprofitable only *lately*?"

"I was engaged on a process of *discovery*, Clare. Morris was merely a useful donkey to bear some bits of the burden. What he has done with it is sheer *folly*. He found others to finance his research, not the least of whom were the good offices of Her Majesty. Rather short-sighted, but they did not understand such a weapon will turn on its bearer as easily as onto Britannia's enemies." Vance's tongue flicked out, oddly colourless, and touched his dry lips. "Or even more easily, as it turns out."

"I see." *Miss Bannon was not told the nature of these experiments. Does the Queen know?* "Her Majesty's government was seeking a new weapon?" He said it slowly, as if not quite convinced.

Vance made a quick, impatient movement. "You are not dim-witted, sir, you understand this very well. Morris convinced a paymaster that such a weapon was efficient and controllable. He is wrong, very wrong. I am not certain whether he believed it himself, but it matters little." Vance had gone still, a flush rising in his cheeks. "What matters is finding a remedy."

"Indeed." Clare's chin dipped. He stood, sunk in deep thought, until Valentinelli's return was marked by a cheerful slam of the door.

"Ah, you must want to start with his eyes!" The Neapolitan thumped his own small well-worn Gladstone onto a free expanse of table, snapping it open with practised movements. "Not where I would choose, *mentale*, but very well."

"Hush for a moment, my dear bandit." Clare's eyelids had dropped halfway, and he longed for a fraction of coja to sharpen his faculties. Vance was still studying him, and the thought that the criminal mentath might be uncertain of Clare's next move was a balm indeed. "Yes," he said, finally. "Yes, we must find a remedy."

Valentinelli made a small spitting sound, and Clare turned his gaze upon him, noting afresh the man's pock-marked cheeks and calloused hands. *A prince? He is certainly noble, and his manners – when he chooses to use them – are exquisite. Very possible. Or perhaps Vance is seeking to misdirect. Either is possible, which one is probable?*

He brought his attention back to the matter at hand. He had noted this before – after a severe shock, sometimes the faculties wandered, taking every route to a problem but the one most direct.

"A remedy," he repeated, and stood straight, dropping

his arms. Vance twitched inside his casing of rope, and the assassin leaned forward. He had produced a knife with a dull-black, tarry substance smeared on the blade, and was examining the bound mentath with a wide white grin likely to cause no few nightmares. "Yes. We must consult Tarshingale."

Chapter Eighteen

How Well I Obey

The worst was landing on a steam ferry's heaving deck, salt spray and screaming. Gryphon claws dug into wood, Emma bruised and bumped about like a pea in a shaken pod, her numb fingers plucking at the buckles. The charm for loosing them almost would not rise past her chapped lips, and she felt *quite* dishevelled, thank you very much.

The screaming quieted as she rose from a tangle of leather. The sky was a sheet of bruised iron, rain slashing down in knife-sharp curtains. Mikal was fully occupied in keeping the gryphons under control as they screeched and beat their wings, and the ship's surface suddenly *far* too small for the chariot, the sailors, the winged beasts and those passengers unlucky enough to have paid only for deck-passage.

The captain hurried forward as Emma spat another charm, a hard bright jet of ætheric force opening like a parasol, shunting aside the restless rain. It was a simple act, but it saved *so* much explaining. Grizzled and bearded in his blue serge jacket and struggling-to-stay-aboard cap, the man opened his mouth to berate her, but shrank back as her status became evident and the gryphons almost bolted free of Mikal's grip.

"Good day," she shouted, over the incredible noise. "In Britannia's name, sir, I require your help."

She glanced behind him, just in time to see one of the deckside passengers edging for the railing. Tall, and wrapped in a long dark high-buttoned coat, the man lifted his hand to cough just as her attention came to rest on the furtive set of his shoulders, and intuition blurred under Emma Bannon's skin.

She flung out a hand as the captain began spluttering, and the gryphons ceased their noise. A great stillness descended upon the heaving ship; Emma pushed herself through air gone thick as treacle, humming a simple descant that nevertheless strained at her control. She was spending ætheric force recklessly, but cared very little. Her rings warmed, and the uneasy wind plucked at her skirts as rivers of charter symbols slid up her arms, circling her throat.

The man, caught in the act of turning, had ruddy, clean-shaven cheeks and a stained collar. His eyes were wide and dark, rolling as a horse's as he strained to reach the railing. In every particular, he matched the description of a certain John Morris, and Emma's throat filled with wine-red fury.

The descant took on an impossible, razor-edged depth, and Time snapped forward again. Only now, she was at his side, and laid her hand upon the man's arm.

"Sir." Very quietly, under the slap of rain and swelling of ocean-breath, the vibration of the steam engines a beast's slumbering rumble underfoot. "What is your name?"

The captain shouted behind her, and Mikal answered with an exceedingly impolite oath. That quieted matters somewhat, and he had the gryphons well under control. They clacked their beaks angrily, but did not cry aloud.

Good. That was rather about to give me a headache.

"*Prima?*" Mikal called, over the muted, returning noise of wind and waves.

Morris stared at her, glassy-eyed with terror. She would have to examine the passenger manifest and his papers, but she was reasonably certain it was he. The descant ended on a snapped note, cut off savagely, and she struck him across the face.

It was not ladylike to behave so. Just at the moment, however, it did not trouble her as much as it should. The weight of psychic force behind the blow knocked him to the deck like crumpled sodden cloth, and she inhaled sharply. *Consider yourself lucky your neck has not snapped, sir. When Britannia is finished with your services, I will find you. But for now . . .* She cast a glance over her shoulder, and every blessed soul on the deck was staring at her. *I am causing a scene. Do I care? No. It is enough that I have not killed him outright. Does Britannia know how well I obey?*

Most likely not. And most likely, she does not care.

For a moment the fury was crystalline, and she saw how easy it would be to shred this ship like a soap bubble, and consign every soul upon it to the Channel's uneasy depths. Child's play, for a Prime. And it would serve no bloody, God-be-d—ned purpose at all.

It would not bring Eli back from Death's domain. Nor would it bring Harry, or Jourdain. Or any she mourned.

There is no remedy for what ails you, Emma. Save service, and protecting what still remains.

Would that she had realised it before this morning, and Timothy Copperpot. Would his shade haunt her as well?

It was necessary. Yet that was the entire trouble with embarking upon a course of lying to oneself, she discovered. It meant one could no longer be so certain what was necessary . . . and what was merely, simply, vengeful pride.

"Madam." The captain stamped across the deck as the gryphons mantled nervously. They could not see her, or else they might strain more against her Shield's control. "I, erm. Yes. Captain James Deighton, at your service, mum." He touched his hatbrim with two calloused fingers, and she smelled tar, sweat and the iron note of charm-laced steam forced through metal throats to power the vessel. Some of the jacktars – no doubt those relieved she was not arriving to pursue *them* for any trespass, real or imagined – openly stared, no few of them conferring behind hands held to shield their mouths.

She gathered herself to deal with this fresh unpleasant-ness. Her throat was raw-scraped as if she had screamed, but it was merely the effort required to keep a civil tone that made it ache so. "Thank you. Miss Emma Bannon, sir, representative of Her Majesty. I require this passenger's records. If he is indeed the man I seek, I shall require any luggage of his brought forth and stowed upon the chariot, and a few of your sailors to bind him and place him on said chariot as well. Then I shall leave you be." She paused, then added judiciously, "You shall be compensated for the inconvenience, as well as the damage to the decking."

This news brightened the captain's outlook considerably, and smoothed the passage of events in a wondrous manner. In short order she had examined the passenger manifest and his papers to verify that it was indeed Mr John Morris, genius of Biology, who lay senseless and bound on the deck. He had not signed the manifest under his own name, of course, but the papers tucked into his folio proved his identity beyond a doubt.

Canny prey, yes. He had perhaps not thought he would be connected to the Alterator, or that Rudyard would be in the country to divulge Copperpot's name.

For a moment something – *oh, call it conscience*, she told herself irritably, *you might as well* – inside Emma twinged afresh, but she set that aside and returned to smoothing Captain Deighton's ruffled feathers. It was not a difficult task, and she turned down his offer of a cuppa as gracefully as possible.

In short order Morris's trunk was secured – there was no other luggage, which was a problem she would solve after she had brought him to Britannia. The unconscious man, his breathing coming laboriously, was placed carefully on Mikal's other side, strapped down like a prize pig meant for market, and Emma suffered the indignity of another jacktar, his bloodless face sweat-drenched even through the spray, buckling her into the straps again. Her bruised body ached, and the cold tingling in her fingers and toes told her she had expended perhaps a bit more force than was wise on this affair.

There was a lurch and a scrape, the gryphons screaming angrily as every sailor and passenger on the deck wisely flattened themselves, and Mikal managed them into the air again. If he was tired, his face gave no sign, and Emma's fingers curled around his ankle once more. The slow bleed of ætheric force through her hand resumed, and she fervently hoped it would drain her past the point of losing consciousness.

She had the uncomfortable idea only such an event would grant her any relief from the way her stupid, bloody, useless, and utterly infernal conscience was contorting.

Chapter Nineteen

A Fineness of Morals

"I do not like it." Valentinelli kept his tone low. The door to Clare's workroom, a sturdy strapping chunk of dark oak, was the only witness to their whispers. That and the short hall before the stairs leading to the hall from the sunroom, which Clare was *certain* had not sported this outgrowth before.

Do not think upon that.

"For the moment, there is much to be gained from his collaboration." Clare suppressed a sigh. "Simply watch him. When Miss Bannon returns, you shall give her an account of—"

"You shall not stir one step beyond this house without me, *mentale.*" Ludovico was *most* troubled – the fact that he had dropped his Punchinjude accent *and* the Exfall crispness clearly said as much. "I am *responsible* for—"

"I am visiting an old friend. Tarshingale is a well-respected man, and he is exceedingly unlikely to put me in any danger, except perhaps the danger of being bored to death when he begins to go on endlessly about the wonders of carbolic." He lowered his voice still further. "I need you *here*, with both eyes on that mentath. Who knows what he will—"

The knob turned, the door's hinges ghost-silent as it swung open. And there, framed in the doorway, stood Francis Vance, arranging his sleeves as if about to sally forth through his own house door.

He had, apparently, shed the ropes binding him.

"Sir. And sir." He nodded to both of them. "Where are we bound, then?"

Valentinelli frankly stared. Clare sighed, a sound perhaps too much aggrieved. The damn man was a nuisance now, instead of an adversary. "I suppose it would be too much to ask for you to remain where I place you, Dr Vance."

"Oh, indeed." His smile was far too merry. "You are quite interesting, Mr Clare. I do not know how I have escaped you so far."

Oh, you are a bastarde, *as Ludo would say. And I shall call you to account for that remark at some other time.* "No doubt it is because of my fineness of morals allowing you an advantage." Bad-tempered of him, and ill-mannered, too. Not worthy of a mentath.

Or a gentleman.

"No doubt." Vance did not take offence at all. "Were it not for such a fineness, sir, you may well be my rival instead of my foil. I repeat, where are we bound? And I answer: to consult the controversial Edmund Tarshingale. You no doubt have an Acquaintance with the gentleman?"

"I do." Clare, nettled, glanced at Valentinelli. "Let us be on our way, then. You may be more useful where I may watch you, sir. And Tarshingale takes his dinner early."

Portugal Street was crowded even at this hour. Holbourne was famous for its taverns and divers entertainments, and additionally for closed-front houses where several fleshly pleasures of the not-quite-legal variety could be found – in a word, ancient mollyhouses, winked at even in Victrix's reign, reared slump-shouldered in the yellow Londinium fog. Their frowning faces were a reminder of their unhappy status, and the laws regarding such sport had not eased much, if at all.

However, since Tarshingale was not at his penitent Golden Square address among the musicians, it was to Holbourne that Harthell was directed to point his clock-horses' heads. And in the carriage Valentinelli glowered at Vance, who was silent, perhaps sunk in reflection.

Or turning some plan on the lathe of his nimble faculties. Who knew?

The tall narrow pile of King's College, its bricks pitted by corrosive rain, rose solemn and frowning as evening gathered in the yellow fog. If Tarshingale was not at home, he was here, treating all patients with polite, Scientific indifference in service to his theories. He was no mentath, charmer or Mender; no, Tarshingale was not even a genius.

He was dedicated, had graduated at the top of his class, and humourlessly insisted on muttering about carbolic at every possible juncture as well as lecturing his fellows about the requirement to serve all, even the meanest of Britannia's subjects, with equal care.

If the gentleman – for so he was, despite his lodgings – *had* been a mentath, his difficulty with Polite Society might have been acceptable. As it was, he was generally held to be a most awful dinner companion. Even his patients did not like him, though he was successful in treating some very odd and dire cases. His papers were marvels of bloodless circuitousness, the most amazing theories and conclusions hidden in a hedge of verbiage dense enough to wall a sleeping princess behind for years.

Considering how those theories and conclusions were hooted at by his colleagues, perhaps it was not so amazing.

The small room serving as his office was deep in the bowels of King's, stuffed with paper and specimens on groaning, ancient wooden shelves. Hunched over his desk, writing in flowing copperplate script on one of his interminable Reports, a full head of black hair gleaming under the glow of a single hissing gaslamp, Tarshingale muttered as the nib scratched the paper. He dipped the pen again, and the wheeze of his asthmatic breathing fell dead in the choking quiet of stacked paper.

"One moment," he murmured, and the first surprise of Edmund Tarshingale was his voice, deep and rich as his breathing was thin. The second, Clare knew, would be when he rose, and rose, and rose. For the good doctor towered over his fellows in his own lanky way, and some of Tarshingale's troubles, Clare privately thought, was that he towered over them in other ways as well.

It would have been much more just if whatever divine clockwork moved the earth had made him a mentath. But Justice, like Fate, was blind to quality, and never more so than when it came to those whose dedication removed them from a pleasant temperament.

Edmund glanced up, taking in the three men with a single passionless glance, and his dark eyebrows rose. However, he returned his attention to his Report, and Clare used the time spent waiting to compare the room to his remembrance of it the last time he had ventured into the clamour of King's. And, not so incidentally, to examine Tarshingale's coat – reasonably clean at this point in the evening, without the coating of blood and matter that would give it the hallowed surgical stink. He would be in a dashed hurry to get on with the evening's rounds once he finished his notes, and Clare would only have a moment or two to interest him.

As if on cue, Tarshingale spoke again. "Clare, isn't it? Mr Clare. A pleasure to see you again. May I enquire what brings you here?"

I have very little time to catch your interest. Still, Tarshie was a stickler for *some* manners. "May I introduce Dr Francis Vance? And this is my man, Valentinelli."

"Sir."

"Sir." Vance contented himself with a slight, correct bow, and Valentinelli was still as a stone.

Clare forged ahead. "I do apologise for my impoliteness, but there is a mystery I believe you may be able to solve. Not only do I believe so, but I have convinced Her Majesty's government of it."

The resultant short silence was broken only by the gaslamp's hissing.

"There are many patients to see tonight," Tarshingale said, mildly. "Surely some of my esteemed colleagues could answer your questions."

"Your colleagues have little experience with the Pathogenic Theory, sir. At least, not enough to be of any use in this particular matter."

"The Pathogenic Theory is not *mine*. It is Pasteur's. And someday it will be shown to—"

Interrupt him before he gains his head. "My dear sir, *I* am convinced. It is the only possible theory to explain what I have observed, and I believe you will be of inestimable help in not only this matter, but also proving beyond a shadow of a doubt some of your refinements. There are lives to be saved, Tarshie."

"Very well." Tarshingale conceded, stiffly. The tip of his nose had reddened, as had his scrape-shaven cheeks. The gap between his front teeth had no doubt been wonderful for whistling, had the young Edmund ever unbent enough to do so. "I can spare ten minutes, Clare. Please, do sit, sirs. And *please* do not call me Tarshie."

It does you good, sir. Clare could imagine Miss Bannon's arched eyebrows and amused smile, but it was not a proper thing for a gentleman to say. "My apologies." He stepped further into the room as Edmund rose, indicating the two spindly chairs set on the other side of his desk. "Let me list for you the symptoms . . ."

Chapter Twenty

An Unseemly Display

The Queen was still Receiving, despite the lateness of the hour. She sat, enthroned, the Stone of Scorn glowing slightly under the northern leg of the jewel-crusted chair, the ruling spirit's attention weighting the shadows in the corners of the Throne Hall. The great glass roof had been repaired, and the stone floor, polished by a few hundred years' worth of hungry feet seeking influence in the sovereign's atmosphere in one way or another, was worn smooth. The roof was a great blind eye, watching everything below with impersonal exactness.

Emma could have perhaps chosen not to hit the Reck Doors at the end of the Hall *quite* so hard with ætheric force, their charm-greased hinges whisper-silent as they swung inwards, the stuffed-leather pads set to stop their motion popping a trifle too loudly to be mannerly.

She further could have chosen not to drag the errant Dr Morris the length of the Throne Hall, his heels scraping the stone and her passage accompanied by crackling sparks of stray sorcery, the simple Work used to ease his dead-weight along fraying at the edges as her temper did. Mikal stalked behind her, wisely keeping his mouth shut, pale and haggard from the effort of controlling two gryphons to the Channel and back. Still, his irises flamed with yellow light, and his appearance was sufficiently disconcerting to have overridden all question or challenge so far.

Her own appearance was likely not decorous enough to inspire confidence. Windblown, salt-crust tears slicking her chapped cheeks, and with every piece of jewellery flaming with leprous green glow, she was the very picture of an angry sorceress.

Which probably explained the cowering among the Court, and the screams.

Her fingers, cramping and cold, slick with seawater, rain, and sweat, vined into Morris's hair and the cloth of his coat equally. Melting ice ran in crystal droplets from her hair, from his skin. Mikal was dry, and his dark hair disarranged; his head came up as some feral current not emanating from his Prima passed close by.

Britannia's attention strengthened. "*Leave Us,*" she whispered, Victrix's lips shaping the hollow coldness of the words, and there was a general move to obey. Emma strode up the centre of the Hall as the Court emptied. Only the Consort remained, his dark eyes round as a child's, his fine whiskers looking pasted on, as if he were a-mumming.

A brush against her consciousness was another sorcerer, a Prime, no doubt, but she was past caring *who* witnessed this. Her arm came forward, and Morris's form tumbled like a rag doll's, fetching up against the steps at the Throne's feet with a sickening looseness.

"He killed my Shield," she informed Britannia, and her voice, while not the power-laden darkness of the ruling spirit's, was still enough to cause every shadow to deepen and shiver. "Justice, Britannia. After You have no use for him, he is *mine*."

Victrix's ring-laden hand, curved protectively over her belly, tensed, but the ruling spirit rose behind her features, settling fully into its vessel. "And you, Prima, are disposed to order Us about?" Sharply, each sibilant edge a knife, just as the gryphons spoke.

Did Victrix ever guess how like her chariot-beasts she sounded, when the spirit of the Isle filled her to the brim?

No more than I know what I sound like, when my Discipline speaks. Emma shook the thought away. "It is no order, my Queen. It is a simple statement of fact." *And you would be wise to understand as much.* Something in her recoiled from the thought . . . but not quickly.

And not far. The sense of another sorcerer, very close and watching, was undeniable but the room appeared empty. Perhaps in the gallery overhead. It mattered little. For right now, Emma Bannon cared only for the woman on the throne and the gasping man on the steps between them.

"Arrogant witchling." But Britannia's smile stretched

wide and white, a predatory V. "We are amused. This is Morris, then."

"In the flesh." But Emma did not lower her gaze and she did not pay a courtesy. *Do you understand what you commissioned from him?*

Did you not think to warn me of the poison, this illness?

Of course not. It was ridiculous. Warn a tool of its breaking, or a sword of its meeting another blade? Who would do so?

And yet even a tool could turn in its master's hand, when used improperly.

I have been so used. But I was willing, was I not? And who am I to question Her?

"We see." Victrix's free hand, resting on the throne's arm, tapped its fingers precisely once, each ring spitting a spark of painful brilliance. Emma's jewellery did not answer – but only because she willed it not to.

I do not challenge Britannia. I serve.

And Eli had paid the price, just as her other Shields had. The warmth of the stone inside Emma's chest, her surety against death, turned traitorous. It was a claw against her vitals, and each of its nails was tipped with a bright hot point of loathing.

Morris coughed, weakly. Both the Queen and the sorceress ignored him. His hollow cheeks were reddened, deadly flowers blooming under the skin. Emma held her sovereign's gaze, Victrix's eyes fields of darkness from lid to lid, strange dry stars glittering in their depths. They formed no constellation a man could name, those stars, and perhaps there was a Great Text that held their secrets . . . but it was not one Emma had ever been privileged to read.

"And this unseemly display, sorceress?" Victrix's tone now held no pity — or, despite her earlier words, amusement.

A hot flush went through Emma, followed by an icy chill. *So you did intend to use him in secret after this. Dear God.* "You wished him returned to you. Here he is." *And that is all I will say before witnesses.*

Morris choked. Blood bubbled in his thin lips, and for the first time he spoke. Or perhaps it was only now that the terrible windrush of fury was no longer filling her ears that she could hear his mumbles.

"*Nomine Patris.*" Bright blood sprayed, and the smell of sick-sweet caramel rose, adding its tang to the sweat, salt and stench of fear. "*Patris . . . et Filii . . . Spiritus Sancti . . .*"

He's a Papist. Inquisition filth. Revulsion filled Emma's throat. She turned her head aside and spat, uncaring of the breach of protocol, and Alberich the Queen's Consort inhaled sharply as he hurried down the steps, as if to render aid to the genius.

He was perhaps a decent man, the foreign princeling. But it did no good. Morris shuddered, his heels drumming the floor as his body convulsed, broken on a hoop of its own muscle-bound making, and a fine mist of blood and fouler matter sprayed.

Emma Bannon watched him die. When the last rattle

and sob of breath had fled the corpse, she returned her gaze to her sovereign's face . . .

. . . and found Victrix unmoved. Perhaps she *had* known the manner of research Morris was engaged upon, and at least some of its dangers. Did she guess Morris had died of the same poisonous filth he had been called upon to produce for the purpose of serving Britannia's enemies with terrible, torturous death? Or did she think Emma had somehow crushed him with a toxic sorcery and brought him here to die?

The uncertain young Victrix, new to the rigours of rule and desperate for any bulwark against those who would make her a puppet, was no more.

Now she was truly a Queen.

Britannia was stone-still upon her Throne, and when Emma turned on her heel and stalked away, her footsteps loud in the echoing silence, her fists clenched in her black-mourning skirts, that Queen – Emma Bannon's chosen ruler – uttered no word.

Perhaps she understood her servant's fury. And whoever was witnessing this scene, what tale would they carry, and to whom?

The Consort, however, said enough for all three. "*Sorceress!*" he hissed. "You shall not *dare* approach again! You are *finished*! *Finished!*"

Emma halted only once. She stared at Mikal's drawn face, and his hand twitched. She shook her head, slightly, and her Shield subsided. She did not turn, but her own voice rang hard and clear as an æthrin-scry crystal.

"No, Your Majesty the Consort. When another death is required, or another black deed is to be performed, I am Her Majesty Alexandrina Victrix's servant. As always." She set her jaw, for what threatened to come hard on the heels of those three sentences was couched in terms she could not make less stark.

And the next time you insult me, petty little princeling, I shall call you to account for it as if I were a man, and this the age of duels.

She strode from the Throne Room, her face set and white, and her Shield followed.

Chapter Twenty-One

A Curative Method

Tarshingale was very still, his eyes half-lidded, his long legs tucked out of sight underneath the desk. There was a commotion in the hall outside – some manner of screaming and cursing, very usual for King's this time of evening. Perhaps a patient requiring bleeding, or some other dreadful necessity. The surgical wells would be full of howling, with those patients fortunate enough to swoon under the assault of medical treatment the only exception.

Finally, Tarshie stirred. "The implications," he murmured. "The *implications*."

For Science? Or for suffering? Clare decided on an answer that was equally applicable to both. "Troubling, yes. And deep."

Vance had subsided into his own chair, watching Clare as he laid forth the bare facts of the case, then judicious applications of his own observations. He occasionally stroked his fair moustache with one fingertip, and Clare caught sight of an irregular inkstain on the criminal mentath's thumb. The mix of dust and paper, the haze of Tarshingale's living heat warring with the cold stone exhalation of the walls, the tang of carbolic and the effluvia of surgical practice, all was as it should be. Even the ghost of Valentinelli's cologne.

So why did he feel so . . . unnerved?

Something is amiss here.

"A rubescent miasma." Tarshingale nodded, as if wrapping up a long internal conversation. "A very bloody illness, this is. A red film over the *ocularis orbatis*. Hmm."

Clare's body grew cold all over. "Tarshie, old chap—"

"Archibald, for the love of God, address me as Edmund if you feel the need to be familiar," Tarshingale snapped, irritably. "*Pray* do not address me as the other."

"A prickly character," Vance interjected. "You were at school together?"

"Two years ahead." Tarshingale rose, pushing his chair back with a weary sigh. The laboured rasp of his breathing evened out. "And he was insufferable even then."

"Pot calling kettle, I'm sure." Vance's tone bordered on the edge of insouciant. "You are not surprised at Mr Clare's tidings, sir. And I detect a breath of sweetness in the still air of this charming hutch, which is *quite* out of place."

"Quite so." Tarshingale did not take offence. "I am afraid I must tell you something very disturbing, Archibald. As your friend has *no doubt* deduced, this contagion has already arrived at King's." He took a deep breath, pushing his shoulders back, and his surgical coat rippled, dried blood flaking from the rough fabric. "We had four sufferers this afternoon. Three died within hours, and the fourth . . . well."

"Dear God." Clare's lips were numb. "You are the foremost advocate of the Pathogenic Theory, Edmund. Do tell me you have some idea of how to combat this bad bit of business."

"No way that does not involve quite a long bit of trial and error." Tarshingale seemed to age in the space of a few moments, deep lines graving his face, and Clare noted with no little trepidation that a faint blush had arrived on the doctor's scrape-shaven cheeks. "Come. He is a drover, our fourth patient, and quite hardy. If he is still alive, we may well have a chance."

"*Damn* it all," Clare breathed.

The ward was full of moaning, shrieking sufferers. It was almost as deadly-chaotic as Bedlam, and Clare's infrequent visits to *that* hell of noise and stench were always more than enough to convince him he never wished to practise the art of Medicine.

The patient – a heavyset, balding Spitalfields drover, carried across Londinium by two of his worried fellows who had left him and a fistful of pence in Tarshingale's care because of Edmund's reputation as a Charity Worker – lay in a sodden lump of blood and other matter, including the foul-sweet pus from burst boils. His empty gaze, filmed with already-clotting red, was fixed on the distant shadowy ceiling, and the indentured orderly responsible for heaving the corpse onto a barrow blinked blearily at the arrival of August Personages, well dressed and obviously healthy, in this pit.

"Joseph Camling." Edmund reached the bedside, and his work-roughened hand covered the staring, bloody orbs. He held the eyelids, waiting until the dead gaze could be for ever veiled. "Do you recall your History, Archibald?"

"I recall rather everything. I am a *mentath*." Clare glanced at Valentinelli, whose attention was fixed on Vance, for all he seemed to be taking no notice of the criminal mentath, whose long fastidious nose was wrinkled most unbecomingly. "Edmund—"

"Some two hundred years ago. You would have had Tattersall for those lectures, I believe." Edmund took his hand away, gazing upon the drover's dead face with a peculiar expression. "My organ of Memory is rather large; though I despise phrenologomancy with a passion as unscientific it is rather useful to be measured at least once. I digress, though. I recall—"

"Tattersall. Lecture one hundred and fifty-three." The blood was draining from Clare's face, he could feel it. There was a disturbing tickle in his throat, as well. A cough caught, or perhaps merely his digestion – excellent as any mentath's, really – was beginning to turn against him. There was, he reflected, very little that could unseat a logician's stomach. But this threatened to. "The plague. But there is no—"

"Nine of the twelve symptoms overlap. It is foolish to discount some things simply because *you* cannot compass their existence." Tarshingale drew himself up. It was his usual, pedantic, insufferable moment of lecturing. "It came to my attention that this was remarkably similar. I spent the afternoon pillaging an excellent library or two, combing for accounts of the Dark Plague and its effects."

A warehouse hard by the Black Wark. A perfect place for research, but . . . Clare's faculties raced, and he almost staggered. Vance's hand closed about his elbow, and the art professor steadied him most handily.

"I say, old chap, what is it?" Did Clare's nemesis actually look . . . yes, he did. It seemed impossible to credit.

Francis Vance looked *concerned.*

"Ludovico." Clare shook free of his fellow mentath's grasp. Tarshingale's mouth was a thin line of disapproval, since he had been interrupted before he could gain his stride. "Hurry, man. Fetch Harthell and the carriage. We haven't a moment to lose."

The Neapolitan, to give him credit, did not hesitate, merely vanished into the throng of indentured orderlies.

Edmund's nostrils flared. "Really, Archibald—"

It was Francis Vance who stepped in now. "Very well. I believe now is the moment for a rather bruising carriage ride. Shall the good physicker be coming along, old chap?"

"Bermondsey." Clare found himself actually *wringing his hands*, and almost shouting to be heard over the sudden jarring noise of the ward, intruding on his consciousness. "A plague pit. Of *course*. We may find the original source of the contamination, and a method or means of stopping it."

Vance stepped forward, as if to shake hands with Tarshingale. Whose pride had been touched now, and roundly, too.

"I am no *physicker*, sir, I am a doctor of Medicine, and I shall thank you to—"

"Very good." Vance's grip was bruising on Edmund's arm, and the doctor of Medicine gasped aloud as the mentath's fingers found a nerve-bundle and pressed home, unerringly. "Dear Archibald requires your services, sir, and we shall do our best to send you home in your original condition when he has no further use of you."

"Do be careful!" *I sound like an old maiden auntie. How Miss Bannon would laugh.* His collar was uncomfortably close, but Clare did not stop to loosen it. "Come. A Curative Method, Edmund? Tell me every particular while we hurry for the carriage. It may not be necessary for you to leave King's." He paused, and a rather horrible, unavoidable deduction surfaced. "I rather think," he continued soberly, settling his hat upon his balding head, "that you shall be needed here very badly, and sooner than you think."

❖ Chapter Twenty-Two

Unlucky Enough to Live

It was a long way, and she was in no fit condition to be seen in public. Still, Emma kept her head down, cracked cobbles ringing under her boots, and Mikal's presence ensured she was not troubled by catcall or jostle even in the crowd. Yellow fog crept between the buildings, threaded between carriage-wheel spokes, touched hat and hair and hand with cold, sinister damp. It was a slog-souper tonight, the fog lit from within by its own faint venomous glow, and even the air-clearing charm every Londinium sorcerer learned early and used daily could not keep its salt-nasty reek from filling the nose.

She alighted from the hansom, Mikal having ridden with her instead of running the rooftop road for once, and brushed futilely at her skirts. Then she had set off, as Mikal tossed the fare to the muffled driver.

I am a needle, seeking north. Except she knew very well what she sought, and it was east. The Eastron End, as a matter of fact. Her jewellery sparked in fitful waves, golden charter charms spinning through metal and stone. Her hair, dressed as well as she could manage without the benefit of a mirror, was still dishevelled enough to annoy her whenever a dangling curl swung into her field of vision. The throbbing pulse-noise of Londinium at night rose and fell, just as the roar of the wind and steady wingbeats had while she was strapped into the chariot.

Mikal must have been weary, but he made no demur. The only mark of their voyage was his windblown hair and his haggard air, his coat hanging from an oddly wasted frame. He would need physical sustenance to repair the damage, and soon.

Still, she walked. The hired hansom had let her loose at Aldgate, where the æther still resonated with the impress of the ancient barrier. The Wall still stood, of course, but the Ald had shivered itself to pieces during one of Mad Georgeth's fits of pique. Sometimes smoke still rose from the blackened cobbles, and traffic – both carriage and foot – was *always* pinched here, no matter the hour.

She hesitated for a bare moment before turning due east, and the buildings rose, the reek thickening at the back of her throat.

Whitchapel swallowed them both, and Mikal drew closer. On a night such as this, even the threat of sorcery might not keep a band of predators, flashboy or other, from trying their luck. The gaslamps sang their dim hiss-song inside angular cups of bleary streetlamp glass, their faint glow merely refracting from the fog's droplets and making possible danger even less visible.

Any carriage or cart rumbling through echoed against cobbles thick with the green Scab, organic matter having long lost its individual character. Excrement – animal and human – foodstuffs too rotted to scavenge, small carcasses, rat, insect, who knew – bubbled as the slime worked at them in its own peculiar fashion . . . there were other less-savoury substances in the coating, and Emma's skin turned rough with gooseflesh as she remembered slipping barefoot through its slick resiliency.

The Scab grew nowhere but Whitchapel, and it thickened at night. It covered a flashboy's footsteps and swallowed a drab's last cries; it clawed up buildings every evening and retreated steaming from the touch of morning sun. If there was any sun to be had, that is, in the alleys beneath frown-leaning slumhouses that almost met over the narrow twist-curved streets. Some bits of Whitchapel were scrubbed by sunshine, and it was those the sorcerously talented unlucky enough to live in the borough clustered in.

Between one step and the next, Emma halted. Her hands, occupied by holding her skirts free of the worst of the muck, trembled. It was a sign of weakness she should not allow, except her traitorous body would not listen.

Mikal was very close. "Tideturn," he breathed into her hair.

A wave of gold rose from the Themis, and the renewal

of ætheric force made her blind for a few precious seconds. The Scab hissed with displeasure as golden charter symbols burned through its hide, and the steam from the touch of Tideturn added another choking layer to the fog.

When her vision cleared, Emma found her hands much steadier and her head clearer as well. Whitchapel seethed about her, an unlanced boil. Someone in an alley was coughing, great hacking retches, and there was the splorch-skim of running feet.

"Mikal?" she whispered.

"Here." An immediate answer. "Prima . . ."

"I feel it." And she did. The disturbance in the æther that was another sorcerer, a vast storm-approach prickling that was another Prime. "Be at ease, Shield."

It stayed with her, the consciousness of being followed. She set off again, and even blinded, she could have found her way.

There is the church. Barred every night, and there the ragpicker's workhouse. There is Jenny Anydill's doss, and the Mercoran brothers lived there. That was a grocer's stall, and there was the market aisle.

Now there was a tavern, spilling raucous screams and gin-fuelled hilarity into the fog-soaked dark. This deep into the Scab, the streetlamps were broken or dying, and the yellow-tinged dark was full of stealthy movement. Flashboys, their Alterations metal-gleaming or blackened with soot, stalked among the alleys, and there were wars fought in the country of these bleak nights respectable Londinium never suspected.

She hurried now, nipping between two buildings, through a space so small her skirts brushed either side. Mikal exhaled softly, his worry a burning dull-orange, and she followed the labyrinth twists without needing to see.

So little changed.

It even smells the same. The Scab, the cheap gin, a breath of rotting brick, something dying, a raft of excrement reek, the boiled odour of piss left in puddles. The years dropped away and she was six again, a thin scrap of a girl with black-burning eyes and an unlucky streak of uncontrolled ætheric potential.

The buildings leapt away as if stung, and she skidded to a halt. The dimensions of the empty space were unseen but felt by instinct, judged by fingertip and echo. Her breath came harsh and tearing, and Mikal's grasp on her upper arm was a sweet pain. It nailed her to the present moment even as she drowned in memory.

The cobble underneath her left boot was broken. She felt its slide as the Scab worked through it; the slop of Whitchapel's skin against her boots would leave acid traceries on the leather, corrosion on the dainty buttons.

She raised her free hand and pointed. Witchlight bloomed, a point of soft silvery radiance. It was good practice to make it so dim, but it still scorched her dark-adapted eyes.

The tiny point hovered uncertainly, then dashed across the courtyard. It came to rest between two barred doors of old, dark wood, daubed with rancid oil to protect them from the Scab.

"Emma?" For the first time in her memory, Mikal sounded . . . very uncertain. His hand gentled on her arm, but whether his grasp was meant to steady her or halt further flight she could not tell.

"Right there." The words rode a soft sipping inhale. *After the throat-slit and the blood, and all the screaming.* "That was where they found me. The Collegia childhunters. I caused . . . quite a disturbance, even so young."

He said nothing, but his fingers loosened further. The other Prime was very close. She could almost taste the peculiar "scent" of another sorcerer, the personality building delicate overlapping traceries within the disturbance of the æther. It was akin to many layers of gossamer fabric with wires underneath: nodes and lines of force under a many-layered shroud.

Come and face me, if you dare. She did not *quite* send the message out in the invisible way available to any sorcerer above Mastery, but the other Prime would feel her quality of attention and remark upon it.

The Whitechapel night held its breath, and Emma let her skirts drop. Pretending she was not mired in filth would gain her nothing. Seeking to become Respectable did not succeed overmuch when one had been born here, and when one's memory held the image of a maybe-mother, her raddled face under a mask of caked powder, her throat pumping bright scarlet blood as the father – or whoever was the father that day – laughed his small whistling laugh, his knuckles greased with grime and blood.

Then he turned his attention to me, and I ran. And here

was where they caught me. I thought they were his *flash-boys, and I bit one of them – the childhunter with the red thread in his hair.* A shudder worked its way through her. *I paid for that.* "Mikal."

"Emma." Again, an immediate response. Was he worried? She was not acting like herself.

Who would I be, then?

"Shall I acquire more Shields?" As if she did not care. She stared at the witchlight, its burning becoming more intense as her attention steadied. "What say you?" Her tone changed, she found the slurring accent that lay beneath every thought. "*I bin a-doight tha' the nanny I get ain' no more; needin' flashboy to dockie m'sweet navskie.*"

So easily, the Whitchapel dialect rolled off her tongue. The amazing thing was not that it was still there. No, the amazement of it was that once she began, she could not fathom why she had been forcing her tongue to respectable upper-crust Englene to begin with.

And, as she had suspected, it drew out the other sorcerer.

"Speaking in tongues?" The voice was cold, lipless, and freighted with a Prime's force. It touched the filthy cobbles, slid along the brick walls and the shivering doors, and was obviously charmed to provide misdirection. "Bannon, Bannon. You are a wonder, Prima."

And youna gen'l'man looksee to fine a drab, roughuntumble from tha sound o'it. She inhaled smoothly, kept herself still and dark as a deadly pool of Scab itself. Had she drawn the other here as part of a plan, or had she merely, blindly, leapt?

Does it matter? It sounded strange to her, the clipped cultured tones of her education. Mikal had gone still as an adder in a dark hole next to her, and he would be waiting for the other's Shields to show themselves.

They did not. The sense of *presence* leached away, and Emma Bannon found herself staring at a sputtering witch-light in a filthy Whitchapel courtyard that held only memories, the Scab burned away from her and Mikal in a several-feet radius of scorched cobble. Had she let her temper loose here? Or had the slime merely reacted?

It is only the past, Emma. It cannot wound you.

But she did not believe it.

"Prima." Mikal was pale, and he had her arm in a bruising-tight grip again. "Who hunts you now?"

I do not know. "Come." She sought to step away, but he would not turn loose. "Mikal. Cease. I am well enough."

"You . . ." But he subsided as she drew herself up, chin lifting and the stink of Whitchapel suddenly fresher. Perhaps it was just that she had forgotten how to breathe in such environs. And remembered only once the dialect had found her throat afresh.

"Take me home." She shut her eyes, let the mothering dark return. "I . . . take me home."

"Yes, Prima." Did he sound satisfied?

And did she imagine the hissing of the sibilant on his tongue, so like the gryphons'?

Oh, Mikal. I do need more Shields.

For she had a strong inkling that Britannia had begun to see the end of a certain Sorceress Prime's use, and had resolved to lay such a tool aside – suitably blunted, of course. And Emma did not intend to be placed in a drawer quite yet – *or* to become unsharp.

No matter how many of her own pawns she would have to sacrifice, in answer to Britannia's gambits.

Chapter Twenty-Three

In Cleaner Places

Clare, shuttered lanthorn held aloft, stood amid the wrack and ruin of Mr Morris's empire, gazing about with bright sharp interest. Miss Bannon, bless her thoroughgoing heart, had provided him with every address she had been availed of for Morris, and he was slightly gratified to find his faculties were not undimmed and that he was most certainly able to deduce which one to visit first.

"Be careful of the glass," he murmured again, and Valentinelli cast him a dark look. "It is, after all, what killed the Shield."

"Really?" Vance, examining a fire-scarred table, very carefully did not remove his hands from his pockets. "Introduction under the skin, I presume. The vestiges left here . . . hrm."

It was not a gentle death. "It seems Morris sought to

remove evidence, or cleanse this place. Though why he would remain a mystery; it is *quite* out of character for him."

"A man's character may have hidden depths." Vance turned in a slow circle, his own gaze roving. "We are here, old chap, because . . .?"

Have patience, sir. All shall be revealed. His fingers found a starched white handkerchief in a convenient pocket, and Clare stepped gingerly, broken glass crunching underfoot. The cloth, wrapped about his hand, was thin insurance, but all he possessed. Traceries of steam rose from their skin – it was a chill night in Bermondsey, and Londinium's grasping oily fog pressed thick against the walls.

Valentinelli had gone pale, and there was a fire in his close-set eyes that promised trouble. He watched Vance rather as he had been wont to watch Mikal during the first days of Clare's acquaintance with the sorceress and her staff; Clare spared an internal sigh and scanned the floor, dim lanthorn-glow filtering through raised dust. "Should be here . . . somewhere. Close."

He carefully toed aside an anonymous jumble of cloth and splintered wood. Nothing in it should slice the leather of his boots, but still. "Aha."

The trapdoor had seen heavy use, if the marks around it were any indication. The thick iron ring meant to provide leverage to heft it was rubbed free of rust, polished by gloved hands. "This is what we are here for."

"Always down." Valentinelli gave a sigh that would have

done an old woman proud. "Why we cannot hunt in cleaner places, *mentale*? Always down in the shite."

"Miss Bannon is far more equipped to hunt in Society." Clare's amusement did not hold an edge, but it was close. *At least, now it is. Her childhood was perhaps entirely otherwise.* "And that is as it should be. Whether we like it or not, my assassin, *we* are more suited to the mire than our fair sorceress." He wrapped his protected hand about the ring and heaved, and was gratified when the trapdoor lifted, a slice of fœtid darkness underneath dilating. It thudded down, and the draught from below the warehouse was an exhalation of disturbed dust, rot, and the peculiar sourness of earth lain beneath a covering, free of cleansing sunlight, for a very long time.

Rickety wooden stairs under the lanthorn's gleam; he eased the shutters as wide as they would go since there was little chance of a night-watchman seeing a suspicious glow *here*. Vance made a small clicking noise with his tongue, and Clare deduced the man was most pleased.

"What have we here?" Vance's footsteps were cat-soft, but the floor still creaked alarmingly. "Oh, Clare. You are a wonder."

"It is elementary, sir." Of a sudden, Clare was exhausted. "I wondered, why *here*? And I bethought me of the past."

Valentinelli shouldered him aside, a knife suddenly visible in one calloused hand. "What down here, *mentale*?"

"Nothing alive," Clare reassured him. "Everything in this excavation is likely to be mummified as the ancient Ægyptios. But here is where Morris found his prime cause, and no doubt considered himself lucky. The plague was a hardy beast two hundred years ago." His mouth was dry, and as Valentinelli tested the stairs and Clare followed, debated the advisability of explicitly mentioning that here was most likely the original source of the illness that had killed Eli and Tarshingale's patients, and decided against it.

There was no profit, as Vance might say, in stating the obvious.

Down, and down, the sour earth crumbling away from the sides of the passage; shovel-marks were still impressed on damp clay soil. Clare's throat was full of an acid clump, and he restrained himself from coughing and spitting by an act of sheer will.

The earthen strata changed colour, and the first skeletons appeared. Valentinelli crossed himself, and Vance made an amused noise.

"The Dark Plague," the criminal mentath breathed. "Quite. The damp eats at dead tissue, but lower down no doubt there are bodies preserved by the clay. And in those bodies . . ."

"The plague. Which Morris set himself to resurrect, to prove the Pathological Theory or merely to show it could be done. I would give much to know . . ." Clare did not finish the sentence. Anything he wondered now was immaterial.

"Archibald." For the first time, Francis Vance sounded serious. "If I may address you thus, that is . . ."

"For the time being, Francis, you may." Clare lifted the

lanthorn, and Valentinelli breathed out through his nose, the only sign of disgust he would allow himself.

"Very good. Archibald, my friend, we are too late. The genie, as it were, has escaped the lamp."

"You have read Galland, I see. Yes. The dreadful spirit is loose in the world, and our task now is to find a second spirit to oppose it." Clare could see the marks where samples had been scraped from the earthen walls; Morris had a fondness for femurs, it seemed. Scraps of ancient flesh hung on yellowed bone, a rat's corpse worked half-free of the wall and stared with a wide-open snarl, other detritus poured into what had been a grave for the many instead of for one.

Even in death, the space a body took up in Londinium was expensive, and obeyed certain laws of supply and rent, as Locke would have it. Smith and Cournot had refined the principle, of course, and Clare suddenly saw the pages of text before him, clear as a bell. It was an effort to bring his attention to the present moment.

I am frightened, he realised, *and my faculties seek to inure me to Feeling*. Did Vance feel this terror? Was a criminal capable of such dread?

"A cure? Dear man, you are an optimist." And yet Vance's amusement might have been a similar shield, for his tone was not quite steady, and he almost tripped on a stair-tread as earth shifted and the rat's corpse twitched. "Ah. Good heavens, not very stable, down here."

"No, Dr Vance. I am no optimist." Clare's fist was damp, for the handkerchief was collecting sweat in his palm. "I am merely a man who sees what must be done. We shall come to Morris's working area very soon, Ludovico. When we do, you shall hold the lanthorn."

And may God and Science both have mercy upon us.

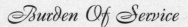 Chapter Twenty-Four

Burden Of Service

Stepping into her own house was tinged with a variety of uncomfortable relief, almost as if she had retired to a bolt-hole. To be Prime was to fear very little, but she was well on her way to seeing enemies in every shadow.

And for all I know, there may be. Especially if Britannia has another sorcerer dogging my footsteps. And the scene in the Hall probably did not inspire confidence or soothe Her. After all, Victrix – and Britannia Herself – could not know what Morris's fevered rantings might have told her.

And there was the question of the two canisters, disappeared. Emma sighed, working her fingers under her hair, leaning against her front door.

Mikal echoed her sigh, his shoulders dropping. He finally

broke the silence between them that had held all the way from Whitchapel. "Another sorcerer?"

"A Prime, no less." Wearily, Emma scrubbed at the skin over her skull. It would disarrange her hair most dreadfully, but she was past caring. *Is Clare here? He should be, if I have to stir one step to seek him out tonight I shall be quite cross.* Even the simple act of concentrating enough to discern who was within her walls seemed far too great an expenditure of precious energy.

The house was awake, in any event, and Mr Finch came stiffly down the stairs, his dusty black making the long thin lines of his gaunt body even slimmer. His indenture collar brightened visibly as he laid eyes on her. "Madam." He showed no surprise at her dishevelment – of course, he was phlegmatic in the extreme, as well as accustomed to the various states of disarray she suffered in Britannia's service. "Mr Clare left, with his . . . guest. Shall I have Madame Noyon . . .?" His eyebrows rose, and his face was truly like a death's head.

Starvation left marks on a man, and Finch was unwilling to let them fade. Or he did not possess the capability of letting such things fade. And, it must be said, neither did his mistress, no matter how successfully she hid the traces of her own private dæmons, real or imagined.

Clare had a guest? For now, though, she was called upon to tend to the responsibilities of a Prime toward her servants. "Yes, please do. I rather require a hot bath. And rouse the kitchen; Mikal requires sustenance." *Who can he have brought home? Not Sigmund, thank God, he's safe enough.* "I shall not stir forth one *step* tonight, Finch, unless there is a dire emergency. And even then, I shall reconsider." *So Clare had better not be in any danger. I may even be* vexed *with the man, and Ludo to boot.*

"Very well, mum. Sir." A half-bow to her, taking in Mikal at the very end, and he vanished down the hall to the kitchens. Waking the house at this hour was all manner of bother and annoyance, but what were such things to servants? Especially indentureds as well-paid and well-treated as her own.

"Is she at odds with you, then? The Queen?"

How was it possible for Mikal to sound so *indifferent?* "I believe her own cleverness stung her fingers, Shield. But she will blame me." *Or does she know exactly what Morris's madness has done? Perhaps I should have kept my temper in order to discern.* A sigh came from a deep well inside her. "Go. I shall be well enough."

He nodded. In the foyer's gloom, gaslamps turned down for the evening and her unwilling to expend more sorcerous force to brighten the air, his yellow irises held a fire all their own. "Emma."

Not now, please. "What?" She sounded ungracious, she realised, as well as peevish.

Well, at least I require no artifice to cover such things. Not with him.

"I am only half . . . what you suspect. The other half is different. The whole is—"

"Mikal—" *Curse you, I do not wish to know!*

He dared to interrupt her. "The whole, Prima, is at your command. Of course." He turned on his heel and strode away, disappearing in Finch's wake as a bell jangled in the depths of the servants' quarters and the susurrus of cloth began. At any moment, Severine and the maids would appear to usher Emma into a hot bath, there would be light refreshment, and she could fall into her bed with a sigh of well-earned relief.

Still, it bothered her. Had Victrix any idea what this "weapon" could do? There was also the little matter of the canisters of poison Morris had taken with him; they must be found and dealt with, and where on *earth* was Clare?

"*Madame!*" There was Severine, in a lace cap, shadows under her coal-black eyes and her plump hands wringing at each other. A dark strand of hair freighted with grey slipped from under the housekeeper's cap, and she negotiated the stairs with most unseemly haste. Behind her, Catherine and Isobel hurried, Isobel yawning and Catherine's curls heavily disarranged. All three wore the powdery-silver metal of indenture collars, lovingly burnished and softly glowing. "You are returned, *bien*! And so tired. Come, come, we shall take good care of you."

"Good evening." Her shoulders dropped for the first time, tension easing. "I hope you will, Severine, for I sorely need it. A bath, and perhaps some *chocolat*."

And I may be able to read half a page of a dreadfully sensational novel before I fall into sleep.

It was by far the most pleasant thought she had

experienced in a few days. Later, of course, she would curse herself for not sallying forth to find a certain mentath. But for that night, Emma Bannon laid down the burden of service for a few hours . . . and was content.

Chapter Twenty-Five

A Congress of War

The following morning began rather inauspiciously.

"What in *God's* name is happening here?" Miss Bannon all-but-barked, momentarily forgetting her usual well-bred tones.

Clare blinked. He had laid his head down on the desk for a bare moment, merely to rest. The stiffness in his back and neck, as well as the uncomfortable crust about his eyes, told him he had instead slept, and quite deeply too.

Valentinelli, his pallet spread near the workroom door, sheepishly slipped a knife back into his sleeve and yawned hugely, stretching. One of his hands almost touched the thunderstruck sorceress's skirts, and she twitched the black silk of mourning away from his fingers reflexively. She was attired as smartly as ever, despite the mourning, and her jewellery – a torc of bronze ringing her slim throat, rings of mellow gold on each finger, her earrings long daggers of jet – rang and crackled with golden charter symbols. Her small arms were full of broadsheets, the ink on them still fresh enough for its odour to penetrate the scorch-throat reek of live experimentation.

Vance had, by all appearances, gone to sleep propped in a corner, very much as an Ægyptian mummy himself. He twitched into wakefulness and caught himself, his gaze distressingly sharp as soon as he rubbed at his eyes. All three men were covered with dust and dirt, the effluvium of a grave below Londinium's surface, and perhaps smelled just as bad as the experiments.

Clare's brow was unbecomingly damp. He coughed, and caught his pen, which threatened to skitter from the desk's cluttered surface. The nib was crusted with dried ink. "I say," he managed, "good heavens. I must have slept."

"There is news." Miss Bannon swept past Valentinelli, and the door moved a fraction behind her, but did not close. "Morris is dead, but his end has been achieved. The broadsheets are full of a mysterious illness spreading with *most* unseemly haste in the lower quarters of town. What *happened?*"

"Morris? Dead?" Vance took two steps away from the wall and halted, his eyes narrowing. "How? When?"

The look Miss Bannon cast at the criminal mentath was chilling in its severity. "Good morning, sir. I do not believe I have had the pleasure." Her tone announced it was a dubious pleasure at best, and her entire demeanour was of the frostiest vintage. "Archibald?"

"Ah. Yes." He cleared his throat again. *This should be quite interesting.* "Miss Bannon, may I present Dr Francis Vance? Dr Vance, our hostess, Miss Bannon."

Clare had very little time to savour Miss Bannon's momentary silence. Vance bowed and his right hand moved as if to lift his hat, forgetting that he wore none. "I am *extremely* pleased to be introduced, Miss Bannon. Mr Clare thinks very highly of you, and your hospitality is simply incredible."

Her response – studying him for a few long moments, from top to toe – lacked nothing in insouciance. "He thinks rather highly of you as well, sir." Her tone managed to express that she did not share such estimation or optimism, and she returned her attention to Clare's quarter with a dark look that promised trouble later. "So. Well. Mr Clare?"

He almost winced. *Oh, dear.* "Suffice to say we are brothers-in-arms in this affair, dear Bannon. The situation is . . . complex. In the lower quarters, you say? Spread of an illness?"

"They are calling it a rosy miasma, and it is spreading quickly enough to make the broadsheets promise another edition at midday. Clare, is it too much to ask for you to grant me an explanation?"

"Not at all. But . . . breakfast. We worked very late last night. I found the original source of Morris's plague. Tell me, what did he die of?"

She all but stamped her tiny foot. "The same poison that killed my Shield. Or is it an illness? This Pathologic

Theory of yours? Really, sir, I *do* require some information at this juncture!"

It rather irked Miss Bannon to be the less-informed of their pairing, Clare thought. Surely it was not quite logical to feel so secretly pleased at the notion. "Breakfast, Miss Bannon. I do not have much of an appetite, but it shall serve as a congress of war. The situation is worse than you may have ever dreamed."

"Lovely." She addressed the ceiling in injured tones. "And now he calls my *imagination* into question. Ludo, if you do not put that knife away *again*, I shall be outright vexed with you. Very well, gentlemen. I expect to see you in the breakfast room soon. Already I have had a request from the Crown for some manner of further explanation, one I cannot give until you share your tidings." Another venomous glance darted at Dr Vance – who looked rather amused again, dash it all – and she spun smartly, twitched her skirt away from Valentinelli again while the assassin stared at her and whistled a long low note, and her retreating footsteps were crackling little snaps of frustrated authority.

Silence fell among the men as they listened to her negotiate the stairs.

"Well." Vance rubbed his fingers together. " A most winning creature, old man, and you have been keeping her all to yourself."

"She singe your fingers, *bastarde*." Valentinelli gained his feet in a catlike lunge. He had, as usual, slept in his boots. "And Ludovico cut them off."

"You're quite a suitor, sir." Vance's laugh carried a note

of calculated disdain, and Clare rubbed at his damp fore-head, where a distressing headache was threatening. "Does your wife know?"

Damn the man. Clare gained his feet, shoving the uncom-fortable wooden chair back, and managed – just barely – to arrive in Valentinelli's way as the Neapolitan leapt for the criminal mentath, whose laugh could have been carved from ice. "None of that!" Clare cried, locking Ludovico's wrist and *twisting*, the knife clattering on the stone floor and his weight driving the assassin back a few critical steps. "*None* of that, Ludo, the man is simply baiting you! Pray do not make it *easier*!"

"Turn him loose, Clare." Vance stood at ease, but with his hands held oddly. Some manner of fighting skill, though Clare did not have enough time to do more than glimpse it, for holding Ludovico back took all his strength and a goodly portion of guile.

Do not force me to harm you. But he could not say it.

Ludovico subsided, though he was sweating, and his close-set eyes were hot with rage. He spoke very low in his Calabrian dialect, and there was no mistaking the import of the words – or their meaning. Not even a threat, merely a promise of retribution.

"Enough." Clare cleared his throat again. He rather wished for a spot of tea to ease the scratching. It would not ease the situation to spit, though. "I shall have Miss Bannon separate you, if you cannot behave as gentlemen. We have *much more pressing* problems, and after this affair is concluded you may duel each other with pistols in

Treyvasan Gardens for all I care. But for now, *cease* this foolishness."

He held no great expectation of soothing either of them, but apparently his invocation of satisfaction at a later point was enough. Vance stepped back, almost mincingly, and Valentinelli shook himself free of Clare's grip, stamping for the door. His footsteps were nowhere near as light or dainty as Miss Bannon's, and they vanished halfway up, as if he had recalled his ability to move silently.

Clare let out a sigh. His brow was really quite moist, and sweat had gathered under his arms as well. Exertion was not a marvellous idea so soon in the morning, and his bones reminded him that he was decidedly not of tender enough vintage to sleep in a chair. "That was ill-done," he remarked, mildly enough. "His possible marriage is rather a sensitive subject."

"They always are. And it is not possible; he had a wife once. You should have deduced as much." Vance, supremely unconcerned, set about adjusting his jacket. "Breakfast, you say? And I hate to be gauche, but a watercloset would do me a world of good, old chap."

Clare throttled the annoyance rising in his chest and nodded, sharply. "Do come this way, sir. I believe some shift may be made for you." His pause was not entirely for effect, for a novel idea had occurred to him. "And do be careful. This is a sorceress's house, and Miss Bannon's temper is . . . uncertain, with strangers."

Perhaps it would make the damnable man behave.

Though Clare, wiping at his forehead and cheeks with a slight grimace, was not hopeful.

Clare's appetite had deserted him entirely, for once. He had suitably freshened himself and changed his clothes, but his back still cramped, reminding him of its unhappiness. His joints had joined the chorus, and the broadsheets, spread over a small table brought into the too-bright breakfast room, did not help.

Morris had done his work well. "The remaining two canisters?"

"Disappeared. Either Copperpot was not truthful, or Mr Morris was not quite honest with the particulars." Miss Bannon's colour was fine this morning, but her small white teeth worrying at her lower lip betrayed her anxiety. "I rather think the latter, if only because of Ludo's fine work."

Clare's stomach twisted afresh. He sipped his tea, hoping to calm his digestion, and turned a page. The ink stained his fingers, but he could not find the heart to be even fractionally annoyed. "The ones left in Londinium are now useless. The genie, as Dr Vance remarked, has left the lamp."

"Ah, yes. Dr Vance." There was a line between Miss Bannon's dark eyebrows. "*This* is a tale I am most interested in hearing, Clare. He is *in my house*."

"I don't suppose there is a method for keeping him here?" Clare blinked rapidly, several times. The words on the pages refused to cohere for a moment.

"I have already attended to that, Archibald." Miss

Bannon glanced across the empty breakfast room as Mikal appeared, his tidy dark hair dewed with fine droplets of Londinium moisture. "Any news?"

"No further dispatches from the Palace." Mikal's lean face was not grave, but it was close. "The borders of the house are secure, Prima."

"Very good. Ludo?"

"At his *toilette*." Grim amusement touched Mikal's mouth, turning the straight line into a slight curve at its corners. "So is our other guest. When shall I kill him?"

"No need for that!" Clare interjected, hastily. "He has a steady pair of hands, and is familiar with the Theory. He will be most useful, and remanding him to Her Majesty's justice at the end of this affair—"

"—will be quite enough to salve your tender conscience?" Miss Bannon's expression was, for once, unreadable. She nodded, and Mikal drifted across the room to fetch her a breakfast plate. The sorceress, settled in her usual chair at the table she shared with Clare when he partook of her hospitality, shook the ringlets over her ears precisely once. "I am gladdened to hear it. But my question remains: what the devil is he doing here?"

"I am not quite certain." Clare forced his faculties to the task at hand, scanning columns of fine print. "Bermondsey, yes. Whitchapel, yes. Lambeth." He noted Miss Bannon's slight movement, slipped the notation into the mental bureau holding her particulars, and continued. "Cripplegate, yes. St Giles. The Strand – why there, I wonder? Ah yes, the Saint-Simonroithe, Morris would of course know the history. And the docks; dear God, it will spread like wildfire. It *is* spreading like wildfire." He exhaled, heavily. "How did he die, Miss Bannon?"

"Of his own creation, sir. I brought him to the Queen's presence; he expired very shortly afterwards." She accepted the plate – two bangers, fruit, and one of Cook's lovely scones – with a nod, and Mikal set to work loading another. "It was unpleasant. Convulsions, all manner of blood."

Clare shut his eyes. For a moment, the idea of swooning appeared marvellously comforting. He was so bloody *tired*. "He died in the Queen's presence? You took him before Britannia?"

"Of course." Puzzled, she stared at him through the fragrant steam wafting up from her scone. "You've gone quite pale."

"Perhaps Britannia will protect her vessel." Clare's lips were suspiciously numb. He gathered himself afresh. "This illness is incredibly communicable, Miss Bannon. The danger is quite real."

"Communicative?" It was her turn to pale as she dropped her dark gaze to her plate. "Infectious? Very?"

"Yes. *Very*. Who else was in the Presence?"

"A few personages," she admitted. "None I care over-much for." Quite decidedly, she turned her attention to her breakfast and began calmly to consume it. "I am still unclear on the exact dimensions of this threat, Archibald. You are to have breakfast and explain. I cannot fend off the Crown's requests for information for very long."

It was, he reflected, quite kind of Miss Bannon that she

did not consider aloud dragging him *and* Vance into Britannia's presence to give an account of the entire mess. "We have found the original source of the illness. Have you studied History, Miss Bannon?"

"My education, sir, was the best the Collegia could provide." But there was no sharpness to her tone. "And I have taken steps to continue it. What part of History's grand sweep do you refer to?"

"Sixteen sixty-six. The Great Plague." *And during it, Londinium burned.*

The silence that fell was extraordinary. Miss Bannon laid her implements down and picked up her teacup, her smallest finger held just so. Mikal settled himself in his usual chair as well, his plate heaped so high it was a wonder the china did not groan in pain.

"A rather dreadful time," she finally observed, taking a small mannerly sip.

"Rather. And we are about to suffer it again, unless Science – in the form of Dr Vance and myself – can effect some miracle of cure. A scrum may be possible, if we are correct."

"And if you are not?"

The door opened and Vance appeared, freshly combed, new linens – charm-measured, no doubt, by the redoubtable Finch and his men – taken advantage of, and his eyes peculiarly dark with some manner of emotion Clare found difficult to discern.

"If we are not," Vance said, "then, Miss Bannon, God help Londinium, and the rest of the globe. Your hospitality is most wonderful, though your servants are peculiarly resistant to any manner of charm or politeness."

Miss Bannon blinked. "They do not waste such things on those . . . visitors . . . I have expressed an aversion to," she replied mildly. "Do come and have breakfast, sir. And mind the silver."

"I am an artist of crime, madam. Not a common thief." He straightened his jacket sleeves and stepped into the room, glancing about him with much interest. "Your Neapolitan is close behind me, old chap. Still in a bit of a temper."

When is he not, nowadays? "Do try not to come to blows at the breakfast table. Our hostess rather frowns upon such things." Clare sighed, heavily, and returned his attention to the broadsheets. Eating was out of the question, at least for him.

"Good heavens." Miss Bannon took another mannerly sip of tea. "Is there anyone in this house you have *not* annoyed, Vance?"

It was, Clare rather thought, a declaration of war. Vance apparently chose not to register it as such. "Mr Clare, perhaps. And I'm sure there is a servant or two who has not seen me. What news, old chum?"

I grow weary of the familiarity of your address. But Clare set aside the irritation. It served no purpose. "Mr Morris fell victim to his own creation, so we are forced to a process of experimentation. Any of his papers or effects detailing his own experiments – Bannon, I don't suppose we could lay hands on them?"

"I have a faint idea where they may be found." Miss Bannon's tone chilled slightly. "I hope the one likely to possess them has not left Englene's shores, or I shall be vexed with *travel* as well. I require as much information as you can give me about the nature of this illness. Perhaps it may yet be Mended."

"If so, I shall be glad of it." Clare closed *The Times* and opened the *Courier,* a most disreputable rag notable for the poor quality of its paper, the hideous shape of its typography, and its absolute accuracy in detailing the grievances of the lower classes. "For I must confess, Bannon, I am not sanguine in the least."

Chapter Twenty-Six

A Gift of Any Sort

Saffron Hill hunched colourlessly under morning drizzle. Emma felt just as dreary, her outlines blurred by a slight glamour – no more than a smearing, a delicate insinuation against the gaze, so that her cloth did not tell against her. Beside her, Mikal was utterly still, studying the end of the street where it devolved into Field Lane, and a more wretched bit of dirt would be difficult to find even in Londinium.

The weight in Emma's left hand was a thin, broken chain of cheap silvery metal. Caught in its links was a thread of dark hair, stubbornly coarse. The tiny brass charm attached very near the break held the impress of a double-faced Indus godling, one of the many who made the subcontinent such a patchwork of competing interests and principalities.

Ripe for exploitation, they are, and Britannia's servants experts of divide and rule. We have done as much since Golden Bess's day. And before. We learned well from the Pax Latium, for all we were slow to apply such lessons.

What instinct had moved her to quietly pocket the broken necklace she had found tangled in Llewellyn Gwynnfud's spacious purple-hung bed on a summer's morning long ago? Their affair had died a fiery death over a certain French "actress"; while Emma was merely unwilling to share, she was outright indisposed to being *lied* to. The tart had been knifed by her "manager" – Emma had borne the accusation of a hand in that manner nobly, considering she was completely innocent – and had been almost, *almost* willing to forgive.

She was no Seer, and the revelation of the necklace's owner – and the source of the coarse dark hair caught in its strands – had been quite surprising. She supposed Llew was catholic in his buggery, in every sense, and so had quietly left his house and returned to her own with the cheap chain burning in her skirt pocket.

And she had never received him again, or sought his company since. Until Bedlam, and the affair that had brought Clare to her notice, and to . . . yes.

To her regard.

Any idiot with ætheric talent knew how to practise a sympathy. And dear old Kim would not be on guard. She had never mentioned that little incident to another living soul. Kim may well have thought Lord Sellwyth had retained the scrap as a memento Llew may not have even known that his dalliance had been discovered or that a piece of evidence had found its way into her hands.

She held it tightly, her gloved fist bound as well with a silken handkerchief Mikal had knotted with exceeding care. It would not do to lose this sympathetic link. She would be forced to resort to other, bloodier, and far more draining methods to find her quarry.

Grey-faced children dressed in ragged colourless oddments slunk in every bit of shade they could find, and the æther here was thick with misery. In Whitchapel there was anger aplenty, but this corner of Londinium had burned through all such fuel long ago and was left with only cinder-glazed hopelessness. It was a wonderful place to hide, if one was a sorcerer; but the ætheric weight would rather tell on the nerves after a while.

If he had any nerves left, that was.

The chain and charm hummed with live sorcery as she caught the rhythm, her throat filling with a strange murmur, heavily accented in odd places. It was a song of spice and incense, the dust of the Indus rising through the cadences, and the brief thought that perhaps Mikal would find it familiar threatened to distract her.

She waited. Patience was necessary, though the consciousness of precious time draining away frayed her nerves most disagreeably. Clare had not looked well this morning, pale and rather moist, but who would look hale when faced with *this*? As well as that distasteful art professor.

The man had looked very much like the worst sort of

disreputable, with a cast to his mouth that was utterly familiar, especially since Emma had gone recently into Whitchapel and peered behind the dark curtain smothering her pre-Collegia memories. She rather disliked those recollections, and endeavoured to put them as far from her as possible.

The trouble was, sometimes they would not stay tamely in their enclosure.

Another twitch, the sympathetic sorcery testing her grasp. Like called to like, and of course he would have defences, some overt, others subtle and more dangerous. Yet he was not on his home ground, and could not risk a heavy expenditure of ætheric force lest it twist in unexpected ways – and, most likely, eat him alive.

Such was not a pleasant end.

Another twitch, more definite, and she pointed with her free hand, a corkscrew-twisted charter symbol spitting and spilling from her right third finger. Mikal had her arm; he guided her across the sludge of the street, old cobbles and bricks slipping and sliding under a thick greasing of muck. It was not Scab, of course, but it was fœtid enough.

She had a vague impression of warped wood and crumbling brick; the consciousness of being all but blind as she followed the inner tugging struck her, hard. Losing breath, the humming tune failing, she shunted aside the force of the triggered defence and inhaled smoothly, the song becoming a hiss-rasp of scales against dry-oiled stone. Mikal's voice, very low – he would be speaking to soothe her if he suspected she struggled with a defensive ætheric hedge.

It was not necessary, but vaguely pleasant nonetheless.

She came back to herself with a rush rather like the humours rising to the head after one sprang too quickly from a sickbed, and her left hand jerked forward and held steady until the connection broke with a subliminal *snap*. Before her rose a crooked door made glue and sawdust, and the narrow, barely lit hall was full of refuse. Somewhere a baby cried angrily, and there was a stealthy noise in the walls – rats, or the poor packed into these rooms like maggots in cheese. Either was likely.

Mikal had drawn a knife. Its curve lay along the outer edge of his forearm, and his eyes were alight with a fierce joy she rarely saw. Her eyebrow lifted a fraction, and he shook his head slightly. He could hear no heartbeat, no breathing behind the door.

Which meant little.

She stepped aside, very carefully, testing the rotting floor before committing her weight. It was her turn to settle herself and nod, fractionally; Mikal uncoiled. The door shattered, a witchlight sparking into being and flaring to distract and disrupt any possible attack, he swept through with her skirts hard on his heels and gave the small hole one swift, thorough glance before turning unerringly toward the makeshift cot mouldering in the corner.

The room was hardly bigger than a closet, its only claim to light or ventilation a small opening near the ceiling. It was barred, but the bars had been worked loose, their softened bases still tingling with ætheric force, torn free of damp-eaten wood. A scrap of black material caught on one fluttered, and Mikal's fingers darted out, catching and tearing it free as Emma braced herself for more traps.

Which were not present.

The room was echo-empty, and a whiff of brimstone and salt drifting across her nose told her someone had been busily cleaning ætheric traces away. "Oh, *bother*," she whispered, in lieu of something less polite. No reason not to act the lady now.

There was a large damp stain on the floor, and despite the chill a lazy bluebottle had found it and was busily investigating. The cot held scraps of white and green, and she cocked her head, openly staring.

A tussie-mussie of jonquil and almond blossoms, a flowerseller's small silvery dust-powder charm keeping them damp and fresh, lay twined with a red ribbon. Underneath, a folio of new, stiff leather lay, still fuming of the solutions used to tan it.

"Blood," Mikal said, grimly. But softly. "Prima?"

"Not enough to consign dear Kim to the afterworld, I fear." She stared at the flowers and the folio. "And it is unlike him to leave me a gift of any sort."

Her eyes half-lidded. The almond blossom was a sign of promise, and the jonquil's pale creaminess spoke of a demand for the return of a certain affection. The red ribbon – blood, perhaps? But Kim Finchwilliam Rudyard would not leave her such tokens.

The other Prime? Perhaps. Probing delicately, she caught no hint or taste of trap. Mikal ghosted forward, waiting for her gesture, and when she sighed and spread her free hand he gingerly touched the nosegay with a fingertip.

Still no trap.

He tucked the flowers under his arm and brought the folio to her; she held it in her free hand while he unknotted the handkerchief and wrapped the broken necklace back into a small efficient parcel, which she slid into a skirt pocket. The folio was so new it creaked, bearing no impress of personality as a well-used item would, and she opened it with a certain trepidation.

Inside, crackling yellow paper, covered in a spidery hand. Her lips thinned as she brought the witchglobe close, uncaring that the sensitised, freshly cleansed æther would hold the impress of even so minor a Work as a simple light for a long while.

And with it, her own presence, like a shout in the night.

Drawings. She riffled through the papers, and her suspicion was verified.

"Well, Clare will be very happy," she murmured. "But I am unsettled, Shield."

"Yes." He held the flowers, gazing at them curiously. Did he understand the message? This was a carefully set stage, and the nosegay had been planned just as the rest of it.

But not, Emma thought, by Rudyard. There was another player at the board. A Sorcerer Prime. One in the service of Britannia? But if so, why would he smooth *her* way?

I do not like this at all.

* * *

Clare blinked, focused through the lenses, adjusting a small brass knob. "Still wriggling. Nasty little buggers."

"Once they are in the blood, they are remarkably resistant." Vance was hunched over his own spæctroscope, his fingers delicate as he fiddled with the *resolutia marix*. "Even a severe temperature change does not alter their rate of progression. Fascinating."

"Quite." Clare restrained the urge to tap his fingertips on the scarred wooden table with frustration. "The cloracemine?"

"No effect, except to cause the iron in the blood to crystallise. Which I really must investigate further, when this is finished. The applications could be— I *say*!"

"What?"

"Nothing. They're still alive, even as the acidity rises. It docs lower their rate of division, but . . ."

". . . not enough," Clare finished. He coughed, wetly, turning his head aside so he did not foul the sample. Traces of steam rose from his cheeks, and he blinked them aside, irritably. It was chill in the workroom, Miss Bannon kindly leaving a charm to keep the temperature fairly steady in order for experimentation to have one less variable.

Valentinelli dozed on a stool near the door. He looked far more sallow than usual, but his scarred cheeks held splotches of bright crimson. His breathing had turned into a whistle, but his dark gaze darted occasionally from under his eyelids, sharp as a knife and more often than not settling on Vance's broad back.

The criminal mentath had taken his jacket off despite

the chill, and his shirt was adhered to his skin by a fine sheen of sweat. He selected another culture and another substance from the racks to his right, deftly sliding the fresh marrowe-jelly full of the original plague organisms into the spæctroscope's receiver. He uncapped the clorafinete powder, measured out a spoonful, mixed it with fresh marrowe-jelly in a small glass bowl, and selected a dropper from the small rectangular *serviette* full of sterilising steam. Two shakes, the dropper cooling rapidly, and the clorafinete mixture was introduced to the original plague. He twisted another knob slightly, and put a bloodshot eye to the viewpiece.

"Blast this all to hell," he muttered.

Clare quite agreed. There was no time, and yet this numbing systematic process was the one that held the greatest chance of working. He himself was no further than wachamile, working from the other end of the elemental pharma-alphabet.

Footsteps on the stairs. The door was flung open and Miss Bannon appeared, high natural colour in her cheeks, her curls disarranged. "Morris's notes!" she exclaimed, holding a creaking-new leather folio aloft rather in the manner of a Maenad brandishing the ivy-wrapt heart of a transgressor.

Such fanciful notions, Clare. But his faculties were in rebellion.

"How on earth did you—" Vance halted abruptly as a charter symbol flashed golden between Miss Bannon's fingers, hissing warningly. The Doctor, already halfway across the workroom, approached the sorceress no further. "Ah. I, erm. Well."

Clare rubbed at his eyes, carefully. *He moves very quickly.*

"Will these help, Clare? I confess I cannot make much of them." It was odd, she seemed almost joyous. "But *you* can. There is another message from the Crown, too. I have not opened it either, but we shall be rather in bad odour if I do not make some variety of explanation soon. The streets are full of coughing, and people collapsing in the road – even respectable people. Why is it so *fast*?"

"I do not know." A thought occurred to him. "Did you happen to see any of the victims with an indenture collar? I ask because your servants have not so much as a cough, yet, and—"

There was a soft thud. Valentinelli had hit the stone floor, and Miss Bannon dropped the folio. In that moment, Clare saw truly what she must have looked like as a young girl, and chided himself for thinking he had ever glimpsed the wonder of it before.

She knelt next to Ludovico, tucking her skirts back, and the assassin cried out weakly in Calabrian. The scarlet flags on his cheeks had intensified, and the shadow under his jaw was a swelling – not yellow, as the new plague, but deadly black, as the old.

Clare's beastly conscience pinched. *He knew the risk, I explained it – there are quite deadly vapours here. How did he contract it, though? Did the plague-pit infect him somehow? But it would have infected Morris too.*

The sorceress's house shivered once. Running feet in its recesses told him the servants heard their mistress's call.

Clare's knees creaked as he bent to pick up the folio. A wave of dizziness passed through him; his faculties noted it, allowed it to recede. He was thinking through syrup. "I will not ask how you acquired these, Miss Bannon. Do make Ludovico comfortable. We shall send word should we require more supplies."

"Very well." She was pale as milk, and he noticed her skin did not steam, even in this chill. "I did see some indentureds among the collapsed, Clare. I . . . perhaps mine are simply hardy."

"Or perhaps you have some natural immunity, Miss Bannon. We cannot be certain." *And should we take a sample of your blood for analysis, who knows what might occur?* He opened the folio, hoping his words did not sound too ponderous. His tongue was oddly thick, and the sweat greasing him was most unpleasant. It smelled of treacle, or something similarly sick-sweet, and they had not managed to discern the mechanism responsible for *that*, either. "Do you feel faint at all?"

"I am *quite* well, thank you. Sorcerers do not suffer some things, perhaps this is one." Her gloved fingers hesitated over Ludo's scar-pocked cheek. For once, she did not draw fastidiously away when he moved. "Clare . . ."

"He is quite durable, and he has not Morris's plague." The false comfort was not worthy of her, but Clare did not have the heart to tell her she was perhaps witnessing the last of Valentinelli's eventful walk upon the weary earth.

There was a commotion as the footmen arrived, and such was the devotion of the sorceress's servants that they did not cavil at carrying another very-ill man about, nor did they make avert signs to save themselves from ill fortune or humour. Of course, an indentured servant could not complain . . . and even cadaverous Finch was in proper health, with not so much as a sniffle.

It was *quite* provoking. He brought his attention back to the folio, and noted Vance's hopeful drawing-near.

Miss Bannon noticed too. A few sharp, instantly forgotten syllables left the sorceress's throat, and Vance hopped back in a most ungainly fashion as the air between himself and Clare hardened, diamond-sparkling for a moment, a concave shield of ice. It slid to the floor, shivering into fragments, and Horace grunted as he hefted Valentinelli's dead weight.

"Mum?" the footman asked, in a whisper.

"Take him to his chamber. Ready an ice bath, I shall be along in a moment." The sorceress rose slowly, Marcus the other footman backing slowly up the stairs with his beefy arms under Valentinelli's shoulders. Strange, how small and thin the Neapolitan looked now. "Doctor, must I warn you further?"

"No, madam." Icily polite, the criminal mentath stepped back to his spæctroscope. "I am dependent upon solving this riddle as much as your Campanian suitor; or rather more, for I have contracted Morris's damnable plague. It may save you the trouble of dealing with me in what is no doubt your accustomed fashion."

"You have precious little idea of my accustomed—" the sorceress began, rather hotly.

Will the two of you cease? "Miss Bannon. Pray leave us to solve this riddle. We shall do all we can. If there is a solution to be found, rest assured you have contributed everything within your considerable powers towards such an end."

She studied him closely and he straightened under her gaze, hoping she could not see the red splotches on his cheeks or the small tremors running through his bones. He did not have much time before he suffered a crueller fate than Valentinelli's.

"Very well." She smoothed her skirts, a woman's nervousness, perhaps. Never mind that she was, in his experience, the female least likely to need such a soothing habit. "Thank you, Archibald."

"Emma." Clare's throat was full. Feeling, the enemy of Logic, was mounting. Inside his narrow chest, the heart she had mended with sorcery such a short time ago settled into a high, fast gallop.

The mentath watched the sorceress leave, took a deep breath, and returned his attention to the folio, ignoring Vance's bright deadly gaze.

Chapter Twenty-Seven

A Finer End

She had never entered the room given over to Valentinelli's use before, and saw no reason to now. Mikal hovered at her shoulder as she held the charming steady, her skirts pulled back from the threshold, and Horace and Marcus lowered the assassin into the ice bath. There was a choked cry and Ludovico's wracked body twisted; Alice the blonde chambermaid and her brunette shadow Eunice worked their homely magic upon the monkish, narrow bed and its linens. Their collars were bright, and they cast darting glances at her; when the footmen heaved Valentinelli free of the slurry of ice and water she made a gesture, a drying charm sparked and fizzed, and he was heaved gracelessly into the waiting bed.

"Mum." Finch's discreet cough. He peered around motionless Mikal. "Messenger from the Collegia. Awaiting your reply."

As soon as she loosed her hold, the assassin began to thrash. She gestured again, and Mikal moved forward, stepping into the room.

An iron rack atop a bureau of dark wood, festooned with cooled and hardened wax, held half-burned candles, their wicks dead and spent. There was a small *tau* corpse upon it, made of pewter with sad paste gleams for eyes and side-wound.

Does he pray?

The same chest she had seen in his other small rooms stood, closed and secretive, at the foot of his bed. He had chosen this room very near Clare's suite, despite its small size, and she had oft wondered what lay behind its door.

Mikal settled at the bedside, yellow irises gleaming in the dimness. He would keep the assassin contained, and make certain he did not strike an onlooker in his delirium.

The gaslamps hissed, and the servants looked to her for direction.

Oh, Ludo. Not like this. You deserve a finer end. There was a dry rock in her throat. She turned her attention to Finch. "From the Collegia?"

"Yes, mum." He did not quite bow, but he did hunch, and she remembered the hungry, sore-ridden wreck he had been long ago, before she had taken him into her service. How Severine had turned up her nose at the distasteful sight, and what had Emma said?

He has performed signal service already, Madame Noyon. Pray do not argue. That had been during the Glastonsauce affair: a newly crowned Queen in dire need of defence against a cabal of creaking ministers and competing interests, not the least of which was her mother's determination to keep Victrix dependent and weak. The affair had taught Victrix to almost-trust the sharp-eyed young sorceress who had entered the game uninvited and turned it to the monarch's advantage.

She gathered her skirts. The jet earrings shivered, tapping her cheeks; she took stock of her remaining resources. There was plenty of ætheric force in her jewellery, and the visit to Rudyard's bolt-hole had not drained her overmuch.

The trouble was, there was nothing she could *do*. Except fend off Britannia's ill-humour, and see what the Collegia was about.

Mikal? He took Shield training, they had plenty of time to notice his . . . distressing talents. They did not. How shall I defend him against a Council of Adepts, one no doubt top-heavy with enemies? Who is likely to be there? What can I muster against them?

And would she surrender her Shield to the Collegia, as the Law might require?

Of course not. Her gaze found Mikal's. He swayed slightly on his chair, a supple movement. *I am Prime. I do not give up what is mine.*

No matter how often she asked herself the question, the answer was unvarying.

Was it more than that? She had undertaken to keep Clare close instead of sending him to Victrix, and undertaken to keep the disagreeable Doctor as well. And there was the matter of a tussie-mussie left for her, and a bloodstain upon a filthy Saffron Hill floor. A promise, and a demand.

From whom? Does it matter?

Finch waited with no sign of impatience or irritation. It was a rare man who knew the value of patience, and who was not bothered by silence.

He was such a man, and had behaved with admirable aplomb in the most dire of circumstances. The indenture collar was in no way sufficient reward, but it had been all Emma could offer him. The safety of her service, and the promise that whatever lay in his past would not pursue him past her doors.

For Finch, it was enough.

"Very well," she said, as if the butler had pressed her. "Show the messenger into the study."

"Yes, mum." He glided away, perhaps relieved.

"Prima?" Mikal, the single word a question. Did he fear the Law? Perhaps not. It was, she admitted, far more likely he feared some manner of duplicity. A missive from the Collegia could bode no good.

"All is well." She was conscious, at once, of the lie. It stung her blocked throat, and Valentinelli moved uneasily, murmuring curses in his native tongue. His eyelids fluttered, and his hands leapt up, fighting a shadow-opponent.

Today, his fingernails were clean. An odd sensation passed through her – a hot bolt of something very much like jealousy. She had never known him to scrape the filth of living away while in *her* occasional service. And yet, he and Clare were wonderfully suited to each other, and she did not have to worry overmuch for either of them when they were about chasing whatever prey the Crown set them at.

Perhaps it is time for worry, Emma. Don't you think so?

The chambermaids fluttered a little. The two footmen were still watching her for directions. How few people it took to crowd a room.

"Be about your duties," she continued, in a far more normal manner. "Except you, Horace – stay with Mikal, and be ready should he require something for Ludo's comfort. Thank you." She turned and swept away, trying not to hear Valentinelli's moaning.

She was braced for any manner of unpleasantness when she opened the door to her study and sallied inside, breathing in the smell of leather, paper, old books and the richness of the applewood fire laid in the grate, a charm whisking the smoke up the flue but leaving the delicious scent.

Anything, that is, except the youngling from the Hall of Mending, his hands wringing together much as Severine Noyon's sometimes did, his charm-smoothed cheeks pale and his tongue twisting as he gabbled out his news.

Thomas the Mender, Thomas Coldfaith, *her* Thomas . . .

. . . was plagued. And he wished to see her, at once. The message was clear.

He did not expect to live.

Interregnum: Londinium, Plagued

First a tickle,
then a choke,
then the red rose
lays a bloke.

*T*he first few cases were ignored. A vast mass seething
in rookeries in several districts – the Eastron End,
hard by Southwark but not within the confines of the Black
Wark, Whitchapel, Spitalfields – swallowed the tiny bits of
poison whole, and the drops altered the composition of the
ocean. They first complained of a cough, red roses blooming
in their cheeks like consumption's deadly flower – and
within hours came the swelling. If the boils burst, blood
and sourpink pus exploding as eyelids fluttered over their
red-sheened eyes, the sufferer might recover. But if the

convulsions started before the boils burst, a winding-sheet was needed.

At first it was called the Johnny-dances, for the convulsions. Then the Red Rose, for the flush in the cheeks, and the Hack, for the thick, chesty coughs. And the sweetbriar sickness, for the sugary smell of the sufferers' sweat. But after a little while, it was simply known as the Red. You caught the Red, hung the Red, danced the Red.

Ships sailed that eve with weakened, coughing sailors; those who were not buried at sea vanished in teeming ports that soon bloomed with deadly roses on hollow cheeks. The Red was a promiscuous mistress. She hopped the backs of gentlemen and hevvymancers alike, and they danced out their deaths in dosshouses and townhouses. Physickers shook their heads in puzzlement, and were often dead as their patients a day later.

And sorcerers fell ill. Some diseases passed the ætheric brethren by, but the Red was not one. In their bodies the Red made illogical sorcery explode in strange ways – one sprouted pinkish fungal growths, screaming as they ruptured his skin, another's body turned to a patchwork of red glass as ætheric force and blood twisted together in an oddly beautiful pattern. Usually so fortunate, the ætherically blessed found the Red invariably fatal.

And some whispered it was only fitting.

Where did it come from? None knew. Charms were no good against it, even those who could afford Mending died under the Red's lash. Some said it was a judgement from on high, others that it was a consequence of Progress and *the filthy conditions of the rookeries and slums of every large city, some few that it was an illness from the hot, newly conquered parts of the globe.*

Only the dead did not speculate. They mounted in piles, and Londinium for the first time in centuries heard the corpsepickers' ancient cry during times of disaster: "Bring out your dead!" The stigma of corpsepicking vanished, for their habit of taking valuables from the dead lost its impetus once there was a glut of said rags and shinies in the shops that would take such traffic. Instead, they carted the creaking barrows full of twisted limbs, and their cheery singing, interspersed with deep chest-coughs, was the sound of nightmare angels.

It was a corpsepicker's duty to sing, while he carted.

And on the Red danced, over the bodies of her victims. She bloomed like the reddest rose of the Tuyedor's device. She grew rank and foul, and there was no cure.

Chapter Twenty-Eight

A Footrace With Death

Genius though he was, Morris had not been *systematic*. The notes were a hotchpotch, records of experiments interspersed with bits of weather observation and snatches of old prayers mixed with hand-drawn observations and elongated screaming faces, lists of foods that interfered with Morris's most delicate digestion and constitution, and some most ugly bits of scurrilousness about Queen and Crown.

Morris had not been turned against his country. No, the genius had merely hated his fellow man with a deep, abiding passion and quite *democratic* uniformity, and found a way to cleanse the world of sinners with almost-invisible contagion – very much the hand of his vengeful God. It was an elegant solution to such hatred, and the drawings of the earlier iterations of the canisters were most intriguing.

But the delivery method did not give enough of a clue to the organism's roots, as it were.

Clare went slowly through the folio as Vance continued his testing. There was some small success with dical-chimide, but it quickly faded. The tiny little beings were incredibly resistant, and Clare had a momentary shudder when his faculties turned to the question of what they were likely doing inside his own veins.

How much time do I have?

His hand stole towards the secret drawer. Inside was a small silver-chased box, and a fraction of the powder inside would make his faculties sharper. Sharp enough to cut this knotted tangle into manageable pieces, as Aleksandr of Makedon once had in a temple, long ago?

What a historical thought.

Near the end, a single, creased scrap of paper drew his attention. The notations on it blurred, and he coughed, thickly. Squinted, cursing the veil drawn over his vision. His nose had dulled, too, for he could no longer smell the experimentation. The thickness of marrowe-jelly, the stagnant reek of disease, the miasma-choke of the autoclave steam-cleansing the eyedroppers. His fingers caressed the knob that would bring the drawer open and reveal the box.

"Nothing with faramide, either." Vance whistled tunelessly, but did not turn. "Do not take your coja, Clare. It will accelerate the illness."

What manner of deduction led you there, sir? But it was immaterial. Clare squinted a fraction more; his faculties seized upon the notations on the crumpled, torn farthing-paper. He could almost *see* Morris hunched at his table, scribbling, incoherent with excitement as whatever vengeful Muse or saint waited upon mad geniuses dropped the solution into his fevered, waiting brain.

"Aha," he breathed. "*Ah*." The fit of coughing seized him, and when it was finished, he spat a globule of bright red. It splatted dully on the floor, but Clare was past caring. "Vance. *Vance*."

"Filistune is also useless. I am here."

"Here it is." Clare forced his reluctant legs to straighten, pushing back the wooden chair with a scrape. "Here is the key. It is the alteration process. By God, man . . . by God . . ."

He did not have to finish. Vance was suddenly there, and the other mentath's sweat was as candy-sweet as his own. Vance took in the scrawled notations with a single glance and shut his eyes, the tear filming down his shaven cheeks tinged with crimson. His own faculties would be working through the ramifications and deductions, and when he opened his eyes again Clare found that their gazes met and meshed with no trouble at all.

It was a moment of accord he could have shared with none other than a mentath.

"Muscovide. And not marrowe-jelly." Vance nodded.

"We must have some method of separating—"

"—and an acidic base. Yes. *Yes*." Vance's fists knotted, and he made a short sharp gesture. As if he felt a throat between his fingers, and he wished to *squeeze*.

"It will take time to prepare, to break the chain of

replication. But by God, man, we can halt this dreadful thing."

"Then we must not stand about." A series of wracking coughs seized Vance's body, and he curled around them, shaking away Clare's movement to help with an impatient violence. When he could draw breath again, he straightened, and another of those piercing looks passed between them.

"Indeed." Clare suppressed the tickle in his own throat. With no further ado, he strode for the table and swept a working space clean with one of his trembling arms. *We are in a footrace with Death. But perhaps we may gain a length or two.*

Chapter Twenty-Nine

One Word

It was a good thing she had not wasted her sorcerous force duelling with the absent Rudyard. She could not take her carriage, or even the smart new curricle, for Mikal was still at Ludovico's bedside. Harthell the coachman paled at the thought of driving to the Collegia, though he was willing enough; *no*, she had told him, *merely saddle the bay mare, properly, and be quick about it. None of the sidesaddle rubbish.*

It meant she could not wear full mourning, but she suspected Eli would understand. And why mourn, when there was death aplenty lurking in the streets? Her least favourite riding habit, in a shade of brown most dowdy and with newly unfashionable mutton sleeves, at least had divided skirts. She could always turn it over to Catherine and Isobel for reworking; Catherine's needle could no doubt change it into something exquisite.

None of her servants had so much as a cough. The likely reason, of course, was throbbing in Emma's chest; a wyrm-heart Stone that granted life and immunity, extending out through the indenture collars. Such protection would not extend where it was most needed.

Mentaths did not indenture.

Wherever Llewellyn Gwynnfud, Earl Sellwyth, was, he was certainly sneering at her.

What would Llew say of this? But she could guess. And it would be nothing she could give credit to if she wished to retain her self-regard.

She gathered the reins, nodded to Harthell, and the bay clockhorse, shining and lovingly oiled, pranced restively. She was a fine creature, deep-chested and beautifully legged, her glossy hide seamlessly merging into russet metal and her hooves marvels of delicate filigreed power. Wilbur the spine-twisted stableboy darted forward to open the bailey gate, and the mare shot forward, hooves striking sparks from the cobbles. The gate clanged at her passage, rather like a mournful bell, and she was very glad Mikal had not come from Ludovico's bedside.

The witchlight before her spat silvery sparks, but she need not have bothered with the warning of a sorcerer's haste. Those on the streets, handkerchiefs clamped to their mouths, scattered as she cantered past, and the few carriages out and about in the Westron End were easily avoided. Those who could afford to stayed inside, those forced out of doors hurried furtively . . . and three of the scuttling pedestrians collapsed as she rode past, their limbs jerking in a deadly dance.

Morris, damn him, had wrought well.

Riding thus absorbed a great deal of her attention, but what remained circled the same few problems as a tongue would probe a sore tooth. They vied for her attention equally – Victrix, the Duchess and her hangman, the face-less sorcerer who had so generously left Morris's notes and quite possibly injured Rudyard severely in the bargain, Clare's flushed cheeks and sweating, fevered brow, Ludovico's restless tossing, Mikal's hypnotic swaying at the assassin's bedside.

What am I to do? How may this be arranged satisfac-torily?

For the first time in a very long while, Emma Bannon had precious little idea. Everything now depended on Clare . . . and on other factors she had little say in. For a sorceress used to resolving matters thoroughly, quietly, and above all, to her own liking, it was a d—d *uncomfortable* state of affairs.

Through moaning, fog-choked, eerily calm Londinium the sorceress rode, and she arrived at no conclusion.

As soon as the bay's hooves touched down on the white pavers inside the Black Gate, Emma tasted the chaos and fear roiling through the Collegia's sensitised fabric. The Great School shook, its white spires flushed with odd rainbow tints and its defences, invisible and barely visible, quivering with distress.

She took the most direct route to the Hall of Mending at a trot, and the Collegia servant who took her horse had a fever-bright glare and an oddly lumbering gait. Emma merely nodded and mounted the steps with a stride a trifle too free to be a lady's, the great Doors opening creak-slowly. She nipped smartly between them, rather as if she were a student again . . .

. . . and plunged into a maelstrom.

The white pennants and hangings had been taken down, and the floor was splashed with scarlet. Cots lay in even rows, then jammed into corners, while Menders and their apprentices hurried from one to the next, seeking to dull the pain of sorcerers who lay twisting and screaming as their bodies warped under a double lash of disease and ætheric eruption. Bannon actually stepped back, almost blundering into a young apprentice who hissed "*Mind* yourself!" and scrambled away, his arms full of bloody rags.

The low sinuous altarstone throbbed as well, flushed with pink as its energies, collected over generations, were now plumbed to aid in Mending.

It did not look as if it was doing much good. As she hurried down the central aisle, looking for a particular set of broad crippled shoulders, a lean hieromancer in his traditional blue jacket thrashed off a narrow cot and screamed a high piercing note of pain, and his body disintegrated under a wave of twisting irrationality. His flesh parted with sick ripping sounds, and the blood that spilled out crystallised into what looked like rubies, gem-bright droplets that chimed as they hit the floor.

Good God. Emma did not halt, ducking the fine mist

of fluid turned to stone and hurrying past as Menders converged, charms flashing valorously but ineffectively. Sweat had collected along Emma's lower back, and she *felt* the death of the hieromancer, brushing her with soft-feathered fingers.

Her Discipline responded, the deeper fibres of her body and mind twitching. She shuddered, and just then caught sight of Thomas Coldfaith.

His regular ungainly walk, shuffling and pulling his recalcitrant clubbed foot, was even more painful; his twisted face florid with Morris's plague and streaks of pinkish rheum streaking his scar-pocked cheeks. His wonderful eyes were bloodshot, and he appeared not to notice her. His Mender's robe was grey, not white, not his usual jay's-bright plumage, and spattered beside with all manner of fluids. He had just straightened from another cot, where a dead body lay slumped, twisting and jerking as it turned itself inside out and spattered the surrounding area with entrails and foul blackish, brackish semi-liquid.

She arrived before him with no memory of the intervening space, the feather-tickles all over her body *most* distracting despite her training's tight reining.

Once or twice before, the Hall of Mending had been full of such suffering. Only then none of Emma's Discipline had been alive to witness it, for those of the Endor had been killed as soon as certain . . . troubling signs . . . were noticed.

Menders, however, had ever been cosseted.

"Thomas." She caught his arm, her gloved fingers

slipping slightly against the slickness coating his robe. "You called for me."

He blinked, bleary, and the red film over his irises and whites turned his gaze to a chilling blankness. "Em?"

"I am here." The same dry rock in her throat. "Thomas . . ."

"And untouched. That is good." A weary nod of his proud, misshapen head. "Though why I am surprised, I do not know."

Her temper and conscience both pinched, but the sea of noise about them overwhelmed both. "There may be a cure. I can bring you to it." *Clare will help. He must be very far along now.* Childish faith, perhaps, but she ignored such an estimation.

More blinking, and Coldfaith swayed, as if undecided.

Enough. She slipped her arm through his and began to urge him along. *They can do without you, Thomas. We need a quiet corner, and I shall . . .*

What was she contemplating? The weight in her chest was terrible. Even more dreadful was the shaking through his body, communicating to hers in a flood of loose-kneed, swimming dismay.

"Em." Coldfaith halted. "I wished to see you, before I did what I must."

All her gentle urging could not move him. She clasped his arm more tightly, set her heels, and pulled a little more firmly. "Come with me. Please."

"No." A terrible clarity bloomed in his dark gaze, behind the film of blood. "Emma."

"Thomas – *Tommy*." As if they were students again, young and bright and struggling. "Come."

He freed himself of her grasp, gently but decidedly. "I wished to see you once more," he repeated. "And to tell you I have not been kind to you. Before our Disciplines, Em, I had . . . thoughts." He murmured something she could not quite catch, and as she leaned closer to him among the buffet of the crowd, he coughed. Bright red spattered along her shoulder, but she did not care. "I . . . I must tell you. Em. Yes, must tell Em . . ."

Another ripple through him, and she caught at his elbow again. A Mender hurrying behind her bumped against her skirt and hissed an imprecation, having little patience for the obstruction it represented. A sea of coughing rose through the Hall's capacious entrance, more screams, and moaning.

Even though the Church held the ætherically talented as doomed to a purgatory at best and deep hellfire at worst, the sorcerers still called for God *in extremis*. Some of them even called for mothers they did not remember, for the Collegia was mother and father once a sorcerous child was taken.

None called for their fathers.

Thomas tacked away, slipping through her fingers with a feverish dexterity. He made for the pink-stained altar-stone, and as he did, a vast stillness descended upon the Hall.

Between one step and the next, Emma froze. She strained against air thick and hard as glass, drawing in a torturous lungful of stabbing air as Thomas reached the stone. He stood, his head down, for a long moment, and she knew what the silence and the difficulty in breathing meant.

Here in the Hall of his Discipline, Thomas Coldfaith was about to open the deepest gates of his sorcery. And Emma, an interloper with stinging eyes and a traitorous stone spike in her chest, was pinned as a butterfly on velvet, unable to act.

No. Thomas, no.

What had he meant to tell her?

He stretched his arms wide, rather as a *tau*-corpse would, and the silence became unbearable. The Hall's light brightened, scouring Emma's skull, nails through her sensitive eyes and her lungs refusing to work, a crushing upon throat and ribs and bones, her dress flapping and ruffling as streams of disturbed æther swirled past, whipping toward the hunchbacked sorcerer.

It was an act spoken of in whispers long after, how the greatest Mender of his generation opened the gates to his Discipline, becoming the throat Mending sang through. How several of the dying writhed before closing their eyes in peace, whatever hurtful blooming of the irrational wedded to the invisible vermin eating their flesh soothed away. How there was a shadow in the midst of the Hall of Mending's brightness, but it fled as Coldfaith cried one Word, the contours of which echoed and rambled through the Hall's nautilus-curved halls and inner recesses for decades afterwards, a Word like a name, full of longing and frustrated love, a depth of passion scarcely hinted at during a lifetime's watching and waiting.

There was only one sorcerer who could have explained the mystery of that Word, but she did not. None would have listened to her talk of Mending, for it was not her Discipline, and in any case, how could she explain *how* she knew?

She knew, for it was her own name: a Word that expressed a thin nervous fire-proud girl with brown curls seen through the eyes of a misshapen boy. The Word rang and rumbled and echoed, and when the door of his Discipline closed, the Menders found one of their own before the now-dark and drained altarstone, bending and coughing great gouts of scarlet blood that stained the pale flooring and would not be scrubbed away by bleach, carbolic, or sorcery.

Mending, as always, had exacted a price. Thomas Coldfaith's body twisted and shuddered as flesh transmuted itself to smoke-dark glass, particles grinding finer and finer until they shredded into dark vapour that streamed out through the vast open doors and dissipated over Londinium.

He failed, but not entirely. Afterwards, the sorcerous of the Empire did not die of irrationality. They simply, merely, died of the plague's convulsions and boils. A small mercy, perhaps, but all the twisted King of Menders (for so he was afterward called) could grant.

And Emma Bannon, Sorceress Prime, left the Collegia grounds on her bay clockhorse. None remarked her presence there that day, and it was perhaps just as well.

For had they addressed her, she would have struck them down with a Prime's vengeance. In each of her pupils the leprous green spark of her own Discipline had strengthened, and that fire would not extinguish easily.

Chapter Thirty

The Island's Heart

The coughing had taken on a wet, rheumy quality that would have been of great concern if Clare was inclined to pay it any mind. The bowl catching their crimson-laced, coughed-up effluvia had to be emptied regularly, else it slopped over onto the stony floor. Even the traceries of steam rising from their skin was tinged with red, or the film over their eyes gave everything a rubescence.

Clare had tossed his jacket and shirt over the desk chair, his narrow chest with its sparse hair visibly sunken as his body, held to its task by his faculties and a mentath's disciplined Will, struggled under the burden. Vance was hardly better, his larger frame scarecrow-wasted and his eyes glittering through the red film. He had stripped down to an undershirt of grey linen, and it did Clare much good to notice the criminal mentath was not quite so fastidious in his underdress as he was in his outer.

They both moved slowly. Past words now, they shuffled about the workroom, its chill that of a crypt. Bubbling alembics as the muscovide was distilled, and they need not culture the new plague, for their own secretions teemed with Morris's deadly gift to mankind. A single glance, or the offer of a freshly sterilised glass dropper, was all they needed.

Outside the workroom, Londinium writhed. The fog, normally venom-yellow, turned grey and greasy with the smoke from the bonfires some of the bodies were tossed onto.

On the fourth day, Miss Bannon appeared. "Clare?" Her gaze was somewhat odd, and he shelved the observation with a mental shudder. He had limited resources, and could not spare them. Not with this matter before him.

Even a mentath's determination would only stretch so far.

"Working." He coughed. "Tomorrow. Come back."

She stood in the door of the workroom, her small hands turned to fists, and after a long while, Clare noticed she had gone. The green pinpricks in her pupils seemed more the product of his fever than of her illogical sorcery. Her house was an island on a sea of chaos, and even the Crown had ceased sending missives.

Britannia, it seemed, was occupied with other matters.

None of the servants took ill, and meals arrived on silver trays and were sent away untouched. They were not quite of the usual quality, but Clare – when he expended any thought on the matter at all, which was briefly at best – realised that Londinium's supplies must be thin indeed at the moment.

An island, yes. But at the island's heart, two small grains of grit, their accretions of bloody phlegm and various odd bits of rubbish from their experiments carted away by pale, trembling servants who nonetheless did not cough and choke, nor grow fevered.

He supposed, when he thought on it – never for very long, there was too much else to be done – that both he and Vance would not live to see the fruits of their labour. There was no word of other mentaths succumbing to the disease, but of course, the broadsheets would not be interested in such things.

On the fifth day, Miss Bannon appeared as he had directed, standing in the door. She wore no jewellery, which was the first oddity; the second was her haggardness, her gaze burning in the peculiar way of sorcerers – as if she had forgotten her very *self*, or some vast impersonal thing was looking out through her skull. It was not the same terrible presence as Britannia peering forth from Her chosen vessel, for Britannia was recognisable in some essential way sorcery was not.

Clare spat at the bowl, accurately. A great deal of practice had refined such an operation – three coughs, deep and terrible, working the weight free of his chest, the roll of the tongue packing the bloody sludge into a compact mass, then the expectoration – just enough of an arc to land it in the bowl with a wet *plop*! It exhausted him, and he leaned against the table, clutching a small glass vial.

Vance swayed. "Muscovide," he croaked. "Who. Would have –" a series of coughs, and he spat as well – "thought?"

Quite. But Clare could not speak. His heart, labouring under the strain, thundered in his ears. He held the vial up, and Vance took it, shook it critically.

"Will it. Work?" The criminal mentath – at least he was, Clare thought hazily, a very fine lab assistant – reached for the spæctroscope. It took him two tries to curl his bloodstained fingers about the dial of the *resolutia marix*.

This was the last test, and Clare's faculties blinked for a moment. He surfaced through a great quantity of clear, very warm water to find himself standing, head down, breathing thickly like a clockhorse suffering metallic rheum, staring as Vance eased a dropperful of the thin red substance from the vial into the scope's dish, where a mass of plague was no doubt writhing and wriggling.

"Suction . . . tube," Vance wheezed. "It must be . . . introduced . . . under the skin."

Miss Bannon said something about a needle, and a Discipline.

"Perhaps." Vance coughed again. "We shall . . . see." His breathing failed for a moment, he swayed again, then leaned down to the spæctroscope's viewpiece.

Clare found his head turning. He stared at Miss Bannon, in her severe black, with no jewels swinging at her ears or glittering at her fingers. You could not tell she was a sorceress except for those green pinpricks in her pupils, the smudges underneath dark as charcoal and her curls more unevenly dressed than he had ever seen them. Had Madame Noyon taken ill?

Her lips moved. Something about Ludovico. Was he dead, then?

A vast weightlessness settled on his chest. The relief was immense, and as his knees failed, Clare realised he was expiring.

It did not hurt. That was the first surprise.

The second was Miss Bannon's wiry strength as she caught him, easing his fall, His field of vision swung to include Vance, who was staring down at him with a peculiar, saddened expression.

Had the cure not worked? But that was *impossible*, every other test had been—

Vance's knees buckled. His fingers were at his trouser pocket, and Clare thought slowly that it was *important*, something about that was vitally important.

Miss Bannon did not move to catch Vance as he folded to the floor. Instead, she bent over Clare, and the sound of her ragged breathing was the last he heard before darkness took him. It was perhaps as well he did not hear what followed.

For Emma Bannon, finally, wept.

❈ Chapter Thirty-One

Unwise and Unbecoming

"**P**ut him to bed." Emma's throat was afire, her eyes dry-burning. She had not slept in days, it seemed, and Mikal was just as haggard.

Ludovico still clung to life; the black boils had burst and he merely lay, weak but still breathing, bandages changed every few hours as the suppurating wounds healed. His dark eyes were those of a captive hawk, sullen and hot with weakness he raged against even as his strength gathered and his body fought off the ravages of whatever dreadful illness he had contracted. It was not the Red, that much was certain; his boils had been *black*, and Clare was in no condition to answer any questions.

Marcus hefted Clare's shoulders. "Light as a feather, he is."

Gilburn grunted, heaving the mentath's lower half. "Not from this end, sir."

It is Clare, do not . . . She could not even finish the thought. Instead, she stood in the fœtid workroom, staring at the heap of sodden cloth that had been Francis Vance. There was a slow-burning ember still clasped in the man's vitals, but it was more than likely the foxfire of nerves and meat slowly leaching of fevered life.

In any case she did not care. "Put that outside. The pickers will take it."

"Yesmum." Finch's face did not wrinkle with distaste, but it might have been a near thing. "Mum?"

Small flames danced under boiling alembics; the floor was a mess of slippery substances perhaps better left unexamined. Papers with odd notations were strewn about, some crumpled, others merely drifting to scatter on the sludge. The water-closet was likely to be a horror. She could charm it clean, and she would.

But not at this moment. It was terrible to see – Clare was normally so *precise*, even when a certain question or series of experiments took hold of his nimble brain. The only time she had ever seen disorder was when his faculties were underused and he began to suffer the mentath's curse.

Boredom. If not trained and used, logic, like sorcery, *turned* on its helpless bearer.

Finch cleared his throat.

She surfaced. The broadsheets were full of wild speculation. And sending any of the servants out into Londinium was becoming problematic in the extreme. "Yes?"

"Another summons, mum. From the Crown." Was there a moment of fear in his tone, a slight catch to the words?

"Yes." She turned, slowly, in a full circle. The walls were flecked and splashed with various substances. Perhaps a flame-scouring would be in order.

And while she was at it, the entire rotting city could be cleansed, could it not? A small matter, for a Prime. One had only to will it, and the entire world could drown in such a flame.

It was *building* that was the difficult bit.

You are not thinking clearly. The heaviness in her chest, the Philosopher's Stone, knocked free of Llewellyn Gwynnfud's dead hands . . . it made her proof against this decay, and was no doubt the reason her servants did not suffer.

But such protection did not extend to Clare. He was not servant or Shield. He was simply, merely . . .

. . . what?

What is he to me? Dare I name it?

Horace and Teague appeared; Finch directed them to lay Vance's body outside the gate for the corpse-pickers. "The Lady wishes it so. Come, hurry along, men."

The Lady wishes it so. "Finch." Rusty and disused, as if she had not spent the past few days roaming her library reciting cantos until her tongue went numb, to keep from unleashing a torrent of hurtful sorcery.

"Yesmum?"

"Have Harthell saddle the bay again, please. If the maids go a-market with Cook, one of the footmen should accompany them – armed. Mikal?"

"Is still at Mr Ludovico's bedside, mum."

"Send someone to watch Ludo, then, and tell Mikal I require him." *Though he will not be happy; I left him like a pin holding a dress-fold and did not return to retrieve him, or give him lee to depart his post.* "No doubt he will wish the black saddled, as well."

"Yesmum. Mum?"

She turned her attention fully onto him, but he did not blanch. A tilt to her head, and she saw the lines graving deeper into his dry skin, the looseness under his chin, the way his collar cut into the papery flesh.

Finch was ageing, too. But *she* was not. As long as she bore the Stone, she would not, and the thought was enough to send a shiver down her spine.

The butler clasped his hands behind his back. "We are grateful to be in your service, mum. There's talk in the servant's quarters, and right glad we are you . . . well, you are our mistress." His laborious accent changed, and it was the slur and slang of his youth wearing through the words now. "Do you close your doons, missan, an' we shall all stay wit'you."

Why, Finch. "I am pleased to hear it. I do not think I shall be required to close the house, though. Britannia dares not imprison me." *For if she did, she would not have me to do certain disagreeable tasks.*

There might be others, though. A sorcerer as invisible as herself, perhaps part of Society, perhaps not, dogging her footsteps and leaving her posies.

"No matter how remiss I have been in answering

summons," she finished. "Thank you, Finch. Please hurry."

He did, and Emma drifted to the door in his wake. She said a single Word, and the lamps dimmed; another, and the flames under the alembics died. She left the workroom in shadow, and when she closed the door, it thudded as a crypt door would, sealing the mess inside.

The pall over Buckingham boiled with the ruling spirit's displeasure. It wreathed the spires of the Palace, it came down almost to the ground, and its thunderstorm-blackness was spangled with flashes of crackling diamond-hard white.

That is quite . . . She could find no words. A coughing groom took her horse, and Mikal's too. Kerchiefs knotted around the lower half of many a face, some soaked in various substances, made Londinium into a city full of highwaymen who sometimes collapsed, coughing bloody sputum and convulsing. The corpsepickers sang, and if not for the grey of the fog – for bodies were burning, and the city full of sweet roasting as well as coalstink – it might have been a pleasant day.

After all, it was not raining.

Haggard Coldwater Regiment guards stood at their posts; she stalked past them despite an attempt to bar her passage. Mikal produced the summons, the paper snow-white and the seal upon it sparking just as the blackness overhead did. The sight of the seal answered all questions, or perhaps it was the expression on her Shield's lean face.

Under the pall, the light was wan and anaemic, and the

corridors of the Palace were oddly empty. Though she could hear motion, scurryings in the walls, as it were, she relied on the guards at each doorway to point her to the Queen's location.

Stalking along, her head high and her dress – mourning, again, but this one much more wilted than her garments were wont to be – rustling as she moved, her hair dressed indifferently and bare of any jewellery, she was an unprepossessing figure at best. The charged atmosphere shivered as she moved through it, a Prime's approach through the thick sensitised æther that of a storm approaching.

Did Victrix feel it?

I hope she does.

The royal apartments, in contrast to the rest of the Palace, were a hive of activity. Physickers and white-robed Menders, a few scarlet-striped Hypatians, more than one Minister in a wig and some of Court grimly determined to be seen as loyal at this extremity, handkerchiefs lifted to their mouths as Emma swept past, Mikal holding the summons aloft as if it were a banner. It was the bedchamber, she found, and though she had a summons, she might be called upon to cool her heels.

Then I will leave. I have other matters to attend to.

As in, watching Clare die? Her skin contracted, a shiver running through her, and she eyed the heavy door to the royal bedchamber, the rose-petalled crest of the house of Henry the Wifekiller worked into the ancient wood and painted over many a time.

"*Bring her in,*" the air whispered, Britannia's tones

shivering through the heads of those assembled without passing through their ears. Emma blinked, but her step did not falter. She passed through the bedchamber doors with her head held high.

Alexandrine Victrix, ruler of Empire, lifted her tear-stained face from the counterpane and fixed Emma with a baleful eye. *"You,"* she said, and the word held a long hiss of displeasure. *"I sent for you!"*

Her eyes were black from lid to lid, the dust over Britannia's glare scorched away, the stars burning in that blackness forming constellations that would make a mortal dizzy if he gazed too deeply. She was on her knees next to a high-heaped bed, and the room was littered with physicker's tools, full of a sweet-burning smell, and tropical-hot. The Queen's pregnancy was more visible now, perhaps because she was merely in a dressing gown, and her dark hair hung in rivulets down her back.

On the bed, under the many blankets – they must have thought to sweat something out of him – lay the Consort, the ruby swellings under his chin grotesquely shiny as the fluid within them strained for release. He coughed weakly, a thick chesty sound, and the bubbling of bloody film at the corners of his eyes was the only colour in the room that did not seem bleached by Victrix's fury.

Emma came to a halt as the door swung shut behind her. Mikal stayed outside; her single scorching look had expressed her desire to face this alone.

"You," Victrix repeated, and it was curious how certain Emma could be that it was the mortal Queen speaking,

though the spirit of rule shone out through her eyes. "*How dare you bring this into Our presence!*"

For a few moments, Emma could hardly credit her ears. Then she realised the nature of the accusation, and her chin lifted. "You sent me to recover Morris, Your Majesty. I did. I even did my best to bring him to you before he expired – at *Your* express command. Had You seen fit to be more open with me about the nature of his filthy '*experiments*', much of this could have been avoided." *There is my gauntlet, Majesty. Return it if you dare.*

For a moment she could not believe she had addressed the Queen so. But the vision of Clare, his sunken cheeks afire and his body held to the task before him with sheer will, rose before her. And it was Victrix's game – the game of empire, of weapons and conquest – that had birthed this monstrosity.

And not only Clare, but Londinium suffered under its lash as well.

"*Our Consort sickens.*" Victrix almost howled the words, and the pall over the Palace rattled ominously with thunder. "*There must be a remedy!*"

She is only a woman, after all, and one with a heart. Something inside Emma's chest cracked slightly. "I am engaged upon—"

It was, she would remember, the last few moments of the Bannon who had sworn service not just aloud, but in the secret chambers of her very self.

Angry colour suffused Victrix's cheeks, less tender now than when they were crowned. "*Engaged?* Engaged?

Engage more thoroughly!" Everything in the room jumped slightly, and Alberich moaned.

Do I look as if I have been taking the waters at Bath? Heat mounted in Emma's own cheeks, and the two women were perhaps just as scarlet-cheeked as the Consort now. "I cannot create sheer miracles—"

"You are a filthy sorceress, what else are you good for?" the Queen cried, in a paroxysm of rage. *"Creeping in corners, a shameless proudnecked hussy airing before her betters!"* She lifted a trembling, ring-jewelled hand, the gems scintillating with fury, and pointed. *"If he dies, if you have killed him, I will punish—"*

Emma inhaled sharply. The ice was all through her, now. The crack in her chest whistled a cold, clear draught right down to her very core. *"I* did not loose this madness upon the world, Victrix. Your own Crown did that, with no help from me. It is unwise – and unbecoming – for you to speak so."

"Get out! Do not return until you have found the remedy, and if my Consort dies I will have your head!"

"You are," she informed the screeching woman, "welcome to try to separate said head from my shoulders." *But it is a task you had best be prepared for the unpleasantness of, and the trouble and expense. I am not some cowering, simpering aristocrat.*

What was she *thinking*?

She did not make a courtesy, either. She turned on her heel, not trusting her voice should she speak further. There were Words crowding her throat and a suspicious looseness at the very lowest floor of her soul – the barred door of her Discipline, ready to open and swallow her whole.

If she loosed it in this fashion, a raging conduit for the power of the Endor, it would not be Thomas Coldfaith's act of sacrifice.

No, it would be . . . otherwise. And the first place that freed sorcery would strike was the suck-sobbing woman crouched at the bedside of her husband, with the ruling spirit watching – coolly, calculating – through her madness.

Victrix beat her small plump hands on the counterpane, and Emma's passage threw the door back, the wood splintering in a long vertical crack as her control slipped a fraction. The material of her dress scorched, a new layer of reek added to the sweetbriar-sickness, the choking atmosphere of the Red.

Mikal's fingers closed about her arm, and such was Emma Bannon's countenance that none dared question or halt them as the Shield, perhaps sensing the danger, ushered her from the room stinking of sweetness and smoke.

Chapter Thirty-Two

A Damned Shame

He did not believe in dæmons. Logic and rationality did not admit such creatures.

And yet, while he burned and twisted, sweat-slick fabric clasped in his wet palms, they were all about him. Black-faced, leering, their white teeth champing, they crowded around the bed and laughed, pointing at him.

Why is this . . . He could not frame the question. His faculties spun, logic mutating, his heart labouring uselessly inside his clogged chest.

Another crisis came, the convulsion tearing through him, his entire body a rod of iron, the star of his faculties a whirling firework inside his aching, too-small skull. He dimly heard himself ranting, shouting filthy words he would never have uttered had he been possessed of his sanity, and the cotton padding in his ears thump-thudded with his heartbeat.

Dying. When the wracking ended, he knew he was. The tide was running away, and once in his childhood there had been the sea along a pebbled beach and his own disbelieving laughter as he saw something so *vast*, and . . .

Miss Bannon's voice. "Clare. *Archibald*."

He was too weak to respond. The sea was all inside him now, its complexity turning to equations, shining strands of logic knitted together so closely they seemed a whole fabric, the vice in his skull and the pounding in his chest dual engines pulling in opposite directions.

"No. Close the door." Miss Bannon, hoarse as if with weeping. "*Close* the door, Mikal."

"What are you—" The Shield, breathless. Another convulsion was coming, and Clare's body was lax in its approaching grip. When its fingers tightened, something in his brain or blood would give way, and the relief would be immense.

Vance. Is he alive?

"Prima . . . no. *No*."

A meaty, bone-crunching, *wrenching* sound. A word he could not quite hear, and Emma's voice, raised sharply.

"It is *mine* to give, Shield! And if you will not obey, I will free you from my service *instantly*." It was a tone he had never heard from her before – utterly chill, utterly level, simply factual instead of threatening.

It was dreadful to hear a woman's sweet voice so. The convulsion edged closer, playing with him, stroking along his body with a feather-caress. The dæmons laughed and twisted.

She does not know, you did not tell her. She does not know.

"Archibald," she whispered, the touch of her breath cold on his slicked cheek. "Dear God, Archibald, forgive me."

There is nothing to—

Then the pain came, and clove him in half. A sudden weight in his chest, as if the angina had returned, and he was never sure afterward if the hellish scream that rose was torn from his own lips . . . or from Emma's.

Archibald Clare fell into a star-drenched night, and the coolness of a summer sea.

Light. Against his eyelids. He blinked, the foulness crusting his eyes irritating as he sought to lift a hand. The appendage obeyed, and he gingerly scrubbed at his face. All manner of matter was dried upon his skin, and every inch of him crawled.

His hand fell back to his side. He took stock.

Weak, but lucid. Again. He blinked several times, and found his familiar bed at Miss Bannon's closed about him. Safe and secure as a little nut in a shell, for a moment he simply savoured the act of *breathing* without obstruction. Such a little thing, and one did not value it properly until it was taken away.

"Alive?"

He did not realise he had spoken aloud until someone wearily laughed, a disbelieving sound. It was Miss Bannon, ragged in a smoke-scored black dress, her hair a loose glory of dark curls falling past her shoulders, tangling to her waist. The hair seemed to have drained its bearer of all strength, for she was wan and hollow-cheeked, the dark circles under her eyes almost painted in their intensity.

Her little fingers were cool against his. Emma picked up his hand, squeezing with surprising strength. "Quite. I worried for you, Clare, but the worst is past."

We do not know that. He let out a long sigh. "Ludo?"

"Mending. Swearing at everyone in sight. Londinium is still plagued. It is rather desperate outside, dear Clare, so if you have any news . . . Dr Vance was quite of the opinion that you have solved the riddle?"

His hand, at his trouser pocket. "The cure – the *cure*. In his pocket. A glass vial . . ."

She actually paled, though he could not see how she could achieve such a feat without becoming utterly transparent. "He . . . Clare, his body was taken by the corpse-pickers two days ago."

"Ah." Clare coughed, more out of habit than anything else. His throat was dry, and Miss Bannon helped to lift him, held a glass to his lips. A wonderfully sweet draught of something tang-laden and cool eased his throat.

Water had never tasted so good.

She settled him back on the pillow. "I can perhaps find his body with a sympathy. It will be—"

"No." Clare felt the smile tilting the corners of his lips. All in all, he had to admit, he felt very fine, considering. A wonderful lassitude had overtaken him, but within it was a feeling of well-being he could not remember ever having before. Perhaps it was simply in comparison to the nastiness of Morris's plague. "I am not a fool, dear Emma. Well, I am in some matters, but not when it comes to Vance. There are extra vials of the cure – they are labelled quite clearly – in the pockets of my jacket, in the work-room." He paused. "Dead, you say? You are quite sure?"

"Dead of the plague." She sounded certain enough, settling back into the chair.

He closed his eyes, briefly. "Shame. A damned shame."

"Well." The single word expressed that she perhaps did not agree, but that she would not argue. Dashed polite of the woman, he thought, a trifle fondly. "The vials hold a cure?"

"And the method for making more is noted quite clearly. I made four copies; one should be in the pockets as well. There is a certain physician – Tarshingale, at King's. He will not only believe, but has the resources to see the cure performed, and can spread the formula and method of manufacture as widely as possible."

"I am told it must be introduced under the skin? Vance mentioned as much, before he . . ."

"Yes. There are many methods . . . I say, Miss Bannon, are you *quite* certain? Of his . . . demise?"

"Very much so, Clare." There was a rustle as she stood. "I shall search your workroom, then, and the matter of disseminating the cure is easy enough. You have done very well, sir."

He nodded, a yawn fit to crack his jaw rising from the depths of his chest. His heart thudded along, sedately observing its beat. Though his ribs seemed a trifle heavy, didn't they? A warmth quite unlike anything he had felt before, but perhaps it was merely a . . .

Miss Bannon breathed a word, the exact contours of which he could not remember as soon as they left the quivering air, and Clare fell into a dreamless, restorative slumber.

❈Chapter Thirty-Three

A Close-Run Race

Tarshingale was easily found, and explanations given; the man's gaze was quite disconcerting and he had given her short shrift until Clare's name was mentioned and the vials and notations – which might as well have been in some tongue of the Indus for all she could make sense of them, though she had prudently retained a copy – shown. She left the man in his bespattered coat with instructions on how to gain admittance to the Palace; no doubt the cure would be administered to Alberich very soon.

If he was not already dead. She had not bothered to check the broadsheets. She told herself it did not matter now.

King's Hospital, bursting at the seams with victims of the Red crammed four to a bed, was also full of moaning and screaming. It reminded her uncomfortably of the one time she had ever braved the halls of Bethlehem Hospital; the cries of Bedlam held an edge of misery this place lacked, though it was a very close-run race indeed. At least the very bricks of King's were not warped as Bedlam's were.

Harthell and Mikal had stayed with the carriage, both were armed with a brace of pistols as well, though the coachman would be of little use except to frighten away the jackals who would prey when the city's forces of order were occupied with other matters.

Besides, she had taken care not to be alone with Mikal since Clare's . . . cure.

The exhaustion was all through her. She had forgotten how weary flesh could become without the bolstering of a wyrm's heart, the Philosopher's Stone granting all manner of immunities.

Even a Prime's strength had limits.

Still, her head came up as her fingers touched Mikal's. Instead of stepping up into her carriage, she dropped his hand and turned swiftly, as if stung, twitching her skirts back and sweeping her hair from her face.

"Penny, madam?" the shambling man asked, querulous, and Mikal moved forward – and halted as her hand, clothed in the tattered rags of a black lace glove, caught his sleeve. "Penny for a poor man? Ha'pence? Farthing?"

The importunate sir was dressed in stinking oddments as well, and under his soft slouching hat the gleam of his changeable eyes was sunken. He had shaved his fair moustache and was far thinner than he had been the first time she had seen him. He halted, and the ghost of amusement on his filthy, crusted mouth was almost too much to be borne.

"Dr Vance." She shook her head, once, sadly. "You rather hoped I would throw your corpse out."

"No other way to leave your tender care, my dear." He had a tin cup with a few thin farthings in it; he shook it and the coins rattled. "We have business, you and I."

She should, she supposed, evince some surprise, but it was useless. "Indeed we have. Pray do enter the carriage, sir. We may at least speak privately there."

He stretched out his legs. Harthell cracked the whip, and Mikal, settled watchfully next to Emma, was tense as a wound clockspring.

As badly as the resurrected criminal's clothes were tattered, he did not *smell*. Which was either an oversight to his costume, a mark of his fastidiousness . . . or the sweetstink of Londinium roasting under the Red had deadened Emma's nose.

"You introduced the cure under your skin in some manner while I was occupied with Clare." She nodded, once, slowly. "You must have been very amused at my questions about that method of applying said cure."

"I expected no less than brilliance from you, my dear, which you have amply demonstrated. I shall be on my way, soon, to sell the lovely cure I helped create at a high price before it becomes common. Profit does not linger."

The missing canisters are in your hands. She was suddenly quite certain of that, though she could not tell if it was intuition or simple logic. *But you had no choice but to work for a cure once you were trapped in my house. Interesting.* "Nor does vengeance."

"I rather suspected you would feel so, yes." He tipped the slouching hat back with one soot-blackened fingertip. "You do not strike me as a forgiving woman."

I have never been. Least of all to myself. "The thought of striking you dead at this very moment amuses me mightily. Why should I not?"

"Because you will calculate that the dissemination of this marvellous remedy, no matter what profit I gain from it, is worth letting me go unhindered. Especially since it has reached the Continent, and no doubt the shores of the New World as well." And d——n the man, but he sounded so very certain.

Just as Clare did, when he knew beyond a doubt what calculation should be attempted to bring the world to rights.

She tapped her fingers on her knee, exactly once. Her back had straightened, and she felt almost herself again, despite the heat of the day. It was uncomfortably *close* in the carriage, and her underarms were damp. Her corset, filthy as it was, scraped against her skin. It had no doubt worn her into a rash. "The satisfaction of knowing you will no longer be a bother may outweigh that philanthropic interest."

"It will not, Miss Bannon. You are a creature of Justice, however odd your method of applying it." He leaned back against the cushions. "I must say, you have a splendid carriage. I quite admire it."

She raised an eyebrow. "Thank you."

The silence that fell was not quite comfortable. Her breathing came a trifle short, but she could attribute that to her damnable corset.

Finally, she sighed. The weariness that had settled on her pressed deeper, into her very bones. At the moment, she very much missed the warmth of the Stone in her chest.

And yet she did not miss the crushing upon her conscience that bearing the Stone had brought her. How Llew would laugh, were he alive to guess such a weakness on her part.

"You shall cease being a nuisance to Mr Clare." She eyed him closely. "Or I shall cut out your heart, sir, and feast upon it." *There is more than enough of your bodily fluids – and your clothing, sir – left at my house for me to practise a nasty sympathy or two upon.*

"That," Dr Francis Vance said, with a wide white smile on his haggard, Red-ravaged face, "is my promise to you, dear lady. Do take care of Clare, he is a giant among mentaths."

With that, he reached for the carriage door and was gone even as the conveyance rolled. Emma caught Mikal's arm.

"Let him go," she said, and surprised herself.

For her pained, unamused laugh turned into a deep, wracking cough, and her forehead was clammy-damp.

Mikal had turned pale, even under his dark colouring. "Prima . . ."

She gestured for silence, and he subsided. Emma studied

his face as the carriage rolled, Harthell gaining as much speed as he dared on the choked thoroughfares, moans and cries and coughs rising in a sea around them. The cup of the city brimmed over, and she found she could not say what she wished.

I am sorry, Mikal. For you shall very shortly be cast adrift, and I am selfish, for I cannot cling to this manner of life any more. No matter my responsibility to you, to them . . . to Her . . .

She coughed again, her fingers in their torn and stained gloves pressing over her mouth, and they came away dripping with red. "Oh, dear," she murmured, and pitched aside, into Mikal's arms.

Chapter Thirty-Four

A Stone is a Stone

The house rang with terror and footsteps. Clare tacked out into the hall, the weakness in his limbs quite shockingly intense despite his rather extraordinary feeling of well-being. He fumbled at his jacket buttons, finally inducing the little beasts to behave, and looked up to see Madame Noyon, her grey-streaked hair piled loosely atop her head and her face tearstained, hurry past with an armful of linen.

"I say," he began, but the housekeeper vanished down the hall. *I say!*

One of the lady's maids – Isobel, the scarred one – leaned against the wall by Valentinelli's door, dumbly staring after Noyon with glittering eyes. Her cheeks were wet, and she had the look of a young woman who had just been rather viciously stabbed in the heart.

"I say," Clare approached her. "Isobel, dear, what is it? What is the—"

"It's Missus," she whispered, through pale, perhaps-numb lips. Her indenture collar was oddly dark, the powdery metal's radiance dimming. "She's taken the ill, she has. We're likely next, she wot was holding it back an'all!"

What? For a moment, his faculties refused to function, despite the tests he had administered to them that very morning, lying in his freshly made bed and quite comfortable at last. He stood very still, his head drooping forward and taking in the girl's feet in their pert, sensible boots.

Bannon does have a weakness for sensible footwear, for herself and her servants alike. He shook his head, slowly. "Ah. Well. There is not a moment to lose, then. I must—"

"*GET OUT!*" It was a scream from the top of the stairs leading to Miss Bannon's chambers. Mikal's voice, and it shook the entire house in quite a different manner than Miss Bannon's return or her anger.

Madame Noyon came hurrying down them, paper-pale and shaking afresh. She babbled in French, Horace and the blonde Eirean maid Bridget behind her chattering in proper but horribly disjointed Englene, and it took quite some time for him to gather a coherent picture of what had transpired.

The Shield had evicted them from his mistress's chambers, quite rudely. While Clare rested himself, Miss Bannon had taken ill; she had passed through the swellings and the convulsions were upon her.

It is too late. The pain in his chest was not angina, it was . . . something else.

He did not have time to discern its source, or so he told himself.

Clare bolted for the workroom.

The stench was terrible. He reeled into the stone room, and it was a very good thing he had not been able to stomach much of any provender lately, for his cast-iron mentath's digestion did not seem to have survived the illness quite as well as the rest of him.

It was dark, and his boots slipped in a crust of God alone knew what on the floor. How had they *stood* it down here?

He found his way by touch to the desk, slipping and sliding. His hip banged a table and something fell, shattering. Perhaps it was a fresh load of plague-freighted marrowe-jelly, but he cared little, if at all.

The drawer slid open, and his questing fingers found nothing but a small jewelled box. He swore aloud, a series of vile terms no gentleman should give voice to, and fumbled more deeply in the drawer, and still his sensitive fingertips found nothing but wood, dust, and the box of coja.

The vials he had hidden here, as well as in the pockets of his jacket . . . gone.

He turned, sharply, snatching up and hurling the tiny box across the room. The crack of its breaking was lost in the sound working free of his throat.

It could not be a sob. Mentaths were not prey to Feeling in such an intense fashion. Feeling was to be examined, thoroughly in some cases, then accounted for and set aside so one could function.

He swallowed something that tasted of iron. Staggered for the door, his legs a newborn colt's. Retraced his route through the house, and found a hall crowded with servants. Ludovico was there too, leaning on Gilburn, haggard and swearing steadily, monotonously, in pure noble Italian. He was pale, his pitted cheeks so thinned his face had become a skeleton's grin. *La strega*, he would murmur, then *demone maledetta*, and finally *donna dolce*, and other terms that would have been quite revealing, had Clare cared to apply deduction to them.

They clustered at the foot of the stairs, Miss Bannon's collection of castaways, the servants making a soft noise every time the light of their indenture collars dimmed. Clare pushed through them, blindly.

No. Please . . . dear God, not Emma. I thought she was immune!

"The Shield," Finch whispered, grabbing at Clare's sleeve. "He is beside himself. He will—"

"I do not care," Clare said, almost gently, and freed himself of the man's grasp. He put his hand to the balustrade, lifted his foot.

He was halfway up and heard it, her laboured breathing and soft choked cries as the convulsions came. The hall stretched away, as in nightmares, and the entire house shivered again, a chill racing through each plank and bit of plaster, from foundations to high lovely roof. The door to her dressing room was open, and gaslamps hissed. The witchlights in their cages of silvery metal dimmed, hissing as well, turning bloody-hued as the indenture collars dimmed, brightening as they brightened.

She fights for life, our dear sorceress. The dry barking sound from his throat had to be a laugh. It could not be otherwise. For what other sound could he make? Mentaths did not weep.

There was another sound – a dry sliding. There was light from underneath what had to be Miss Bannon's bedroom door. An odd scent, too – smoky and musky, a resinous incense, perhaps, but of no kind Clare was familiar with. And the sweetness of Morris's plague, its sickening candy-touch burning through her slight body.

Even a will as indomitable as hers could not stave off this catastrophe. Clare's knees weakened. He forced them to straighten, and later he was vaguely surprised that he had been inside her dressing room . . . and not seen a single thing other than that door of pale wood with a stripe of violent yellow light leaking from underneath it.

The sound became a slicing, a wet noise as if flesh was pulled from flesh in a slaughteryard. Clare shuddered, reaching before him for the handle. He was weaving as if drunk, his feet leaving dark crusted prints. The incense smell turned thick and cloying, and he heard Mikal's voice, singing in a queer atonal hissing manner.

What is he doing?

There was another cry, and this one raised every hair

on Clare's shivering body. The bright yellow light stuttered, thundering as a runner's pulse, and Clare found himself on his knees, shaking his head, not quite aware of what had happened.

Silence, thick and velvet.

The hinges creaked slightly as the pale door opened. Behind it, all was dark. A viscous blackness as if of an Indus midnight, its face a sheer wall, almost . . . alive.

Staggering out of the gloom came the Shield. For a moment he looked oddly . . . transparent. His eyes burned, a yellow fire brighter than Londinium's usual fog, and the reek of musk-burning smoke was so strong it nearly knocked Clare flat.

"*Nå helaeth oavied, nagáni.*" The man stumbled, caught himself, and swept the door closed behind him with such violence it almost splintered. He leaned back, his shoulders meeting it with an oddly light thump, but as he slid down to sit on the carpeted floor he gained solidity.

Clare blinked. It had to be a trick of his recovering vision.

Mikal's eyes half-lidded, their yellow gleam dimming for a moment. "Ah." He coughed, but it was a dry sound, not the wet thickness of the plague. "Clare." As if reminding himself who the mentath was.

Clare's breath caught in his throat. "Emma," he whispered. The silence was deathly. 24½ Brooke Street held its breath, too.

"She . . . will live." He flinched as Clare leaned forward, though there was a great deal of space between them. "*Do not touch me!*"

Clare subsided. Below, at the foot of the stairs, a susur-ration. Sooner or later they would creep up – Valentinelli first, most likely – to see what had transpired here.

"Mikal." He wet his dry lips, settled back on his dirty heels. Winced as he thought of what he had tracked over the carpets and flooring. "What . . . what did you . . ."

The man's grin was a feral baring of strong white teeth, the canines curved and oddly distended, and Clare recoiled from its cheerful hatred. For a moment, the Shield's pupils appeared . . . different, but when Clare examined him afresh, he found they were circular, and normal.

Only a trick of the light. Only that. The witchlights strengthened in their cages, losing their deadly sputter-hissing and growing steadily more brilliant.

"Mentath." Mikal shut his yellow eyes. His calloused hands, empty and discarded, lay to either side of his body. "Remember what I am about to tell you."

"I hear you," Clare muttered numbly.

"There is a proverb among my kind." Another dry half-cough, but he was already looking better, his colour improving. "*A stone is a stone, and a heart is a heart.*" A long pause. "Do you understand?"

What on earth . . . "No," he admitted. "No, I do not."

"Good." Mikal settled more firmly against the door. "Tell them she lives, she *will* live, and not to come up the stairs. Or I shall strike to kill."

He cleared his throat. "Erm, yes. Well, they will be relieved, but—"

"Go." Mikal's frame twitched once, terribly, as if his skin were merely a cover over something not . . . quite . . .

Clare did not remember gaining his feet. He recoiled, and stumbled down the stairs. They caught him at the bottom, and he managed to give his message. And afterwards, he remembered nothing more until he awoke two mornings later in his own bed.

"You told Her Majesty?" She was propped on several pillows, wan and too thin, her hair loosely pulled back but still glossy and vigorous. There was an uncomfortable vitality burning in her gaze, but Clare ascribed it to the tonics Madame Noyon insisted on dosing her with at two-hour intervals, from Tideturn dawn to Tideturn dusk.

"That the missing canisters had been attended to? Yes, quite." *Though I do not know where you found time to attend to that detail. You are a wonder, Miss Bannon.* "I *also* told her I shall cease chasing chimeras," Clare continued, settling into the chair. Miss Bannon's hands lay in her lap, and the dressing gown was quite pretty, a froth of pale lace at her neckline. He tried not to glance too obviously about her bedroom, fighting back a quite uncharacteristic smile as he saw the stack of sensational novels on her nightstand, next to a globe of what had to be malachite in a brassy stand. The books had dust upon their covers; Miss Bannon had not been at leisure to read much lately.

Near the door, Mikal lurked. He kept himself to a patch of convenient shadow, and Miss Bannon's gaze often wandered in his direction, as if he were a puzzle she sought to solve.

"Chimeras," she repeated, softly. It was not quite a question, but Clare made a *hrrmph* noise as if it were.

"Since Dr Vance is dead, of course. I did not tell her so; it would only create . . . questions. I have been settled with an estate or two, I gather; signal service in saving the Consort's life. He is still sickly, but shall recover."

Miss Bannon's upper lip curled slightly. "Britannia rejoices," she commented, quite properly. But there was an edge to the words.

He fought back the urge to raise an eyebrow. "Indeed. The method of cure is spreading with as much speed as possible. Tarshingale is quite the man of the hour. Publicly, of course, it is *his* triumph. I am content for it to remain so." He lifted the package from his lap. "And this . . . Her Majesty sent it for you, expressly. She was quite concerned for you."

For a long moment Miss Bannon examined the linen-wrapped item. It was heavy, and no doubt a costly gift of thanks from royalty. He would have expected the sorceress to be pleased. Instead, she studied it as if it were some manner of poisonous creature, one she rather feared was about to strike.

Finally, her fine little hands moved, and she took it from him . . . and set it, unopened, on her nightstand. "Thank you, Mr Clare. I shall no doubt pen a note of immense gratitude to Her Majesty."

"Well, that's that, then." But he made no move to depart

her bedroom. He found himself wondering what had transpired between Queen and servant while he lay unconscious. It must have been an event of surpassing magnitude . . . but he had a different question that required answering. "Miss Bannon."

She settled a little more comfortably, and her gaze met his. The quality of directness she possessed was even more marked now, and her earrings – dangles of amethyst in silver filigree, matching the small simple necklace that nonetheless glowed with charter symbols – swung slightly as she did so, then nestled lovingly against her curls.

It was very good to see her so accoutred again. And none of her household had taken ill.

There would never be a better time to ask.

He cleared his throat. "You performed some feat upon me while I was fevered, Emma. Do not bother to deny it."

She did not, merely regarded him levelly. Finally, a hint of a smile crept onto her childlike features, but still she did not speak.

So he was forced to. "I have been most exercised upon the problem, and cannot find a solution."

Her dark eyed positively danced. Did she look . . . why, yes.

The sorceress looked *relieved*, and she finally spoke.

"I shall tell you in twenty years' time, sir."

Dash it all. "I am not a young man, Emma. I may not be in a position to hear such news at that time."

Her smile broadened. "Oh, I think you will be. What can I tell you of illogical sorcery? For all you know, I had the method of the cure from dear departed Dr Vance, and introduced it under your skin in some fashion." Was she . . . yes. Her dark eyes danced, and the merriment lurking in her expression was quite out of character. "I would be *quite* vexed to lose you, Mr Clare."

The heat in his cheeks was like the plague-fever, and he stood in a hurry, clearing his throat. "Likewise, Miss Bannon. I shall be along now, I have a workroom to tidy, and some fascinating avenues of enquiry to apply myself to." *For example, the Alderase reactions. Very intriguing.*

"Very well. I believe I shall see you at dinner, sir. In very short order, I shall be quite well." Damn the woman. She *was* laughing, now. It did her a world of good, thin and pale as she was. Still, she looked . . . yes, younger. Though how he could draw such a conclusion Clare was not certain, for she had always seemed childlike, to him.

Then again, Clare himself felt younger and lighter, as if the plague had burned away age and infirmity. No doubt the feeling would fade. His hair seemed to have gained new strength as well, or perhaps the looking-glasses in Miss Bannon's house were ensorcelled. "Delighted. Very well, then." He shook his head, treading by Mikal's shadowed form with a light step. He passed through the dressing room, Madame Noyon bustling in the opposite direction with a covered tray, and halfway down the stairs, he began to whistle.

extras

orbit

www.orbitbooks.net

about the author

Lilith Saintcrow was born in New Mexico, bounced around the world as an Air Force brat, and fell in love with writing when she was ten years old. She currently lives in Vancouver, Washington. Visit her website at www.lilithsaintcrow.com

Find out more about Lilith Saintcrow and other Orbit authors by registering for the free monthly newsletter at www.orbitbooks.net

if you enjoyed
THE RED PLAGUE AFFAIR

look out for

SOULLESS

by

Gail Carriger

CHAPTER ONE

In Which Parasols Prove Useful

Miss Alexia Tarabotti was not enjoying her evening. Private balls were never more than middling amusements for spinsters, and Miss Tarabotti was not the kind of spinster who could garner even that much pleasure from the event. To put the pudding in the puff: she had retreated to the library, her favorite sanctuary in any house, only to happen upon an unexpected vampire.

She glared at the vampire.

For his part, the vampire seemed to feel that their encounter had improved his ball experience immeasurably. For there she sat, without escort, in a low-necked ball gown.

In this particular case, what he did not know *could* hurt him. For Miss Alexia had been born without a soul, which, as any decent vampire of good blooding knew, made her a lady to avoid most assiduously.

Yet he moved toward her, darkly shimmering out of the library shadows with feeding fangs ready. However, the moment he touched Miss Tarabotti, he was suddenly no longer darkly doing anything at all. He was simply standing there, the faint sounds of a string quartet in the background as he foolishly fished about with his tongue for fangs unaccountably mislaid.

Miss Tarabotti was not in the least surprised; soulless-ness always neutralized supernatural abilities. She issued the vampire a very dour look. Certainly, most daylight folk wouldn't peg her as anything less than a standard English prig, but had this man not even bothered to *read* the vampire's official abnormality roster for London and its greater environs?

The vampire recovered his equanimity quickly enough. He reared away from Alexia, knocking over a nearby tea trolley. Physical contact broken, his fangs reappeared. Clearly not the sharpest of prongs, he then darted forward from the neck like a serpent, diving in for another chomp.

"I say!" said Alexia to the vampire. "We have not even been introduced!"

Miss Tarabotti had never actually had a vampire try to bite her. She knew one or two by reputation, of course, and was friendly with Lord Akeldama. *Who was not friendly with Lord Akeldama?* But no vampire had ever actually attempted to *feed* on her before!

So Alexia, who abhorred violence, was forced to grab the miscreant by his nostrils, a delicate and therefore painful area, and shove him away. He stumbled over the fallen tea trolley, lost his balance in a manner astonishingly graceless for a vampire, and fell to the floor. He landed right on top of a plate of treacle tart.

Miss Tarabotti was most distressed by this. She was particularly fond of treacle tart and had been looking forward to consuming that precise plateful. She picked up her parasol. It was terribly tasteless for her to be carrying a parasol at an evening ball, but Miss Tarabotti rarely went anywhere without it. It was of a style entirely of her own devising: a black frilly confection with purple satin pansies sewn about, brass hardware, and buckshot in its silver tip.

She whacked the vampire right on top of the head with it as he tried to extract himself from his newly intimate relations with the tea trolley. The buckshot gave the brass parasol just enough heft to make a deliciously satisfying *thunk*.

"Manners!" instructed Miss Tarabotti.

The vampire howled in pain and sat back down on the treacle tart.

Alexia followed up her advantage with a vicious prod between the vampire's legs. His howl went quite a bit higher in pitch, and he crumpled into a fetal position. While Miss Tarabotti was a proper English young lady, aside from not having a soul and being half Italian, she did spend quite a bit more time than most other young ladies riding and walking and was therefore unexpectedly strong.

Miss Tarabotti leaped forward – as much as one could leap in full triple-layered underskirts, draped bustle, and ruffled taffeta top-skirt – and bent over the vampire. He was clutching at his indelicate bits and writhing about. The pain would not last long given his supernatural healing ability, but it hurt most decidedly in the interim.

Alexia pulled a long wooden hair stick out of her elaborate coiffure. Blushing at her own temerity, she ripped open his shirtfront, which was cheap and overly starched, and poked at his chest, right over the heart. Miss Tarabotti sported a particularly large and sharp hair stick. With her free hand, she made certain to touch his chest, as only physical contact would nullify his supernatural abilities.

"Desist that horrible noise immediately," she instructed the creature.

The vampire quit his squealing and lay perfectly still. His beautiful blue eyes watered slightly as he stared fixedly at the wooden hair stick. Or, as Alexia liked to call it, hair *stake*.

"Explain yourself!" Miss Tarabotti demanded, increasing the pressure.

"A thousand apologies." The vampire looked confused. "Who are you?" Tentatively he reached for his fangs. Gone.

To make her position perfectly clear, Alexia stopped touching him (though she kept her sharp hair stick in place). His fangs grew back.

He gasped in amazement. "*What* are you? I thought you were a lady, alone. It would be my right to feed, if you were left this carelethly unattended. Pleathe, I did not mean to prethume," he lisped around his fangs, real panic in his eyes.

Alexia, finding it hard not to laugh at the lisp, said,

"There is no cause for you to be so overly dramatic. Your hive queen will have told you of my kind." She returned her hand to his chest once more. The vampire's fangs retracted.

He looked at her as though she had suddenly sprouted whiskers and hissed at him.

Miss Tarabotti was surprised. Supernatural creatures, be they vampires, werewolves, or ghosts, owed their existence to an overabundance of soul, an excess that refused to die. Most knew that others like Miss Tarabotti existed, born without any soul at all. The estimable Bureau of Unnatural Registry (BUR), a division of Her Majesty's Civil Service, called her ilk *preternatural*. Alexia thought the term nicely dignified. What vampires called her was far less complimentary. After all, preternaturals had once hunted *them*, and vampires had long memories. Natural, daylight persons were kept in the dark, so to speak, but any vampire worth his blood should know a preternatural's touch. This one's ignorance was untenable. Alexia said, as though to a very small child, "I am a *preternatural*."

The vampire looked embarrassed. "Of course you are," he agreed, obviously still not quite comprehending. "Again, my apologies, lovely one. I am overwhelmed to meet you. You are my first" – he stumbled over the word – "preternatural." He frowned. "Not supernatural, not natural, of course! How foolish of me not to see the dichotomy." His eyes narrowed into craftiness. He was now studiously ignoring the hair stick and looking tenderly up into Alexia's face.

Miss Tarabotti knew full well her own feminine appeal. The kindest compliment her face could ever hope to garner was "exotic," never "'lovely." Not that it had ever received either. Alexia figured that vampires, like all predators, were at their most charming when cornered.

The vampire's hands shot forward, going for her neck. Apparently, he had decided if he could not suck her blood, strangulation was an acceptable alternative. Alexia jerked back, at the same time pressing her hair stick into the creature's white flesh. It slid in about half an inch. The vampire reacted with a desperate wriggle that, even without superhuman strength, unbalanced Alexia in her heeled velvet dancing shoes. She fell back. He stood, roaring in pain, with her hair stick half in and half out of his chest.

Miss Tarabotti scrabbled for her parasol, rolling about inelegantly among the tea things, hoping her new dress would miss the fallen foodstuffs. She found the parasol and came upright, swinging it in a wide arc. Purely by chance, the heavy tip struck the end of her wooden hair stick, driving it straight into the vampire's heart.

The creature stood stock-still, a look of intense surprise on his handsome face. Then he fell backward onto the much-abused plate of treacle tart, flopping in a limp-over-cooked-asparagus kind of way. His alabaster face turned a yellowish gray, as though he were afflicted with the jaundice, and he went still. Alexia's books called this end of the vampire life cycle *dissanimation*. Alexia, who thought the action astoundingly similar to a soufflé going flat, decided at that moment to call it the Grand Collapse.

She intended to waltz directly out of the library without anyone the wiser to her presence there. This would have resulted in the loss of her best hair stick and her well-deserved tea, as well as a good deal of drama. Unfortunately, a small group of young dandies came traipsing in at that precise moment. What young men of such dress were doing in a *library* was anyone's guess. Alexia felt the most likely explanation was that they had become lost while looking for the card room. Regardless, their presence forced her to pretend that she, too, had just discovered the dead vampire. With a resigned shrug, she screamed and collapsed into a faint.

She stayed resolutely fainted, despite the liberal application of smelling salts, which made her eyes water most tremendously, a cramp in the back of one knee, and the fact that her new ball gown was getting most awfully wrinkled. All its many layers of green trim, picked to the height of fashion in lightening shades to complement the cuirasse bodice, were being crushed into oblivion under her weight. The expected noises ensued: a good deal of yelling, much bustling about, and several loud clatters as one of the housemaids cleared away the fallen tea.

Then came the sound she had half anticipated, half dreaded. An authoritative voice cleared the library of both young dandies and all other interested parties who had flowed into the room upon discovery of the tableau. The voice instructed everyone to "get out!" while he "gained the particulars from the young lady" in tones that brooked no refusal.

Silence descended.

"Mark my words, I will use something much, much stronger than smelling salts," came a growl in Miss Tarabotti's left ear. The voice was low and tinged with a hint of Scotland. It would have caused Alexia to shiver and think primal monkey thoughts about moons and running far and fast, if she'd had a soul. Instead it caused her to sigh in exasperation and sit up.

"And a good evening to you, too, Lord Maccon. Lovely weather we are having for this time of year, is it not?" She patted at her hair, which was threatening to fall down without the hair stick in its proper place. Surreptitiously, she looked about for Lord Conall Maccon's second in command, Professor Lyall. Lord Maccon tended to maintain a much calmer temper when his Beta was present. But, then, as Alexia had come to comprehend, that appeared to be the main role of a Beta – especially one attached to Lord Maccon.

"Ah, Professor Lyall, how nice to see you again." She smiled in relief.

Professor Lyall, the Beta in question, was a slight, sandy-haired gentleman of indeterminate age and pleasant disposition, as agreeable, in fact, as his Alpha was sour. He grinned at her and doffed his hat, which was of first-class design and sensible material. His cravat was similarly subtle, for, while it was tied expertly, the knot was a humble one.

"Miss Tarabotti, how delicious to find ourselves in your company once more." His voice was soft and mild-mannered.

"Stop humoring her, Randolph," barked Lord Maccon. The fourth Earl of Woolsey was much larger than Professor Lyall and in possession of a near-permanent frown. Or at least he always seemed to be frowning when he was in the presence of Miss Alexia Tarabotti, ever since the hedgehog incident (which really, honestly, had not been her fault). He also had unreasonably pretty tawny eyes, mahogany-colored hair, and a particularly nice nose. The eyes were currently glaring at Alexia from a shockingly intimate distance.

"Why is it, Miss Tarabotti, every time I have to clean up a mess in a library, you just happen to be in the middle of it?" the earl demanded of her.

Alexia gave him a withering look and brushed down the front of her green taffeta gown, checking for blood-stains.

Lord Maccon appreciatively watched her do it. Miss Tarabotti might examine her face in the mirror each morning with a large degree of censure, but there was nothing at all wrong with her figure. He would have to have had far less soul and a good fewer urges not to notice that appetizing fact. Of course, she always went and spoiled the appeal by opening her mouth. In his humble experience, the world had yet to produce a more vexingly verbose female.

"Lovely but unnecessary," he said, indicating her efforts to brush away nonexistent blood drops.

Alexia reminded herself that Lord Maccon and his kind were only *just* civilized. One simply could not expect too much from them, especially under delicate circumstances such as these. Of course, that failed to explain Professor Lyall, who was always utterly urbane. She glanced with appreciation in the professor's direction.

Lord Maccon's frown intensified.

Miss Tarabotti considered that the lack of civilized behaviour might be the sole provenance of Lord Maccon. Rumor had it, he had only lived in London a comparatively short while – and he had relocated from Scotland of all barbaric places.

The professor coughed delicately to get his Alpha's attention. The earl's yellow gaze focused on him with such intensity it should have actually burned. "Aye?"

Professor Lyall was crouched over the vampire, examining the hair stick with interest. He was poking about the wound, a spotless white lawn handkerchief wrapped around his hand.

"Very little mess, actually. Almost complete lack of blood spatter." He leaned forward and sniffed. "Definitely Westminster," he stated.

The Earl of Woolsey seemed to understand. He turned his piercing gaze onto the dead vampire. "He must have been very hungry."

Professor Lyall turned the body over. "What happened here?" He took out a small set of wooden tweezers from the pocket of his waistcoat and picked at the back of the vampire's trousers. He paused, rummaged about in his coat pockets, and produced a diminutive leather case. He clicked it open and removed a most bizarre pair of gogglelike things. They were gold in color with multiple lenses on one side, between which there appeared to be some kind of liquid. The contraption was also riddled with small knobs and dials. Professor Lyall propped the ridiculous things onto his nose and bent back over the vampire, twiddling at the dials expertly.

"Goodness gracious me," exclaimed Alexia, "what *are* you wearing? It looks like the unfortunate progeny of an illicit union between a pair of binoculars and some opera glasses. What on earth are they called, binocticals, spectoculars?"

The earl snorted his amusement and then tried to pretend he hadn't. "How about glassicals?" he suggested, apparently unable to resist a contribution. There was a twinkle in his eye as he said it that Alexia found rather unsettling.

Professor Lyall looked up from his examination and glared at the both of them. His right eye was hideously magnified. It was quite gruesome and made Alexia start involuntarily.

"These are my monocular cross-magnification lenses with spectra-modifier attachment, and they are invaluable. I will thank you not to mock them so openly." He turned once more to the task at hand.

"Oh." Miss Tarabotti was suitably impressed. "How do they work?" she inquired.

Professor Lyall looked back up at her, suddenly animated. "Well, you see, it is really quite interesting. By turning this little knob here, you can change the distance between the two panes of glass here, allowing the liquid to—"

The earl's groan interrupted him. "Don't get him started, Miss Tarabotti, or we will be here all night."

Looking slightly crestfallen, Professor Lyall turned back to the dead vampire. "Now, what *is* this substance all over his clothing?"

His boss, preferring the direct approach, resumed his frown and looked accusingly at Alexia. "What on God's green earth is that muck?"

Miss Tarabotti said, "Ah. Sadly, treacle tart. A tragic loss, I daresay." Her stomach chose that moment to growl in agreement. She would have colored gracefully with embarrassment had she not possessed the complexion of one of those "heathen Italians," as her mother said, who never colored, gracefully or otherwise. (Convincing her mother that Christianity had, to all intents and purposes, originated with the Italians, thus making them the exact opposite of heathen, was a waste of time and breath.) Alexia refused to apologize for the boisterousness of her stomach and favored Lord Maccon with a defiant glare. Her stomach was the reason she had sneaked away in the first place. Her mama had assured her there would be food at the ball. Yet all that appeared on offer when they arrived was a bowl of punch and some sadly wilted watercress. Never one to let her stomach get the better of her, Alexia had ordered tea from the butler and retreated to the library. Since she normally spent any ball lurking on the outskirts of the dance floor trying to look as though she did not want to be asked to waltz, tea was a welcome alternative. It was rude to order refreshments from someone else's staff, but when one was promised sandwiches and there was nothing but watercress, well, one must simply take matters into one's own hands!

Professor Lyall, kindhearted soul that he was, prattled on to no one in particular, pretending not to notice the rumbling of her stomach. Though of course he heard it. He had excellent hearing. *They* all did. He looked up from his examinations, his face all catawampus from the glassicals. "Starvation would explain why the vampire was desperate enough to try for Miss Tarabotti at a ball, rather than taking to the slums like the smart ones do when they get this bad."

Alexia grimaced. "No associated hive either."

Lord Maccon arched one black eyebrow, professing not to be impressed. "How could *you* possibly know *that*?"

Professor Lyall explained for both of them. "No need to be so direct with the young lady. A hive queen would never have let one of her brood get into such a famished condition. We must have a rove on our hands, one completely without ties to the local hive."

Alexia stood up, revealing to Lord Maccon that she had arranged her faint to rest comfortably against a fallen settee pillow. He grinned and then quickly hid it behind a frown when she looked at him suspiciously.

"I have a different theory." She gestured to the vampire's clothing. "Badly tied cravat and a cheap shirt? No hive worth its salt would let a larva like that out without dressing him properly for public appearance. I am surprised he was not stopped at the front entrance. The duchess's footman really ought to have spotted a cravat like *that* prior to the reception line and forcibly ejected the wearer. I suppose good staff is hard to come by with all the best ones becoming drones these days, but such a shirt!"

The Earl of Woolsey glared at her. "Cheap clothing is no excuse for killing a man."

"Mmm, that's what you say." Alexia evaluated Lord Maccon's perfectly tailored shirtfront and exquisitely tied cravat. His dark hair was a bit too long and shaggy to be de mode, and his face was not entirely clean-shaven, but he possessed enough hauteur to carry this lower-class roughness off without seeming scruffy. She was certain that his silver and black paisley cravat must be tied under sufferance. He probably preferred to wander about bare-chested at home. The idea made her shiver oddly. It must take a lot of effort to keep a man like him tidy. Not to mention well tailored. He was bigger than most. She had to give credit to his valet, who must be a particularly tolerant claviger.

Lord Maccon was normally quite patient. Like most of his kind, he had learned to be such in polite society. But Miss Tarabotti seemed to bring out the worst of his animal urges. "Stop trying to change the subject," he snapped, squirming under her calculated scrutiny. "Tell me what happened." He put on his BUR face and pulled out a small metal tube, stylus, and pot of clear liquid. He unrolled the tube with a small cranking device, clicked the top off the liquid, and dipped the stylus into it. It sizzled ominously.

Alexia bristled at his autocratic tone. "Do not give me

instructions in that tone of voice, you . . ." she searched for a particularly insulting word, " . . . puppy! I am jolly well not one of your pack."

Lord Conall Maccon, Earl of Woolsey, was Alpha of the local werewolves, and as a result, he had access to a wide array of truly vicious methods of dealing with Miss Alexia Tarabotti. Instead of bridling at her insult (puppy, indeed!), he brought out his best offensive weapon, the result of decades of personal experience with more than one Alpha she-wolf. Scottish he may be by birth, but that only made him better equipped to deal with strong-willed females. "Stop playing verbal games with me, madam, or I shall go out into that ballroom, find your mother, and bring her here."

Alexia wrinkled her nose. "Well, I *like* that! That is hardly playing a fair game. How unnecessarily callous," she admonished. Her mother did not know that Alexia was preternatural. Mrs. Loontwill, as she was Loontwill since her remarriage, leaned a little too far toward the frivolous in any given equation. She was prone to wearing yellow and engaging in bouts of hysteria. Combining her mother with a dead vampire and her daughter's true identity was a recipe for disaster on all possible levels.

The fact that Alexia was preternatural had been explained to *her* at age six by a nice gentleman from the Civil Service with silver hair and a silver cane – a werewolf specialist. Along with the dark hair and prominent nose, preternatural was something Miss Tarabotti had to thank her dead Italian father for. What it really meant was that words like *I* and *me* were just excessively theoretical for Alexia. She certainly had an identity and a heart that felt emotions and all that; she simply had no soul. Miss Alexia, age six, had nodded politely at the nice silver-haired gentleman. Then she had made certain to read oodles of ancient Greek philosophy dealing with reason, logic, and ethics. If she had no soul, she also had no morals, so she reckoned she had best develop some kind of alternative. Her mama thought her a bluestocking, which was soulless enough as far as Mrs. Loontwill was concerned, and was terribly upset by her eldest daughter's propensity for libraries. It would be too bothersome to have to face her mama in one just now.

Lord Maccon moved purposefully toward the door with the clear intention of acquiring Mrs. Loontwill.

Alexia caved with ill grace. "Oh, very well!" She settled herself with a rustle of green skirts onto a peach brocade chesterfield near the window.

The earl was both amused and annoyed to see that she had managed to pick up her fainting pillow and place it back on the couch without his registering any swooping movement.

"I came into the library for tea. I was promised food at this ball. In case you had not noticed, no food appears to be in residence."

Lord Maccon who required a considerable amount of fuel, mostly of the protein inclination, had noticed. "The Duke of Snodgrove is notoriously reticent about any additional expenditure at his wife's balls. Victuals were probably not on the list of acceptable offerings." He sighed.

"The man owns half of Berkshire and cannot even provide a decent sandwich."

Miss Tarabotti made an empathetic movement with both hands. "My point precisely! So you will understand that I had to resort to ordering my own repast. Did you expect me to starve?"

The earl gave her generous curves a rude once-over, observed that Miss Tarabotti was niccly padded in exactly the right places, and refused to be suckered into becoming sympathetic. He maintained his frown. "I suspect that is precisely what the vampire was thinking when he found you *without a chaperone*. An unmarried female alone in a room in this enlightened day and age! Why, if the moon had been full, even I would have attacked you!"

Alexia gave him the once-over and reached for her brass parasol. "My dear sir, I should like to see you try."

Being Alpha made Lord Maccon a tad unprepared for such bold rebuttals, even with his Scottish past. He blinked at her in surprise for a split second and then resumed the verbal attack. "You do realize modern social mores exist for a reason?"

"I was hungry; allowances should be made," Alexia said, as if that settled the matter, unable to understand why he persisted in harping on about it.

Professor Lyall, unobserved by the other two, was busy fishing about in his waistcoat for something. Eventually, he produced a mildly beaten-up ham and pickle sandwich wrapped in a bit of brown paper. He presented it to Miss Tarabotti, ever the gallant.

Under normal circumstances, Alexia would have been put off by the disreputable state of the sandwich, but it was meant so kindly and offered with such diffidence, she could do nothing but accept. It was actually rather tasty.

"This is delicious!" she stated, surprised.

Professor Lyall grinned. "I keep them around for when his lordship gets particularly testy. Such offerings keep the beast under control for the most part." He frowned and then added a caveat. "Excepting at full moon, of course. Would that a nice ham and pickle sandwich was all it took then."

Miss Tarabotti perked up, interested. "What do you *do* at full moon?"

Lord Maccon knew very well Miss Tarabotti was getting off the point intentionally. Driven beyond endurance, he resorted to use of her first name. "Alexia!" It was a long, polysyllabic, drawnout growl.

She waved the sandwich at him. "Uh, do you want half of this, my lord?"

His frown became even darker, if such a thing could be conceived.

Professor Lyall pushed his glassicals up onto the brim of his top hat, where they looked like a strange second set of mechanical eyes, and stepped into the breach. "Miss Tarabotti, I do not believe you quite realize the delicacy of this situation. Unless we can establish strong grounds for self-defense by proving the vampire was behaving in a wholly irrational manner, you could be facing murder charges."

Alexia swallowed her bite of sandwich so quickly she partly choked and started to cough. "What?"

Lord Maccon turned his fierce frown on his second. "Now who is being too direct for the lady's sensibilities?"

Lord Maccon was relatively new to the London area. He had arrived a social unknown, challenged for Woolsey Castle Alpha, and won. He gave young ladies heart palpitations, even outside his wolf form, with a favorable combination of mystery, pre-eminence, and danger. Having acquired the BUR post, Woolsey Castle, and noble rank from the dispossessed former pack leader, he never lacked for a dinner invitation. His Beta, inherited with the pack, had a tense time of it: dancing on protocol and covering up Lord Maccon's various social gaffes. So far, bluntness had proved Professor Lyall's most consistent problem. Sometimes it even rubbed off on him. He had not meant to shock Miss Tarabotti, but she was now looking most subdued.

"I was simply sitting," Alexia explained, placing the sandwich aside, having lost her appetite. "He launched himself at me, totally unprovoked. His feeding fangs were out. I am certain if I had been a normal daylight woman, he would have bled me dry. I simply had to defend myself."

Professor Lyall nodded. A vampire in a state of extreme hunger had two socially acceptable options: to take sips from various willing drones belonging to him or his hive, or to pay for the privilege from blood-whores down dockside. This was the nineteenth century, after all, and one simply did not attack unannounced and uninvited! Even werewolves, who could not control themselves at full moon, made certain they had enough clavigers around to lock them away. He himself had three, and it took five to keep Lord Maccon under control.

"Do you think maybe he was forced into this state?" the professor wondered.

"You mean imprisoned until he was starving and no longer in possession of his faculties?" Lord Maccon considered the idea.

Professor Lyall flipped his glassicals back down off his hat and examined the dead man's wrists and neck myopically. "No signs of confinement or torture, but hard to tell with a vampire. Even in a low blood state, he would heal most superficial wounds in" – he grabbed Lord Maccon's metal roll and stylus, dipped the tip into the clear sizzling liquid, and did some quick calculations – "a little over one hour." The calculations remained etched into the metal.

"And then what? Did he escape or was he intentionally let go?"

Alexia interjected, "He seemed perfectly sane to me – aside from the attacking part, of course. He was able to carry on a decent conversation. He even tried to charm me. Must have been quite a young vampire. And" – she paused dramatically, lowered her voice, and said in sepulchral tones – "he had a fang-lisp."

Professor Lyall looked shocked and blinked largely at her through the asymmetrical lenses; among vampires, lisping was the height of vulgarity.

Miss Tarabotti continued. "It was as though he had never

been trained in hive etiquette, no social class at all. He was almost a boor." It was a word she had never thought to apply to a vampire.

Lyall took the glassicals off and put them away in their little case with an air of finality. He looked gravely at his Alpha. "You know what this means, then, my lord?"

Lord Maccon was not frowning anymore. Instead he was looking grim. Alexia felt it suited him better, setting his mouth into a straight line and touching his tawny eyes with a determined glint. She wondered idly what he would look like if he smiled a real honest smile. Then she told herself quite firmly that it was probably best not to find out.

The object of her speculations said, "It means some hive queen is intentionally biting to metamorphosis outside of BUR regulations."

"Could it be just the once, do you think?" Professor Lyall removed a folded piece of white cloth from his waistcoat. He shook out the material, revealing it to be a large sheet of fine silk. Alexia was beginning to find the number of things he could stash in his waistcoat quite impressive.

Lord Maccon continued. "Or this could be the start of something more extensive. We'd better get back to BUR. The local hives will have to be interviewed. The queens are not going to be happy. Apart from everything else, this incident is awfully embarrassing for them."

Miss Tarabotti agreed. "Especially if they find out about the substandard shirt selection."

The two gentlemen wrapped the vampire's body in the

silk sheet. Professor Lyall hoisted it easily over one shoulder. Even in their human form, werewolves were considerably stronger than daylight folk.

Lord Maccon rested his tawny gaze on Alexia. She was sitting primly on the chesterfield. One gloved hand rested on the ebony handle of a ridiculous-looking parasol. Her brown eyes were narrowed in consideration. He would give a hundred pounds to know what she was thinking just then. He was also certain she would tell him exactly what it was if he asked, but he refused to give her the satisfaction. Instead he issued a statement. "We'll try to keep your name out of it, Miss Tarabotti. My report will say it was simply a normal girl who got lucky and managed to escape an unwarranted attack. No need for anyone to know a preternatural was involved."

Now it was Alexia's turn to glare. "Why do you BUR types always *do* that?"

Both men paused to look at her in confusion.

"*Do* what, Miss Tarabotti?" asked the professor.

"Dismiss me as though I were a child. Do you realize I could be useful to you?"

Lord Maccon grunted. "You mean you could go around legally getting into trouble instead of just bothering us all the time?"

Alexia tried to keep from feeling hurt. "BUR employs women, and I hear you even have a preternatural on the payroll up north, for ghost control and exorcism purposes."

Lord Maccon's caramel-colored eyes instantly narrowed. "From whom, exactly, did you hear that?"

Miss Tarabotti raised her eyebrows. As if she would ever betray the source of information told to her in confidence!

The earl understood her look perfectly. "Very well, never you mind that question."

"I shall not," replied Alexia primly.

Professor Lyall, still holding the body slung over one shoulder, took pity on her. "We do have both at BUR," he admitted.

Lord Maccon elbowed him in the side, but he stepped out of range with a casual grace that bespoke much practice. "But what we do not have is any *female* preternaturals, and certainly not any gentlewomen. All women employed by BUR are good working-class stock."

"You are simply still bitter about the hedgehogs," muttered Miss Tarabotti, but she also bowed her head in acknowledgment. She'd had this conversation before, with Lord Maccon's superior at BUR, to be precise. A man her brain still referred to as that Nice Silver-Haired Gentleman. The very idea that a lady of breeding such as herself might want to *work* was simply too shocking. "My dearest girl," he had said, "what if your mother found out?"

"Isn't BUR supposed to be covert? I could be covert." Miss Tarabotti could not help trying again. Professor Lyall, at least, liked her a little bit. Perhaps he might put in a good word.

Lord Maccon actually laughed. "You are about as covert as a sledgehammer." Then he cursed himself silently, as she seemed suddenly forlorn. She hid it quickly, but she had definitely been saddened.

His Beta grabbed him by the arm with his free hand. "Really, sir, manners."

The earl cleared his throat and looked contrite. "No offense meant, Miss Tarabotti." The Scottish lilt was back in his voice.

Alexia nodded, not looking up. She plucked at one of the pansies on her parasol. "It's simply, gentlemen" – and when she raised her dark eyes they had a slight sheen in them – "I would so like something useful to do."

Lord Maccon waited until he and the professor were out in the hallway, having bid polite, on Professor Lyall's part at least, farewells to the young lady, to ask the question that really bothered him. "For goodness' sake, Randolph, why doesn't she just get married?" His voice was full of frustration.

Randolph Lyall looked at his Alpha in genuine confusion. The earl was usually a very perceptive man, for all his bluster and Scottish grumbling. "She is a bit old, sir."

"Balderdash," said Lord Maccon. "She cannot possibly have more than a quarter century or so."

"And she is very" – the professor looked for a gentlemanly way of putting it – "assertive."

"Pah." The nobleman waved one large paw dismissively. "Simply got a jot more backbone than most females this century. There must be plenty of discerning gentlemen who'd cop to her value."

Professor Lyall had a well-developed sense of self-preservation and the distinct feeling that if he said anything desultory about the young lady's appearance, he might actually get his head bitten off. He, and the rest of polite society, might believe Miss Tarabotti's skin a little too dark and her nose a little too prominent, but he did not think Lord Maccon felt the same. Lyall had been Beta to the fourth Earl of Woolsey since Conall Maccon first descended upon them all. With barely twenty years gone and the bloody memory still strong, no werewolf was yet ready to question why Conall had wanted the bother of the London territory, not even Professor Lyall. The earl was a confusing man, his taste in females equally mystifying. For all Professor Lyall knew, his Alpha might actually *like* Roman noses, tan skin, and an assertive disposition. So instead he said, "Perhaps it's the Italian last name, sir, that keeps her unwed."

"Mmm," agreed Lord Maccon, "probably so." He did not sound convinced.

The two werewolves exited the duke's town house into the black London night, one bearing the body of a dead vampire, the other, a puzzled expression.